The Reluctant Series

Book One: Lovestruck
Book Two: Bargains
Book Three: The Wild Ride

RELUCTANT

Book One: Lovestruck

By Karen Renee Krebs

Cover Illustrations by Kate Henriott-Jauw

Copyright© 2022 Karen Renee Krebs
All rights reserved
ISBN-

Cover Art © Kate Henriot-Jauw

Acknowledgments

There are so many people in our lives whom we meet and every one of them has some impact on who we are and whom we become. You never know what word, sentence, or idea you share will have a huge impact on another person's life. A smile or a hug at the right moment can change a person's life. So can a harsh word or an insult. I am sure I have been guilty of both.

I'd like to thank my partner, Denise Hodgden, for her love and encouragement. I would also like to thank her for her technical expertise in helping me get my novels off of the Windows 95 computer with no back up drive I was using and into the twenty-first century. That and for putting up with me!

I'd like to thank Delight Lester, my oldest and dearest friend, for her help in getting these books out there. You are a beacon of love and light and you have always been there for me.

I'd like to thank Dr. Joy Ochs, a professor at Mount Mercy University, for taking the time to be the first to read the rough draft of the novels and for her constructive ideas and encouragement. I cherish your friendship!

I'd like to thank Sister Shari Sutherland, a Sister of Mercy, for not only her encouragement but also for being there for me when things were dark and hope was just a dream. Your beautiful heart shines as a testament to your faith, Sister!

*Dedicated to my boys,
Charles and Jack*

Reluctant: Part One-

Lovestruck

1

As I stood on the rim of the Grand Canyon I looked down into the abyss and realized that if there was ever a metaphor for my life, the Grand Canyon must be it. Like me, it was very interesting but also vast and empty. Unlike me, it was incredibly beautiful. So was the woman who stood a dozen feet away staring into the canyon! I couldn't help but stare at her as she was the most beautiful woman I had ever seen! Her long curly blonde hair seemed almost radiant as it reflected the sun's rays. The same rays penetrated her white summer dress accentuating the curves of her near-perfect body. Then she turned and looked past me and I saw the bluest eyes I'd ever seen and when she smiled it turned my heart to mush. I wanted to walk over and say something but realized there wasn't anything to say. She was way out of my league.

So, I cinched up my daypack and headed past her, smiling and nodding as I did. I walked up a trail and headed to one of the many lookout points where I planned on spending the day staring into the abyss. According to the park map, there were a dozen short side trails leading to lookout points. I chose one near the middle figuring I'd have the best chance at finding it empty and succeeded on my first try. I found a nice rock in the shade of a comfortable tree, sat down, and relaxed. Not that I had anything to relax from!

That was kind of the point. As I stared across the expanse at the North rim, I felt just as distant from any ambitions. I was literally adrift in America with no focus other than where my next campsite was going to be. But I realized that my money, while still fine, was not going to last forever. I estimated that it would hold out through the summer, but by Labor Day I had better start looking for a job. But what that job would be and where it would be was completely unknown. When I was a kid, I wanted to be a fireman or a doctor or whatever. But at this point in my life, I didn't want to be anything other than to be in love, and more importantly, to be loved. After working in a machine shop, I was pretty sure I could handle any kind of work, but without someone to share my life with what would be the point? What was the point of life anyway? Live, work, and die? Without love, life had no purpose at least as far as I could see.

I had traveled for three months and camped and hiked in some of the most beautiful country I'd ever seen but had no one to share it with other than an occasional hitchhiker. Nightly I recorded my thoughts in a beer-stained journal, but there was never anyone to look over at and say, 'Isn't this beautiful?', to. Mom always said I'd meet my soul mate someday, but I doubted it, or if I did they'd probably already be married. Just my luck!

So I spent my day lying in the hot sun contemplating everything and deciding nothing. Well, that's not true, I decided to go to Vegas. I had been debating that over and over again as it wasn't exactly the place to camp, but I figured any town that honors drunks the way Vegas does was a place I would probably be welcome in. Besides, sometimes I needed a dose of the city. So, I decided to splurge on the cheapest room I could find for a couple of nights and spend a night on the town. I was looking forward to it as I headed back to my car late in the afternoon.

As I exited the trail and turned towards my car, I was surprised to see that the beautiful young lady I had seen earlier was standing next to my car. I hurried over to her, but she was gone by the time I got there. But when I looked at my dust covered window, I realized she had written the number '17' in the dust. I sat in my car and drank a beer as I stared at that number. Was she telling me her age? If not that, then what? I was terribly confused. But as the beer relaxed me, I was determined to find her!

That night and for the whole next day I bounced from hotel to restaurant, checking gift shops, the park service buildings, and generally hanging around looking for my mystery woman. At first it was frantic and then methodical, but the results were all the same. I saw a dozen women who looked close, but I couldn't find my angel. My heart dropped lower into my stomach each time I failed as I realized I would never see her again and that made me sad. After sleeping in my car and spending a long day looking for her I found myself sitting on the rim of the canyon as I sighed and gave up. I watched the sun set as light and shadows completely changed the way the canyon looked. As darkness crept in I returned to my car and after topping off the ice in my cooler I headed west and on to Las Vegas. I camped in the mountains near the Arizona border.

I stopped at Hoover dam and as I stood on it I was amazed at its height. The Hoover dam provided enough electricity for Las Vegas and did it without burning carbon fuels or splitting atoms, just good old-fashioned gravity and a whole lot of turbines. I know that dams aren't great for fish, and they're even worse for the animals that lived in the canyon before they flooded it, but in my mind, they are a whole lot better than some of the other ways we make electricity. Pretty impressive to see as well!

I found a cheap hotel in Vegas called the Flamingo Ranch Motel, paid forty bucks for one night, and headed to the casino. I was careful to only bring a single hundred-dollar traveler's check with me and kept the rest locked in my motel room safe. When the money was gone my night was over. First, I drove up and down the strip looking at all of the famous casinos and the stars that were performing. I ended up at Caesar's because it was one of the last of the old casinos. It was everything you could expect from a bastion of hedonism. The cocktail waitresses wore skimpy white togas, and they were all beautiful. There were tall bulky men in breastplates, helmets, and capes. There were thousands of flashing lights and hundreds of slot machines making plinking and ringing sounds. The casino floor buzzed with a rhythmic excitement as tables of craps players cheered or groaned.

Frankly, it was too much to take in. I had never gambled before and certainly never won anything, but just being there was intoxicating. I had played a lot of poker with my grandpa when I was growing up and he would visit but knew better than to go to the poker parlor where the sharks waited for a fish like me. I knew nothing about the game of craps other than it was played with dice and the same was true with most of the games. But before I could partake in anything, I needed some money. I went to the cage and cashed my traveler's check and got two rolls of quarters. I decided you didn't have to be a genius to pull a handle.

I was wrong. After my second pull, the old woman with white hair sitting a few machines away leaned over, smiled, and said, "You're going to be awfully sorry if the jackpot comes up and you only have one coin in!"

"Huh?" I asked.

"First time?" she asked. I nodded. "Thought so! I'm Mildred and let me give you some tips!"

She came over and sat next to me as she explained how to read a machine. Apparently, each machine was different, but none of them paid the full jackpot out unless the maximum coins were played. But each machine took from three to ten coins to get to the jackpot. Also, some of the machines paid the jackpot on only one of the lines, while others paid it out on any line. At first, it was a bit crazy, but I quickly caught on and thanked the lady who wandered off. I found a machine that Mildred would approve of and went to work. I held my breath with each spin and got excited when something actually lined up and the machine's bells went off. I was even more excited when the Roman Goddess cocktail waitress brought me a Heineken! I tipped her a buck and she came back regularly.

I was halfway through my first roll of quarters when I got triple bars and won two hundred quarters, more than doubling the coins I started with. I was excited and continued to pump money into the machine. But I went into a long period where the machine took a lot more than it gave and so I kept pumping quarters into it. Quickly my winnings were gone and I was back to using the rolls of quarters I had bought. But I had been playing for close to two hours and had consumed four Heinekens, so based on the bar cost of imported beer, I figured I was about even. When I ran out of quarters, I turned on the change light and a pretty young girl sold me two more rolls of quarters. The machine paid out twenty and occasionally fifty coins, but the big jackpot wasn't quite in reach. I was only into my fifth Heineken when I was halfway through the fourth roll. I was either going to have to drink quicker or gamble slower I reasoned.

I popped three more coins into the machine and pulled the handle, then lit another cigarette. I reached down for the ashtray when the bell went off and was surprised to see that the sevens that had been popping up regularly were neatly aligned on the center row. I looked up the machine at the payout display and saw that I had won five thousand coins. I quickly did the math and almost peed when I realized that I had just won over twelve hundred dollars. The coin girl came up and called her supervisor who came up, turned his key in the machine, and left. A few minutes later he returned and counted out twelve hundred-dollar bills and one fifty into my hand. Someone took my picture. I gave the change girl the fifty.

I went to the bathroom to compose myself and get rid of some of those Heinekens and after splashing a little water on my face I felt a whole lot better. I treated myself to a steak dinner and sobered up a little. The truth was I was elated. I now had as much money as I had started with three months ago and could keep up my vagabond lifestyle indefinitely. The waitress brought the check, and I laughed when the total was $17.17. I had a vision of the mysterious woman writing on my car. 'Mystery solved', I thought and laughed.

    I decided to get it while the getting was good when I saw her, the girl from the Grand Canyon. She was working the roulette wheel or at least it looked just like her and her smile beckoned me over. The table was empty as I sat down, and I tried to play it cool even though I didn't know what I was doing. I handed her two hundred-dollar bills, and she handed me forty blue chips each worth five dollars. I learned quickly that Kathy, the dealer, had not been to the Grand Canyon recently and was not my mystery woman. But she was pretty as well as nice and her friend Colette was a cocktail waitress who brought me more Heinekens on a regular basis, so I stayed and played.

    I played small low odds bets like odd/even and black/white as I studied the board. Roulette is a game of pretty true odds if you don't take into consideration 0 and 00, which screw up the odds in the houses favor. If you ignore the 0 and the 00, there are thirty-six numbers and the pay out for a single number is thirty-five to one. Like I said, true odds. I settled on choosing a block of six, which paid five to one and I got lucky three times in a row. So, I started playing five chips at a time and after losing twice I won four times in a row. I was having so much fun I hardly noticed when Kathy had left. I pushed the bet to ten at a time and watched my pile started to dwindle until I hit six in a row. I pushed the bet first to a hundred then to two hundred and my stack grew. I lost a few more times and realized that I was pretty drunk, so I cashed out. She handed me a stack of chips. I tipped the dealer and was going to leave when I heard the blackjack dealer behind us call out, "Dealer has a seventeen!"

I realized I hadn't played the mysterious lady's number yet so I approached a different roulette table and placed most of my stack of chips on number seventeen. The dealer called the pit boss over and everybody watched as the little ball spun around the wheel. I hadn't even counted the chips I had bet. I was lighting another cigarette as the ball dropped into the slot, but I heard the pit boss gasp. I looked over as the dealer placed the marker on top of my chips. He counted my stack of chips that I thought were hundred-dollar chips carefully and then counted out and handed me fifty-two black one thousand-dollar chips and five one-hundred-dollar chips.

"How much did I bet?" I asked.

"You had ten black and five blue chips sir. You bet ten thousand five hundred dollars on that spin."

I almost fainted. Another player leaned over and whispered that if I cashed them all in at once that I would have to pay taxes, but if I cashed them in amounts under seven thousand dollars that I didn't have to fill out any forms. I already had a thousand in cash in my pocket, so I stuffed the chips into my jacket and headed back to my room. On my way I stopped at the bar, had one last beer and tipped the bartender heavily. Before I left, I asked him when the shift changes for the cage were. He willingly told me the information.

    I returned to the Casino every eight hours for the next three days until I had cashed in all my chips. When I was done, I had a stack of hundred-dollar bills that added up to almost sixty grand! It was to be an endless summer! First, I visited a dozen banks and purchased two thousand in traveler's checks at each bank, so that half of my money was in travelers' checks. I bought new tires, a tune up, oil change, alignment, and had a brake job done on my car. I bought a new sleeping bag, new hiking boots, and replaced my leaking cooler. Then I headed west before the temptation to return to the casino caused me to lose the money. I hid the traveler's checks and the remainder of the cash in plain white envelopes in Ziploc baggies in a shoebox that I placed in the spare wheel compartment under the trunk. With this kind of cash, I could be a vagabond forever!

    I spent almost a month in Yosemite and could have spent more. While Yosemite Valley was magnificent, I fell in love with Tuolumne Meadows and spent weeks hiking in the backcountry and climbing domes for spectacular views. But as the month went on, I kept having a dream about the girl at the Grand Canyon and she kept telling me to hurry. Hurry where? I would wonder when I woke up since I had no idea where she would be waiting for me. All I could tell was that there were big trees and a lot of mist. It was very confusing.

Finally, I headed for the coast, my ultimate destination. I camped on the shores of the Pacific at a place called Halfmoon Bay and dipped my toes into the Pacific. It was very cold. Then I had to decide whether to turn right or left. The fact that it was late August, and it was a hundred and ten in the shade in LA convinced me to turn north, so I headed up the coast. I ended up going to Marin County north of the Golden Gate Bridge and found a campground not too far after passing the bridge. I was surprised to discover that there was a large renaissance festival going on at the park and there were thousands of costumed characters running around. Joining them I ate turkey legs, threw knives and battle axes at targets, shot arrows, drank ale, and had a grand old time watching jousting, sword fighting, and even a life-size chess match. By late afternoon I had drunk a number of ales and decided to lie down under a tree in the shade to rest. Drowsy from the ale, I lay back and fell asleep.

I don't know how long I slept but when I awoke the sun was lower in the sky and I felt considerably soberer than when I had lain down. As I lie there smoking a cigarette a herald walked down the nearby path calling out, 'Make way for the Goddess'. I leaned up on one elbow to see a procession winding up the path. At the center of the group, there was a woman with beautiful curly blond hair, all dressed in white and when I looked at her I almost flipped out. It was the girl I had seen at the Grand Canyon. At least she looked like her. But I had also seen her face in Kathy's face in the casino, in the face of a Park Ranger in Yosemite, and in the face of a young surfer at Half-moon Bay. So instead of making an ass of myself for the fourth time I just leaned up on one elbow and watched the circus pass. As it did, she turned her head to look right at me and for just a second seemed surprised. Our eyes locked and my heart was pounding as we gazed at each other. But the moment passed as she smiled, and she nodded her head. I smiled and nodded back as the procession passed by.

That evening I was sitting by my fire staring at the coals when a young woman entered my campsite and stood across the fire from me. I looked up at her and almost fell off the camp chair I was sitting in. It was her, the Goddess from earlier, but instead of dressed in white she was wearing camp shorts and a hoodie.

"I'm glad you finally made it Quentin!" she smiled.

"Thanks," I replied when a chill went up my spine as I realized she knew my name. "How did you know my name?" I asked but she only smiled.

"I know a lot of things Quentin. How did seventeen work out for you?" I stumbled to my feet.

"It is you!" I said. "But how?" I couldn't even find words to ask about my confusion.

"Later, buster, we have to get moving." She said looking around.

"Moving?"

"Yes Quentin, moving. We're not safe here! How long before you can break camp?"

"We're not safe? Now c'mon, you're kidding, right?" Just then I heard a sound like a wolf in the distant. She looked alarmed.

"Shit, they're coming. Do you have any weapons?"

"Weapons? Like what, a gun or something?"

"A silver sword would be more useful?"

"Right!"

"Look Quentin, we don't have much time. You have some money, don't you?"

"Yeah, how much do we need?"

"Bring ten grand!"

"Ten grand?"

"Yes, and hurry." I went to the trunk and removed ten envelopes. "Come with me." She said as she grabbed my hand and dragged me through the woods.

"Um yeah, but where are you taking me?"

"You'll see. I'm Sharon."

"Uh, nice to meet you, mysterious Sharon. How did you know my name?"

"Because Quentin, you're the reason I'm here. Now be quiet." She led me to a large tent illuminated by candlelight. A large man armed with a long blade guarded the door. He looked as if he wouldn't hesitate to use it.

"Is Omar in?" she whispered, and he nodded and opened the tent flap as I made my way out of the twenty-first century and into what appeared to be the twelfth. The smoky interior of the tent was lit by candlelight as an old, scarred swordsmith sat polishing a jewel-encrusted sword. When Sharon entered the tent, he rose and bowed. Sharon quickly went up to him and they whispered together. Twice the old swordsmith looked over at me and shook his head both times. Finally, he nodded and led her to a large locked cabinet. Drawing a key from around his neck he opened the cabinet and revealed a number of special jewel-encrusted swords with sharp keen edges. I was beginning to wonder when I would wake up.

Sharon called me over and handed me a short sword that I almost dropped when she handed it to me. It was heavier than it looked.

"You know how to use that, don't you?" she asked as tried a variety of swords.

"Um, slash, parry, stab, something like that right?" I said sheepishly.

"You left out die!" Omar said sarcastically. What could I say, the closest I'd been to being in a real sword fight was fighting it out with my brother with the cardboard tubes from the Christmas wrapping paper. That and video games.

"I can't imagine what circumstances could occur that would necessitate me knowing how to use a sword!" I said bewildered. They both looked at me with incredulous looks on their face. Was that really such an unreasonable statement to make, I ask you? Sharon just shook her head and chose a variety of swords, daggers, and other weapon-like things I had no idea what they even were. Roger carefully loaded the weapons into a bag and added a couple of bows and a handful of quivers full of arrows. Finally, I paid him six thousand and started to drag the bag back to camp.

Sharon helped me carry the heavy bag and looked at me with disgust on her face. This made me begin to wonder when I was going to wake up. But I didn't because apparently, I was awake. Every time I tried to ask her about why I needed a sword she hushed me but as soon as we got to camp, she began to arm us both. It was weird having blades strapped to my calves, arms, and waist, but when she was done I was wearing four different knives that couldn't be seen. Then she strapped the sword around my waist and as silly as I felt, it kind of turned me on when she reached around me to tie the scabbard. After she was finished, I drew the blade and had to admit it felt pretty good in my hand. It was perfectly balanced and didn't seem too heavy when I swung it. I slid the sword back into its scabbard. "Tell me again why I need a sword?" I asked.

"Cause you can't kill everything that needs killing with a gun!" she said as I looked at her.

"Um, hold on, girl, who said anything about killing? I'm a pacifist, I hate killing anything but time."

"Cute Quentin, but we don't have time for this. If we don't pack up and get moving, you're either going to get killed or have to do some killing. Do you understand?"

"No! I don't understand anything. I don't understand how you know my name and why I just spent six grand buying medieval weapons! I don't understand how you knew to write seventeen on my car or how I won playing it for that matter. But most of all I don't understand why I can't get your beautiful face out of my mind and my dreams. I see your face everywhere." She actually blushed and smiled for a second before her scowl returned.

"What time is it?" She asked.

"Eleven thirty, why?"

"Because Quentin, if we're not out of this park in thirty minutes, we're both going to die. Do you understand that?" She said. In the far distant I heard a strange animal cry that sent chills up my spine. In an instant, her sword was out. I found my hand on my own sword and a terrible fear in my heart. "Quentin," she said, and she sounded terrified, "we have to go, NOW!"

I quickly broke camp, rolled up my tent and threw everything into the trunk and the back seat. In ten minutes, we were on the road as the screams of the banshee grew closer. Usually, I would have laughed but Sharon was frightened to tears and never let go of her sword. I drove as Sharon directed me and we finally, just before twelve, left the boundaries of the park. As soon as we did, Sharon visibly relaxed.

"Okay Goddess, disaster averted. Now where?"

"Just keep driving north. We've got a lot of work to do. And whatever you do, don't stop for hitchhikers." With that she laid back and went to sleep. I tried to ask her questions, but she just lay there and snored.

As usual on long quiet trips I grew introspective. I wasn't quite sure what was going on but I was amazed that I found myself in my car with Sharon. Okay, so I never figured I'd be wearing knives and carrying swords, but hey, she was here. Why she was here was beyond my ability to grasp! But I was excited to be near her and I frequently looked over at her. Inside I felt many things but love, at first sight, seemed the best way to describe it. Well, not love, but infatuation. But it was more than that. It was like meeting an old friend even though I had just met her. I felt our destinies were tied together. I wondered about the number seventeen, the money, the swords and well, everything. But that only made it more enticing to me as I had been bored for a long time.

The truth is I have never been that enamored with the life I've been given. Oh, I make the best of what I've been given and I'm relatively healthy if you ignore a few of my unhealthy habits liking occasionally smoking pot or getting hammered. It's just that things never clicked with me in life. I was the second and last son of four kids. My older brother Jerry was the first born and could do no wrong. My sister Anne was the first girl and could do no wrong. My little sister Irene was the baby and could do no wrong. Me? I was chopped liver and all I could seem to do was wrong! It didn't help that I had a restless soul. Of course, I could have been A.D.D. but they never tested me for that. Mom said I was too smart for my own good. Dad regularly called me a dumb shit or a smart ass, so I was getting mixed messages from the beginning!

It didn't help that we moved around a lot! No, dad wasn't in the military, he was an accountant in a national accounting firm and he was climbing the corporate ladder one miserable rung at a time. We moved five times between second grade and the time I graduated from high school. As a result, I didn't really have a hard time making friends; I just couldn't keep them. The longest I ever knew anyone was about two years, then I would have to start over. Being the new kid could be a good thing if you were handsome, strong, and athletic, as it gave you an air of mystery. Of course, if you're just normal and maybe a little short and thin it just made you the weird new kid. So, I always had a few friends but never a close one. And as for girls, forget about them. For the most part they wanted nothing to do with me and I was pretty inept when it came to the courting ritual. It didn't help that my parents named me Quentin either. I'd pay a million dollars to have been named just about anything else.

And for some reason, I was cursed with bad luck. Whenever my brother and I received identical gifts, mine was always broken, scratched, or damaged in some way. And if it wasn't it was always the first to break. My parents claimed I was just rough on things, but I thought God just hated me. Everyone thought that Jerry was the smartest of us all and his nickname was 'Brainiac', a cross between a brain and a maniac.

He was always taking things apart and putting them back together again, sort of, although he always seemed to have had a few extra parts left over when he was done. He studied hard and got good grades. Me, I was allergic to studying and coasted through school. I changed schools so many times and there were so many gaps between the schools that a lot of my education fell through the cracks. It seemed like I was always learning something I had already learned or was finding out that something I didn't know had been taught last year. But I was great at taking tests so somehow, I got through school.

The truth is, I learned later that I was actually a lot smarter than anyone let me know. Only when I was going through some papers as I was packing my things after high school graduation did I discover the truth. All through school we had to take those aptitude tests that lasted a couple of days. Since I tested well, I actually enjoyed the break from the boring lessons. As I was packing I discovered a pile of them in a file in my dad's office. Jerry's scores were in the low eighties, meaning that he tested better than eighty percent of the students taking the test. My scores were no lower than a ninety-seven and most were ninety-nines. If the tests were a measure of intelligence, I was certainly smarter than my brother was. No wonder my teachers were always saying I was working below my potential. But my parents were always satisfied with my mediocre grades, so why should I work harder? Truth is, I only did homework when it was absolutely necessary.

Not that I didn't learn anything. When I was interested in a subject, I was all over it like a cheap suit! In seventh grade we studied American Indians and I ended up reading dozens of unassigned books on the subject. I did the same with most of my history classes. I also read a lot books that were science fiction and fantasy. Each summer I would pick an author and read all of their works. Shakespeare was the hardest to read at first, but after a while I got used to his style. When I read Hemmingway, I could almost sense the inevitability of his dark and tragic end. Twain's sarcastic style was my favorite and I wondered about Edgar Allen Poe's state of mind. My problem in school wasn't my ability to read or write it was that I just preferred to control my own content.

I think I was in second grade the first time I fell in love, and you can imagine how that went over when I sent her a love letter. The day after I handed her the perfume scented letter she transferred to another class. I fell in love again in fifth grade with Janet Cartman and she actually seemed to like me as well. Unfortunately, Tom Gilmore, the boy who lived across the street from her, had a different idea. They had grown up together and their parents always talked about how they would probably get married someday and Tom was planning on crushing anyone who stood in the way of that happening. That would have been me, of course. My brother and I always wrestled and fought, but Tom's father had taught him the art of boxing and he wasn't shy about using it. I learned that the first day of school when I was talking to Janet at the bus stop. We were fifth graders and Tom was in the fourth grade because he had been held back. After school he informed me that I was not allowed to speak to Janet. Then he beat the shit out of me.

Ah, love makes us do funny things. The thing was that Janet and I connected and we loved to sit and talk for hours about things. One day she needed ferns for a project and after describing what she wanted I headed into the woods. Hours later, in the dark, I knocked on her door and she was surprised to see the handful of ferns I had brought her. We had many magical days lying on our backs and laughing as we described the shapes of the clouds. I was in love and didn't know what to do about it. I should have just kissed her. It would have made everything worth it. As it was, the only thing I got for my trouble was black eyes, bloody noses, and sore stomachs. I always wondered why he didn't knock a few teeth out. It turns out his dad was a dentist and had taught him to avoid the teeth. Apparently, he didn't want to get sued. So regularly I'd be sitting and talking to Janet and Tom would show up and challenge me to a fight. I'd say I rather not and he'd fight me anyway. It usually didn't last long and then I would stumble away bleeding or dizzy. Janet put up with it, the bitch!

The first time I got beat up I went home which was a big mistake. They all laughed and made fun of my bloody nose. Dad said it would build character! How does getting the shit kicked out of you build character? I think that's just one of those things they say. So, from then on, after Tom had worked out on my face, I hid in a tree. Yes, a tree. In the lot next to my house there was this tall tree, and I learned every branch of it. I would climb all the way to near the top where I would sit in the place where three branches split off to make up the very crown of the tree. It was comfortable perch and the whole top of the tree swayed in the breeze as I sat up there for hours. Tom was afraid of heights, so I felt safer up there than I did on the ground. So, I spent a good part of that year sixty feet off the ground in a tree.

I didn't realize it then, but from the safety of the tree, I learned perspective. For an ADD person to sit calmly in the top of a tree for hours looking down on the world was no less than amazing. But up there I learned to quiet my mind and look at the big picture. It was in the tree that I realized that Janet really was to blame for tolerating and in some ways getting off on Tom's violence. Looking back, I wonder if later in life she was ever on the receiving end of one of his 'gifts'! People who think with their fists aren't too far away from domestic violence. But I never knew because we moved away, which broke my heart but saved me a whole lot of ass-whippings!

After that, my luck with women didn't improve much and as a result, neither did my skills. Jerry seemed to have had a girlfriend since birth. Me, the closest I came was a girl at a party in eighth grade who was drunk and trying to see how many boys she could French kiss in one night. I was sixteenth out of twenty-two. She stopped when she threw up on Bobby

Derkowitz, number twenty-three. I told him he should have avoided the onion dip! I always seem to fall for a girl who just wanted to be friends. On the other hand, it wasn't like I was getting any offers either. Jerry was always being chased by at least a few girls, but I was unaware that any girl ever had a crush on me. I was a virgin when I left high school and would have stayed that way except for Cheyenne.

Cheyenne was the older sister of my friend Jackson from high school and we met during Spring Break of my sophomore year in college. She was a welfare momma with a three-year old daughter and she latched on to me like a remora. Jackson had a party the last night of spring break and Cheyenne dragged me into their parent's room and deflowered me. I didn't last long but was relieved when it was finally over. But it wasn't. Cheyenne showed up on my campus a week later and we spent a lot of time together, most of it having sex. She was a demanding woman in the bedroom and had zero problems telling me what she liked and how I was doing. Jenny was her beautiful little girl and I enjoyed telling her stories and taking her to the park. Then one day when I was home for the weekend my brother Jerry pulled me aside and lectured me about using condoms. The next time I was with Cheyenne I insisted we use a condom and she broke up with me a few days later. Jackson told me later that she confided to him after we broke up that she was trying to get pregnant because she was about to lose her welfare benefits. Sure enough, six-months later he told me that she was three-months pregnant. I was just glad it wasn't mine.

I started college three weeks before 9/11 and watched in horror as the world I lived in changed in a moment. I was angry and confused but never afraid the way others around me were. This kind of shit had been happening in the rest of the world for decades and I figured it was just our time. I tried to remind people that the real lesson of 9/11 was three out of four. Once people on the planes figured out what was happening, they no longer were passive. But the people in power had whipped the country into a frenzy, so I learned to keep quiet about the subject.

I dropped out of college after my sophomore year. It was kind of a mutual decision. While I maintained a solid 'C' average I did it by acing half my classes and failing the other half. But the second term of my sophomore year, distracted by my new discovery of sex, everything kind of fell apart and my average slipped below a 'C'. They pounced on me the first chance they got and demanded that if I returned, I would have to be on social probation. Okay, so I was a bit of distraction to the other students. I liked to party and apparently the fact that I encouraged others to join me was a problem. Since alcohol was illegal for anyone under twenty-one, we needed fake ID's and I knew a guy who could make them. This was the closest thing to popularity I had ever experienced. In my defense, I never made a penny on the transactions. And I didn't give up my source when I got busted and would have gone to jail if the cops hadn't bungled the case. I didn't go to jail, but the college jumped at the chance to force me out.

So, I moved home, got a job in a machine shop and saved money. Dad was always telling me to get my own place, but I was done with Detroit. Bored and depressed, I drank regularly and planned my escape. Over the next year I fixed up my car, bought a new tent, backpack, sleeping bag, cooler, and cook stove. The following Spring, after I got my income tax refund, I split. Mom freaked and Dad praised the Lord when I left. I loaded the trunk of my car with my camping gear, a box full of canned soups and stews, a couple of boxes of granola bars, and a few dozen mini cans of juice and headed west. In the back seat I had a cooler with beer, cheese, milk, butter and a few other necessities. The food lasted a month before I had to replenish it. When I needed to I replenished the beer, cheese, and milk and sometimes picked up some chicken or hamburger to grill up.

I had a road atlas that conveniently had every state and national park and forest campground marked on it. When I got tired of driving, I would pull out the atlas, find a park and camp for the night. As a tent camper, I paid almost nothing. If I liked an area, I would stay a few days and explore and if I didn't like the area I would move on down the road. I traveled through northern Wisconsin and Minnesota and marveled at the stars. At the Teddy Roosevelt National Forest in North Dakota, I was stranded on a road as a herd of buffalo surrounded my car. No, I mean a big herd, like a thousand strong. It smelled like shit and scared the hell out of me. Not a great place to be if a stampede starts, so I turned off the car and waited for them to pass.

When I got the chance, I picked up hitchhikers and we talked about our lives. I wasn't that much different than they were only I had a car. I picked up dozens over my travels, but they were all on the way to get somewhere and I was going nowhere. My heart raced as I climbed into the Rockies in Montana and saw the mountains for the first time. In Yellowstone, one of the park workers led me to a hot springs where we lay naked in hot sulfur water as the river rushed by a few feet away. A couple of elk came by to drink from the river. The Great Salt Lake was large, flat, salty, shallow and smelled, but the mountains beyond Salt Lake were beautiful. There was still three feet of snow on the ground when I hit the North rim of the Grand Canyon and it was a hundred degrees on the South rim.

During my travels I often parked the car, loaded up my backpack and headed into the woods. I enjoyed the quiet solitude of the woods and still climbed to the tops of trees for the view. It took me three months to make my way across the country to the Grand Canyon and I hadn't slept inside a building the whole time. To be honest with you I preferred the solitude of state and national forest campgrounds more than I did the state and National Park ones. The best features and attractions were always in the parks, but so were the crowds. They were often full and when they weren't they were overcrowded, overused, dirty, and noisy. And the parks often charged up to twenty-five dollars a night to camp there, while many of the forests charged under ten, if anything at all. So, I stuck to the woods and avoided the crowds whenever I could. Somehow all of that had brought me to Sharon.

  I drove for about two hours before I started getting groggy and pulled over into a pullout that overlooked the ocean. I covered her with a blanket, grabbed my sleeping bag, locked the doors, and lay down on a flat area not far from the car. I don't know why I did it, but I brought the sword and placed it in my bag with me. It made me feel a little safer, I guess. Sharon had made me nervous. I was asleep in minutes.

  I had been sleeping in the woods for almost five months and I had grown accustomed to the night sounds around me. I no longer awoke to the scampering of a squirrel or chipmunk, but the unmistakable grinding of the human foot had me awake in an instant. I lay still in my bag as I listened as someone slowly circled my car trying to look into the foggy windows. Apparently, they didn't know I was out here. Muffling my sword with my body, I slowly pulled the scabbard down to the bottom of my bag and removed the sword. It felt warm in my hand, kind of like an old friend even though I had only held it once. Then I felt a little silly as I realized that more than likely it was the local ranger or state trooper checking on the car. But he circled the car until he was next to her window and suddenly he raised a club.

"Hey!" I shouted as I sprung up, sword in hand. "What in the hell do you think you're doing to my car?" I ran up to the car. He turned and bellowed at me and I almost shit myself. He was tall, over six feet and on his forehead were two small horns and his legs were hooves. "What the hell are you?" I screamed but instead of answering he raised his club and swung at me.

I dodged his club and swung with my own sword and missed. The club swung around and came right at my head, so I swung at the club with all my might and it cleaved in two. Whatever it was that I was fighting looked almost as surprised as I did.

"Now get on the ground or you'll get it," I said waving the sword in front of him. He looked carefully at the sword, bellowed loudly and charged. I could see a dagger in his hand as he charged at me, so I rammed the sword into his gut. I figured that would stop him, but he kept swinging his blade at me as the blade went deeper. So, I pulled the blade out and took a step back and swung at his blade arm with the sword. Only I swung high and I accidentally decapitated the beastly fellow. Then he stopped! My blade was covered with thick black blood that I wiped first on him and then with some grass before I put it away. I casually retrieved my sleeping bag, rolled it up and put it in the car. I got in the car, started it up and turned the car around. As my headlights swung across the corpse I noticed that the body was slowly fading into mist. Great, I thought!

I was down the road about a mile when I reached in the cooler with a shaking hand and grabbed a cold beer. I took a long drink from it and slowly began to relax. Sharon just sat there biting her thumbnail nervously.

"Why did you stop?" she finally asked in a panic. I reached back, grabbed another beer and handed it to her. She opened it and took a long drink.

"Better?" I asked and she nodded.

"So Quentin, why did you stop?"

"For the same reason you slept the whole trip. I was tired."

"But you left me!" There was just enough panic in her voice to let me know she had been frightened.

"Sorry! I just wanted to stretch out. I had no idea Lucifer was after you."

"After us!" she stated.

"Right. Only to be honest with you Sharon, up until this evening, even though I have been sleeping outside for six months, I've never actually been attacked by anything worse than a hoard of hungry mosquitoes and certainly not a demon full of black blood carrying a club and a knife. Funny how you never own a sword your whole life and the day you buy one you need it! Who'd have thought it?" She laughed at my sarcasm. "Any chance you know what the hell that thing was back there or even better, why it is chasing you or even how the hell it found us?"

"Yes and no. I don't really know what it is, some kind of demon I guess, but I do know why it's chasing us."

"Look Sharon, I think you are the most beautiful woman on earth and I just killed a demon thing back there for you so would please explain to me why I'm driving north at three o'clock in the morning?"

"We have to go see a pot grower!"

"Right, a guy who grows marijuana?"

"Yep, only the guy is a girl whose name is Rikki and she's going to help us."

"Help us do what Sharon?"

"Save the world?"

Of course," I said smugly, "what else? Another beer darling?" I said as I reached back into the cooler.

2

We had breakfast in a small diner on the highway just before dawn. Sharon said that where we were going we wouldn't want to drive up in the dark unless we wanted to get shot. I found that quaintly reassuring. She pointed out that a well-armed place was just what we needed to get a good night's sleep. I was beginning to have doubts about my dream girl.

Rikki was a blond tanned goddess herself as she stood with hands on her hips on the porch of her beautiful log home. Windmills turned behind the house and a rushing stream could be heard behind the house. From all appearances, the place appeared to be a normal ranch, other than a lot of No Trespassing signs around the entrance. Normal that is until she brought out a joint and I smoked the best weed I'd ever smoked in my life. I was completely paralyzed in my chair as Sharon told Rikki about our little camping experience. Her eyes widened and looked at me as Sharon told the story.

When it was over Rikki turned to me, smiled and said, "Thanks for protecting my friend." All I could do was giggle. "Don't worry Quentin; it will ease off in a few minutes. Hungry?"

I nodded. Cheetos sounded really good for some reason! Rikki and Sharon left me sitting there and went to fix some lunch. I sat, stoned to the bone, and tried to contemplate the ridiculousness of my situation.

A few weeks ago I meet, no, I see a beautiful woman on the rim of the Grand Canyon and she apparently writes the number seventeen on my car. Now, only a few weeks later, I'm sitting at a pot farm with the same girl after having killed some ugly demon. With a sword, no less! That's where the whole thing gets a little weird and fuzzy. What the hell was that thing? Its body just dissolved. But I was kind of a badass with that sword! I realized how Dorothy felt when she opened the door of her house to Oz or how Alice felt when she went down the rabbit hole. I was hoping I'd get some answers that I could understand, but secretly I knew that I probably wouldn't be happy with them anyway. Slowly the pot slacked off and I began to breathe again. I took a long drink of water and felt immediately better when Rikki handed me a beer. But the beer only relaxed me and the lack of sleep had me nodding out. Rikki led me to a bedroom where I flopped out and slept like a baby.

I awoke a few hours later feeling tired and groggy. When I looked out the window I saw Sharon in the garden. She was sitting there and it looked as if she were talking to someone. I followed her eyes and saw her talking to a rabbit and damned if that rabbit didn't seem to be paying attention. I went into the bathroom where I noticed Rikki had left me a clean towel and some soap. I was grateful and slowly stripped and laughed when I realized I was still wearing four blades. I wondered if they would be considered concealed weapons. Probably! A long hot shower did me wonders and clean clothes even more. I didn't think twice about re-strapping all four blades back onto me before I dressed though. When I looked back outside, Sharon was gone.

Rikki was puttering around the house when I awoke and informed me that Sharon was showering and would join us shortly.

"So do you know what's going on, Rikki?"

"Kind of sweetie, but I can't say. You'll know everything in a short time. In the meantime, do you want a tour?"

I agreed and she toured me around her large California ranch-style mansion. She walked me into her bedroom and into her walk-in closet. There were dozens of boxes with shoes in them and she opened one and pressed her thumb to a pad. The back of the closet slid open and we were facing a narrow staircase that led down into the dark. She placed her hand on another pad and a light scanned her hand. Only when the flashing red light turned green did we head down the stairs. The closet wall slid quietly back into place behind us as soft lighting came on in the stairwell. At the bottom of the stairs she reached into a box at the bottom of the stairs and handed me a pair of wrap-around sunglasses. Once they were on she placed her hand on another pad and the door swung open and I was amazed at the glare.

I swear I heard a symphonic up swell when I walked into that room as I had a near religious experience! The room itself was half the size of the house and filled with lights but what caught my attention were the rows of plants in various stages of growth. The temperature was in the eighties and the humidity level high. The place reeked of pot. A couple of gray-haired, tie-dyed, hippie throwbacks trimmed the leaves of the plants around buds the size of a cob of corn. It was a pot smoker's wet dream.

Rikki carefully explained that the floor of the enormous room was at least twenty-five feet beneath the surface. Above the room there was a three foot thick concrete slab, insulated foam, ten feet of dirt and then the house. As I examined the plants up close she gave me the low down. They only kept the female plants she explained as she showed me how they prune them and nurture them until the plants are ready for harvest. She led me to a large hot room called the drying room where cultivated plants hung upside down to dry. Then she took me to another room where the buds were harvested, placed into garbage bags and the bags weighed.

"So what do you as the grower get?" I asked Rikki.

"Depending on the buds, the market, competition and the feds, I can get from anywhere from two to four thousand a pound. I get a pound for about every ten plants once it's dried and trimmed and harvest about a hundred plants a week." Twenty to forty grand a week sounded pretty slick to me.

"Aren't you afraid of getting busted?"

"Of course, but we've taken a lot of precautions. Besides being deep underground to hide our heat imprint we're covered by the house and all venting is done through the barn. It keeps the animals warm in the winter and their smell masks the pot smell. We also supply all of our own power through water and wind turbines, solar panels, and even solar shingles on the roof so we barely appear on the grid. The harvested weed is taken by tunnel to the barn where it is taken to the city once a week by a close friend. I deal with one guy who pays on time and I've known him for years and he only deals with a few people. No money changes hands and once a month a deposit is made into an account I keep in the Caymans for consulting fees. We've been doing it for over ten years."

"How did you get into this business?" I asked curiously.

"I was raised around here. Before I was born my parents started growing pot in their backyard long before the feds started using helicopters. When they did in the early eighties my dad became a pioneer in using hydroponics for pot and growing indoors. He was always one step ahead of the law mostly because his cousin was a cop and notified him whenever people started sniffing around. By the time I was born it was the Reagan era and dad was an outlaw pot grower. Mom died shortly after my birth and my dad raised me. While most kids were mowing the lawn, I was clipping leaves and trimming buds. My dad built this place in the nineties and left it to me when he died in two thousand. I added the turbines and solar stuff to keep the feds off my back. So far, so good," she said as she knocked on wood. "Of course if the feds did try to break-in they'd be in for a big surprise!"

"Why?"

"Long before dad was a pot grower he was in Vietnam in a Special Forces unit in the early seventies. He was kind of messed up when he got home but he had made a lot of friends over there and a few of them were able to get him whatever he needed. If the feds raid this place and try to get past our security, the whole place is rigged to blow. That's if they make it up the hill. But I wouldn't try to sneak onto this property. God knows what you'll find out there!" She smiled and winked. Good to know!

Sharon was waiting for us when we returned. "So Quentin did you like the tour."

"It changed my life," I smiled.

"Good, just don't smoke anymore! You need a clear head."

"Hey, I was tired, for Christ's sake."

"Nonetheless. Now Rikki, we need to buy a pound of your finest. Quentin, pay the lady."

"First you tell me not to smoke it and then you want me to buy a pound?"

"It's not for us, silly, it's an offering."

"For who?" I asked stunned.

"The Hermit!" she said as if I was stupid.

"Right," I said, "the Hermit, of course. And the Hermit doesn't take cash, only the finest weed Humboldt County has to offer. And he doesn't need an ounce of it; he needs a whole pound, of course!"

"Now you're getting the hang of things, Quentin," Rikki smiled. I still felt like Alice down the rabbit hole as I handed her four grand and she handed Sharon a gallon-sized Ziploc baggie of giant purple buds. She also slipped a full sandwich baggie into my jacket pocket and winked. "Now Sharon, do you need anything else?" Sharon nodded. "After your story I thought so. Come on."

We returned to her bedroom and walked down the long stairs. At the bottom, instead of entering the door to the greenhouse, Rikki opened another panel and the rock to our left slid away revealing a dark passage. The lights came on when the rock slid shut and we came upon a new door that she opened with her palm print. When the door slid open, I was amazed at the sight. It was a weapons depot. The storeroom was lined with racks and crates and there was almost every kind of gun imaginable. "Oh Quentin, did I mention daddy also liked guns." Rikki laughed.

It was an understatement. The large room held racks of automatic weapons, rifles, crates of handguns and hand grenades, and enough ammo to start your own war. It was truly impressive and frightening all at once. I wandered around the room staring at the variety of guns as the ladies went to work. Rikki provided a long canvas duffle bag that Sharon proceeded to fill with a variety of weapons. Rikki produced and packed into the bag boxes of ammo for each gun Sharon selected. I was amused as Rikki explained the various weapons to Sharon like an appliance salesman at the local Sears. I saw handguns, shotguns, rifles, machine pistols, Uzi's and even a dozen grenades go into the bag along with dozens of extra clips and ammo. Before last night I couldn't imagine a world where I would need a gun. Now, they didn't seem all that unappealing.

When the bag was loaded they dragged me into the next room which was a padded lounge overlooking a long indoor gun range. Sharon placed the bag on a table and carefully removed each weapon while Rikki sorted ammunition and clips. I watched in fascination as Rikki carefully loaded clips and Sharon locked the clips into place. Rikki handed us each a pair of headphones and then Sharon was happily blasting away at targets. Who was this woman shooting targets with a bloody Uzi and what the hell was I doing here? But then she let me fire it, giving me instructions as we went. I had to admit it was kind of fun. I spent the next six hours learning to load, fire, and clean every weapon in the bag. I felt like freaking Rambo!

After we had cleaned all the weapons, we carefully reloaded all the clips as well as all the extra clips Rikki had provided. She even taped some of the larger clips together like they do in the movies. Rikki was as comfortable around guns as she was around her pot farm. Me, I was terrified and excited all at once. I was much too reckless as a youth to be trusted with guns and my parents didn't like them anyway, so up until that afternoon my only experience shooting a gun was at Boy Scout Camp where we shot twenty-twos. But the difference between a twenty-two and an Uzi is like the difference between a rowboat and a jet boat! While I still wasn't sure if I could actually aim at a living creature, I loved shooting up the targets and it turned out I was a pretty good shot once I got used to the weapons.

Rikki carefully reloaded the bag, replaced the ammo we had used up, and added an extra metal ammo box with additional boxes of ammo. As we were hauling everything up to her room I casually turned to Rikki and asked her, "So Rikki, how many years will I get if we get caught carrying this much hardware and a pound of weed?"

"You have hand grenades, Quentin. I wouldn't really worry about the weed at all. As too how many years, well, let's just say you might as well go down shooting." She laughed. "Besides, the cops are the least of your worries." That wasn't exactly reassuring to me. The total for our new arsenal and the pot was close to twelve thousand. Since she didn't take travelers checks I gave her cash for the balance. If we kept spending money like this, I was going to have to cash some traveler's checks.

Over dinner, Rikki asked me how I got there. "I don't really know. I was at the Grand Canyon and saw this beautiful woman I desperately wanted to meet but didn't really know what to say to her. Later when I came back from my day of staring into the void, I saw her writing something in the dust on my windshield. It was the number seventeen. Ever since then that woman has been in my dreams. I went to Vegas and ended up playing number seventeen on the roulette wheel and won about fifty grand. After a month in Yosemite, I came to the beach and wandered to Marin where I found a bizarre Renaissance fair, drank too much, and passed out. I'm hoping to wake up at any time now because if I'm not dreaming, well then I'm on the run with Patty Hearst, I killed a demon with a sword, and am now armed like Neo in the Matrix. And as all of this is happening I have absolutely no idea why. But you know what the most amazing thing is Rikki? I'm doing it all because I'm so pathetically lonely that I'll chase the barest glimpse of a beautiful woman halfway across the country and slay a demon, just so I can talk to her." I slumped back in my chair and held my head in my hands.

"Look Quentin, you made her blush!" Rikki said. I looked over and Sharon looked down and Rikki was right. "Well boy, you're here, she's here, so talk."

"Yes, uh, right, um...I'm sorry. It's just that in most of my previous dreams this conversation doesn't actually take place after an afternoon of munitions training. Anyway, I'm Quentin, although the fact that you knew that before I met you bothers me immensely. I am strongly attracted to you despite your fearful hobbies of knives, swords and guns. Since until last night I haven't been attacked by anything worse than my older brother and a jealous juvenile delinquent, I'm going to assume that whatever I killed last night was after you. I just wanted you to know that whatever happens, I'm by your side, but I don't rob banks." They both laughed.

"Thanks Quentin, that's sweet. I didn't ask for any of this any more than you did. I'm sorry for dragging you into it, but I really didn't have any choice."

"So I'm here on purpose?" I asked even more surprised.

"Yes. It was me at the Grand Canyon?"

"But why me? How did you know me?"

"I didn't, I knew your car."

"My car?"

"Yes, I knew that I had to be at that place at that time and that at exactly 4:30pm Pacific Time I would look at my watch and write seventeen on your window. I didn't actually know why I did it, but I knew that I if I didn't do it I would die. So I went and followed my vision. It all came true."

"What about the dealer in Vegas and the Park ranger in Yosemite?"

"Not me, but the suggestion that was planted when you saw me and saw the number seventeen had you looking for me. Since then I have visited you occasionally in your dreams to hurry you here."

"You were in my dreams?"

"Only a few of them."

"Which ones?"

"The ones where I'm dressed!" she said teasingly and this time I blushed. "Rikki can you help me, this is hard? Rikki was the one who helped me understand."

"Understand what?" I asked.

"Quentin, what do you know about the Goddess?" Rikki asked.

"That in every major religion there is a goddess figure, like the Virgin Mary in Christianity and Isis in Egyptian lore. Unless you're specifically referring to the Goddess in the Druid lore in which case not much is actually known about that since not much that was written back then survived."

"Well you're right on all accounts. The goddess was there in druid times and she was also Isis, the Virgin Mary, and a dozen other women throughout the years. She appears throughout history whenever the need arises. And whenever the Goddess arises she finds a woman to channel her work through. Sharon is the vessel of the goddess and is the Goddess on earth. She is also Sharon. The Goddess shares her wisdom, but she also tells her to do things but doesn't tell her why. The Goddess told her to write seventeen on your window but she didn't know until later that it would bring you here."

"Last month the Goddess told me where I would find you and that if I didn't I would die. You saw us buy those weapons last night, but she actually chose the blades, not me. She said you would be tested, but I had no idea what that thing that attacked us was or why it really attacked. I also saw that I would come here and that we would go to see the Hermit. If we survive, he will show us our path."

"Survive?"

"Yeah, well my visions aren't always complete. Sometimes I can see the outcome, but sometimes I think the outcome is going to be up to us. Like that thing that attacked us. You killed it so we get to go to the next step."

And if you die?"

"I guess the Goddess would have to find a new channel, but that would give the enemy time."

"Yeah, about that, who is the enemy?"

"The goddess has come to Earth many times to fight and usually the same type of foe, someone who doesn't belong here. The creature that attacked us was some sort of dark demon called from the depths. Apparently such things have simply not been seen on earth in a long time, so the Goddess fears our enemy is waking the old dark spirits. She says the Hermit will know for sure."

"Great. Say, did I see you talking to a rabbit and it seemed to be listening?"

"You saw that? Oh well, yes as the Goddess I was negotiating with the rabbits."

"Negotiating? What did they kidnap someone?" I joked.

"No silly, they've been helping themselves to Rikki's garden."

"Pesky little critters." Rikki added. "Dad used to trap and skin them but that's not my style. Still, they've been cleaning me out."

"Yes, so I negotiated with the rabbits who agreed to leave the crops alone if Rikki left them something as a replacement. A rabbit has to eat!" Sharon said and I laughed.

"Sounds logical. So if you're the Goddess, then who am I?"

"Quentin, whenever the goddess appears she always has a champion to advance her cause and protect her. You are the goddess' champion." I looked at them both like they were crazy. I mean, I'm five ten on my tippy toes, only weigh about a hundred and sixty pounds, okay seventy, and have no specific skills that would make me a good choice. Rikki must have noticed the look on my face.

"Don't worry Quentin, nobody made a mistake. Last night when you killed the demon you proved that you were the hero. Sharon said you handled the sword like a pro. And you just learned how to strip, clean, assemble, load, and fire a dozen different weapons in only six hours. But I bet if I handed you any one of those weapons you could field strip it in a second. No one is born with hero skills but they are always quick learners. Just like Sharon has come to accept and follow her visions, you will learn to accept and use your unique skills that you will continue to develop."

"So what's this dark force and why the hell is it in California? What could require the return of the Goddess?"

"Hopefully the Hermit will tell us!" Sharon grimaced.

"And if he doesn't?"

"We'll probably be dead." She stated rather matter-of-factly.

"Jesus Sharon, does everything always have to end up in death with you?"

"Sadly, Quentin, it's always seems to be one of the options." She said quietly

"Yeah, well so is they lived happily ever after!" I said and Rikki laughed.

Later, when alone with Rikki, I asked her a private question. "Rikki, does the hero ever get the girl?"

"Sometimes, if he lives."

"I get the feeling I'm a pretty big disappointment to Sharon. I mean I can see why and all."

"Don't worry about it kid! We all have our allusions. I'm sure you're a little disappointed in Sharon now that you've met her."

"Not really, Rikki. I don't know what it is about her, but I'd do anything for her just to catch her eye. There's something about her. When I look into her eyes I see a depth that is filled with love and understanding. I don't know if it's Sharon or the goddess or both but I sense a great capacity for love and that is even more attractive to me than her beauty. "

"Wow, she's a lucky girl. Look blue-eyes, I'll make you a deal. If when this whole thing is over you're alive and she won't give you the time of day, you come back and see

Rikki! You are a hopeless romantic and I've got a real soft spot in my heart for selfless people. If she doesn't appreciate you then you come back to someone who will!"

"Thanks Rikki, but can we stop ending every sentence with 'if I live!'"

"Sorry!

Before settling down we carefully packed our car with our new munitions. I pointed out to Sharon that the felonies were piling up, but she didn't seem to mind and every time she smiled my heart melted. But I had to do something about the weapons. With the car loaded down as it was there was a good chance we'd go to jail before anything had a chance to kill us. So I made a call to Frankie Rollins. Frankie was my buddy from college who had moved to the Bay Area a year after I got busted to avoid any chance of prosecution. Rikki had cautioned me about saying anything I didn't want overheard on the phone so I was very careful. Frankie, paranoid since birth, was surprised to hear from me, but as we traded stories he warmed up and agreed to meet me the next day for lunch. Sharon was furious.

"Are you kidding me, the world hangs in balance and you want to go drink beers with your fraternity brother? We have to get to the Hermit!"

"Look Sharon, we'll go to the Hermit, but first we make a stop. Now maybe you think you can go waltzing around like it's the middle ages, but if you have any desire to accomplish your mission, then let me work a little of my own magic, okay."

"What's Frankie going to do for us?"

"Frankie has one great skill. He can make illegal things legal."

"How?"

"By creating plausible paperwork. Who are you?"

"Um, Sharon Falstaff."

"But I only know that because that's what you've said. If you said your name is Gladys Peabody and you had a driver's license, social security card and birth certificate that said that, well then who would know? Have you ever had your fingerprints taken?"

"Me? No!"

"Good, that means your prints aren't on record. Mine were, but I got them removed when they dropped the charges on me. So as far as the cops are concerned, we are whom our ID's say we are, get it?"

"Not really."

"Don't worry about it, Sharon its brilliant!" Rikki was smiling.

"She gets it!" I said and pointed to her. "To spell it out for you, I'm going to ask Frankie to create two new identities for us and preferably two that will make all our weaponry plausible, like rare weapons and gun collectors or dealers. He can create and provide for us concealed weapons permits, gun permits, business cards, you name it. It won't fool the cops for long, but possibly long enough to make bail and disappear."

"Whatever Quentin, just don't make it take too long."

"Rikki, can I use your computer?" I asked and she led me over to it. I took a picture of each of us and scanned the pictures onto her computer. Then using a password I logged on to a special VPN tunnel that Frankie maintained. Soon we were in contact.

"Um Quentin, I'm not sure that's secure."

"It is the way I logged on, it's encrypted. Now I know you heard what I said on the phone to Frankie, but we have our own language. When I said, 'drink some beers, do some of the things we used to do' he knew this was business. Frankie only drinks scotch and single malt at that. When I said I wanted to buy him a great big steak dinner he knew it was a big cash deal as he is a vegetarian. When I said I wasn't going to be in town long he knew it was a rush job. He was waiting for me when I logged on."

I sent the pictures and then started a list of what I needed. I sent him our weapons list and he freaked so I told him my girlfriend's uncle died and left her all this stuff and she wants to sell it but we need to dummy up some paperwork for it. The keyword was 'dummy up', because that was our code word for please don't ask. We spent a few minutes coming up with a plausible plan and then I signed off. Rikki was impressed.

"So he can do all that overnight?"

"Frankie was one of my only friends when I was in High School and we attended the same college. Frankie was a worse student than I was, but he was a genius at both computers and creating fake ID's for his fellow students. But what nobody else knew, except for me and another close associate, was how good Frankie really was. Not only will he create fake permits, but he'll backdoor them into the system. That clean weapon will have a fake pedigree that will keep them scratching their heads for a long time."

"How?"

"Data is just as real as things are. Insert data and it exists. By tomorrow each of those weapons will have been owned by someone who never knew that they owned them and sold them to a dealer who sold it to another dealer who sold it to us. Each of those people can be traced to an address that they used to live at but had moved from and left no forwarding address. And none of it is real as it will all exist as simply data. But when a cop runs the guns through the system, bingo, it's there and legal."

"You're saying that by tomorrow we will be carrying all this legally?" Sharon asked.

"I don't know about the grenades!" I admitted. "I was a little nervous about telling Frankie about them?"

"Why?" Rikki asked.

"Wrong guy! Frankie was a terror with firecrackers. I can't even imagine him with a grenade and if he heard we had some he would want some for himself. He loves blowing shit up!"

"Nice guy!" Sharon said sarcastically.

"Not one you would willingly turn your back on, but yeah Sharon, he is a nice guy. At least he never cut anyone's head off!" I said a little hurt.

I have to say that a good night's sleep did me wonders and it seemed to renew Sharon as well. She practically glowed as she swept into the kitchen, and it took my breath away. Once again, she was the gorgeous girl at the rim, before the swords, guns and mayhem. I couldn't help but stare. It annoyed her to no end.

"Are you going to stare at me for the rest of our trip?"

"If you always look like that I will."

"I'll have to remember to dress down for you." she said cattily. I shook my head and looked down. She came over and sat next to me, "Look Quentin, can't we just be friends?"

Those five words were like a knife running through me. I had heard them often enough in my life to understand their meaning. It meant she wasn't interested, period. So why was I here? Was I crazy enough over her to risk my life, knowing she would never be interested? My heart lay in tatters as I grimaced and replied, "Sure Sharon, that would be swell!" She seemed annoyed as I turned away and busied myself.

"What's your problem?" she asked.

"Jesus, Sharon," Rikki stepped in, "do you ever actually listen to yourself?"

"What?" She said defensively.

"What? The guy is infatuated with you, saves your life, offers to protect you, and then you say 'can't we just be friends'!"

"Well, I just didn't want him to get the wrong idea!"

"You crack me up! You find a guy willing to risk his life just to talk to you, willing to risk his life to protect you, and follow you on some bizarre quest, and you're looking for something better? Girl, you got real high standards!" Then she walked right up to me and took my hands in hers. "Quentin, I'm serious about what I said. You come back when this is all over, because I do appreciate who you are!" She put her arms around me and kissed me long and hard in ways that I hadn't been kissed in a long time. I was embarrassed that I got hard immediately. After a long kiss she stared into my eyes and then smiled, winked, and let me go. I glanced over to Sharon who stood there with her mouth open.

"Let's go!" I said and walked out. Rikki didn't move as she watched me leave.

As I was walking out the door I heard Rikki say to Sharon, "Take care of him Sharon!" Sharon came out in a bit of a daze.

It was a quiet drive to the city. Frankly my head was spinning. I was extremely attracted to Sharon who hasn't treated me very well. Yet after the taste of Rikki's kiss, I found her much more attractive than I had noticed before and she had always been nice to me. Okay, so she was a serious train wreck waiting to happen with her pot and guns, but for the first time in my life I actually felt like maybe someone liked me for who I was. And knowing that warmed my heart.

Finally Sharon broke the ice. "Sorry."

"For what?"

"For hurting your feelings." She said meekly.

"No problem, it was inevitable. One of the most important lessons you can learn in life and one that I learned early, is that just because you like someone doesn't mean they'll like you. So no matter how much you like someone if they aren't attracted to you you're going to eventually get the 'let's be friends' speech. So don't worry about it. Besides, a lot has changed lately."

"Why, because Rikki kissed you?" she almost sounded jealous.

"Yes and no. Yes, when Rikki kissed me I guess it made me realize that I had some value, that maybe someone saw me for who I really am."

"So now you're not in love with me and you're in love with Rikki?" I could hear something behind her tone.

"Frankly I realized that I really don't know either one of you. Could I wake up and stare at your face every morning for the rest of my life? Yes Sharon, I could but not if that face is going to ridicule me and be nasty to me. I doubt if Rikki's offer was anything more than a confidence booster for me but she was warm and caring and I could wake up to that for the rest of my life as well."

"I can be warm and caring." She said meekly.

"Good for you." I spit out before thinking about what she said.

"You don't even know me. This isn't who I am! I've just been stressed with this whole goddess thing."

"You don't have to apologize for your feelings, Sharon. It's just I've been down this road before. Look Goddess, I'm your guy. I'll do my best to protect you and keep you alive because I believe you and because Rikki believes in me. But I also understand that I'm not the guy, not your guy! You may have been the girl of my dreams but I am not the man of yours and its okay; maybe in the next life. So let's get some new papers, go see the Hermit, kick some Nubian ass, and get on with our lives."

"It sounds like you've been hurt before." She said quietly.

"Only because I was foolish enough to care about someone."

"Why do you say that?"

"Sharon, you're a beautiful woman and even though I don't know you I can guess that you've rejected a lot more boys than have rejected you and more than likely you always had a few in the wings waiting for a chance. My whole life has been a rejection. Of the four of us kids, I was the one who was always never good enough. All through school they praised me for getting 'C's because I passed and do you know what I found out when I graduated?"

"What?"

"That I'm a fucking genius! My IQ is a hundred and sixty-six, I tested in the top one percent in the country and nobody ever fucking told me. Instead they said I was doing the best I could! Why?"

"Because I wasn't good enough! You know what, when enough people tell you you're not good enough you start to believe them, so I got in my car and left home forever. So when I hear a girl say 'can't we just be friends' all I'm hearing is that I'm not good enough! Well you know what my one wish in this world is?"

"No?"

"To meet someone who actually thinks I am good enough! Rikki is the first person who ever treated me that way and it felt good!" It was silent the rest of the way to the city.

Sharon was in a funk and was angry at, well, everything. For the last year she had been blessed with the presence of the goddess and had been led on quite a journey. But sometimes that blessing was a curse! When the Goddess told her that she would be meeting the champion she had anticipated some Herculean hunk torn right off the page of a calendar. When the Goddess pointed the Champion out to her she looked over and saw a boy lying on the ground on one elbow with a stupid drunk look on his face. Surprised and perhaps a little disappointed was her reaction at the time. Then the Goddess told her that if she didn't get the Champion armed and out of the park by midnight they would all die. Sharon had never faced death before and the seriousness of the Goddess' warning had her terrified to her core. But the Goddess was also an anchor for her and she was able to get the boy moving.

Okay, she had to admit to herself, it was kind of fun watching Quentin squirm as she revealed that she had written seventeen on his car window but nothing she saw in him gave her any relief from her own nightmarish fears. The goddess was firmly in control as she led the boy to get themselves armed which was good because she was so far out of her own bailiwick that it seemed surreal. She had trained with both swords and knives in the last year but wearing them as well as needing them was new to her. As she watched the boy drag the bag she began to wonder about her 'protector'. In disgust she helped him carry the bag back to camp and helped arm him. He was practically hopeless. Until of course she awoke to him yelling at something right outside the window. The Goddess was screaming a warning and she was terrified and maybe a little impressed as Quentin killed the Demon in short order. Suddenly she wasn't quite as scared as she had been earlier.

Being told your pretty or beautiful occasionally can warm a girl's heart, Sharon thought, and it was nice to be appreciated but Quentin's constant mentioning of it but also annoyed her. In her politically correct post-feminist view it reduced her to being just that and nothing more and she was much more. She was distrustful of the idea of love at first sight because she believed that love was and should be deeper than just physical attraction. While attraction is important, so is how they think and feel and in the end that becomes even more important. Besides, they had a job to do and she remembered the goddess' warning.

'Sharon, when a young lady such as you meets the Champion there is a natural tendency to fall for the guy which I would advise against.'

'Why?' Sharon asked. It was weird holding conversations in her head but it was one of the many things she had grown used to over the last year.

'He is your protector and that means that you cannot allow your judgment to be compromised by personal feelings. The time may come when you have to send him to his death in order for us to succeed and the less attachment you have the better off you'll be.'

All this talk of death bothered Sharon but taking the advice she held Quentin off at every approach. She didn't want to give him the wrong idea and so she gave him the 'let's be friends' speech. She didn't think he'd take it so hard though? What was up with that? And what was Rikki playing at? She had to admit to herself that she felt at least a tiny bit jealous when she kissed Quentin and had no idea where that was coming from. Quentin was right though; they really didn't know each other that well. He acted like she was some experienced lover when the truth was she hadn't had very much luck in that department. Despite Quentin's belief, there was never a line of suitors waiting to court her. She had boyfriends but nothing serious. Glancing over at the boy who was lost in his own thoughts she thought that she really didn't know this strange boy and maybe she should take the time to change that.

We met Frankie at a coffee shop and went for a long walk in a local park. Once in the park he frisked us and scanned us to make sure we weren't wired. Then he handed me a briefcase.

"Look 'Q', let's make this quick. This is the scariest thing I've ever done."

"I know, buddy, thanks." I handed him ten grand in an envelope. Then he pulled me aside.

"Look man, I don't know what you've gotten yourself into, but if you want out I can help. You're dealing with some pretty scary stuff."

"Remember when we used to play Dungeons and Dragons?"

"Shit yeah, best fun I've ever had!"

"Well somehow I'm caught up in the real thing." I lifted my sleeves and showed him the knives. "All I know is that I have to protect this woman and something very dark and evil is trying to kill her."

"Now you're bullshitting me!"

"I know it sounds farfetched, but like thirty some hours ago this six foot thing with goat legs and horns attacked us with a club and a knife. So I cut its fucking head off with a sword and it disappeared into a mist! So I don't know what I've gotten into, but you can see why having a little firepower might not be a bad thing."

"Jesus Q, a mist? What was it, a demon or something?"

"All I know is when you cut its head off it disappears into mist and it scared the piss out of me."

"Well, I was going to offer to help, but I think I'll pass. Good luck!" He shook my hand.

"Thanks Frankie, it was good to see you!" He turned back to Sharon.

"Ya know, sweetheart, you're lucky you found this guy. He don't look like much, but he's been through a lot and he's strong inside. He had the opportunity to give me up to the cops to save his ass but he was ready to go to prison and ruin his life to protect his friend. You may not approve, but that's loyalty and in my book he's a stand up guy. You're lucky to have him on your side. Later 'Q'!" and he was gone.

"Q?"

"We watched a lot of James Bond movies in high school."

I dragged the bag back to the car and quickly drove out of the city. Stopping in a rest area I opened the case and reviewed and sorted the papers. Thirty minutes later our actual IDs were hidden and we each had a new identity as well as concealed weapons permits. The rest of the bills of sale and permits I left in the case. We packed it in the back seat and headed west.

"So what's the deal with this Goddess thing, Sharon?"

"Huh?"

"How does it work? Does she talk to you in the shower?" I asked and she laughed at that.

"Sometimes! She came about a year ago and I thought I was nuts. She explained who she is and then she started teaching me some cool things. I found that I knew things I didn't know I knew. Like shooting! I never shot a gun in my life before I first visited Rikki last winter but could hit the bull's-eye every time. With a bow and arrow as well even though I'd never pulled a bowstring before. Her memories string back to the beginning of time and she has the knowledge to do everything from fight with swords to make plants grow and what she knows I know. If she shares it with me, that is."

"It's possible," she continued, "that she could very well know exactly what's going on and not tell us. Sometimes she asks me to do things and I don't know why I'm doing them and I don't always get all of the vision. Like only after I wrote the number on your car could I see your face."

"So how do you know when it's coming from the Goddess and not just your own thoughts?"

"It's this warm feeling inside and then she talks. God, at first I thought I was crazy."

"You said Rikki helped you. So besides being an outlaw what's her connection to this?"

"She's actually a Druid Priestess. That Renaissance Fair looked like fun and games but some people use it as a cover for their organization."

"Are you a member?"

"I wasn't."

"Boy, I bet that pissed them off!"

"What?"

"Here they keep a tradition alive for like a thousand years and the Goddess chooses an outsider."

"God, you're probably right." She laughed.

"So why did the goddess choose you?" I asked. She looked at me and then looked forward.

"That's one of the things she hasn't told me!"

We took I-80 east into the foothills and turned north at Auburn. Slowly we climbed into the mountains. Every once in a while she would tell me to turn here or there and I did as requested. The shadows began to grow as the early evening sun started to dip below the horizon. Every time we went into a shadow she got nervous and looked around and only relaxed when we came back into the sun.

Sharon enjoyed talking to Quentin and had been impressed with the whole Frankie experience. While it seemed stupid at first she had to admit that she was a bit relieved to have 'legal' paperwork for all of their weapons. The fact that Quentin even knew somebody who could make that happen made him seem a little more mysterious and even dangerous. As they talked she found him to be smart and witty and he had a great sense of humor. But in the back of her mind she reminded herself they were supposed to be a team and not a couple.

When Quentin asked why the Goddess chose her she didn't have an answer mostly because she hadn't ever been given one despite asking the question herself many times. She was a normal girl growing up but not exceptional. She always had a circle of friends and a best friend who she shared her thoughts and feelings with. Rhonda Simmons was her best friend in grade school. They slept at each other's houses almost every weekend all the way through middle school until one day in high school she caught her boyfriend making out with Rhonda. She felt terrible and betrayed as it ended the relationship with her boyfriend and her friendship with Rhonda. Stripped of her confidence and bitter from the betrayal she had a hard time dealing with the jealousy and insecurity it brought on.

So she joined the track team and ran from her troubles. She dated off and on but nothing serious and nothing even that interesting. When the Goddess came it was a wonderful addition to what had been a boring life. The Goddess began teaching her about healing and nature and she loved everything she was learning. Even more she felt like she was doing something important and felt needed and that helped her confidence. She only wished she had been told everything.

She hated it when things just happened, like how she suddenly knows there's a good chance they might die. 'Oh Shit!' She thought.

"We're not going to make it!" She said in a near panic.

"We'll be fine, Sharon. How far do we have to go?" I said

"I don't know!" she was shaking.

"Sharon," I spoke in a very soothing and calm voice. "Please listen to me. Close your eyes and concentrate, how far do we have to go?"

"A few more miles."

"And where is the danger, behind us or in front of us!"

"In front of us!" Now she was panicked.

"You're doing great sweetie, now can you sense what were up against."

"They are gathering!" She said I slowed down and stopped. "What are you doing?" she screamed.

"Relax." I got out and opened the trunk and brought the weapons bags into the back seat of the car.

"Can you drive?" I asked as I opened the bags and began to remove weapons and clips.

"Yes. What are you going to do?"

"I'm working on it Sharon. Tell me everything you can about what's ahead."

"All I know is it's a test before we can reach the Hermit."

"I understand, but do I need swords or guns?"

She closed her eyes for a while and then spoke. "The Goddess says you're going to need both!"

"Great." I said and she looked really scared. "Don't worry Sharon, I told you, I'm great on tests!" she laughed. I carefully had guns and ammo stashed and strapped everywhere and my sword was handy. I dug around my stuff for some rock climbing gear I had bought in Yosemite and clipped a couple of slings around the doorposts and then clipped them to my swami belt, which I wrapped around my waist. I tested it and found that with my feet braced against the seat and leaning against the slings, I could lean pretty far out the window without using my hands to hold on. But the window scraped my ribcage so I put my pillow there to cushion it. Sharon laughed.

I checked my Uzi as she started easing the car forward. She had a machine pistol in her lap and the car was loaded with weapons. Both of our attentions were focused forward. "We're getting close. The gate is only a few hundred feet past where they are gathered," she announced.

"Okay, Sharon, here's the plan. When we get there you go for the gate. I break us through, but whatever you do or whatever happens, don't stop. Just listen to my instructions and I'll get you through! Okay?"

"Yes. It's just ahead!" My heart was racing!

"Here goes!" I said as I braced myself and leaned out the window.

We came over a small rise and she suddenly stopped the car. I looked through a pair of field glasses Rikki had thrown in and could see that a car was blocking the narrow road ahead. Behind the car I could see four humans with guns, but closer inspection showed them to have a possessed look on their faces. Three of the ugliest things I've ever seen in my life were standing right behind them. Two were over six feet tall and the third one was shorter but thick. One was just like my friend from the other night and he carried a spiked club and knife. The second one was just as tall but had the head of a panther and he carried a short sword. The last one was about my height but looked like he weighed over two hundred and fifty pounds, all muscle! He had a vultures head and carried a sword and a small mace.

"The three in the back need sword action." Sharon said.

"Got it! I reached into the bag and produced a few additional swords and knives. The boys behind the car let out a volley at us but their bullets fell far short. I was terrified, but was thinking clearly as I marked the distance their bullets traveled before they hit the road. I felt the wind and looked at the setting sun. Then I took a moment and thanked the Great Spirit for my life. "Ready!" I said as I leaned out the window.

Sharon gunned the car and the wheels spun in the dirt as the car lurched forward. I kept my eye on the spot where the bullets landed and held my fire until I got past there. "Stay left!" I shouted and she swerved to the left side. I now had a clear line of sight and she was better protected. They opened fire long before we were close enough and their bullets danced in the dust in front of us. As soon as I reached the spot I had been watching I carefully unloaded a clip aiming just above the door line of the car. I saw one guy spin and fall as the others dove for cover. I popped and reversed the clip and emptied it right at the gas tank of the car. The gas tank ruptured and exploded and the car lurched three feet to the right. Sharon gunned it and aimed for the gap between the car and the trees. I picked up the other Uzi and let loose with a volley at the back of the car. At least one of the men was burning and the other two were down on the ground.

I aimed at the beasts and didn't seem to have an effect as they were lumbering to fill the gap. So I dropped the gun and grabbed my swords. As I was pulling the swords from their sheaths one of them must have brushed the slings and when I leaned back out the window the sling gave way and I fell out of the car just as we approached the monsters. Luckily for me I hit one of them at forty miles an hour to cushion my fall. Sharon jammed on the brakes to stop, so I rolled off of the groaning demon and shouted, "Go!" and the car took off. Then I turned to meet my fate.

I guess it was lucky that I ran over goat boy, because the panther and vulture wanted my ass bad. At first I came out swinging like a champ, but I quickly found myself doing a lot more parrying than thrusting. I had two swords, one in each hand, and that made it possible to do two things at once. I was consumed with the idea of staying alive so I carefully blocked their attempts and waited for opportunities. One came when Panther guy swung and I ducked and he went sailing past me. Vulture boy was surprised and was even more so when I came up sweeping my sword upwards and neatly removed his head. I was turning to face panther boy who was charging when I felt wind near my ear. I ducked quickly and felt the first guy, now recovered from being hit by me, swing his club where my head used to be. I swung up and around and removed his head as well.

Then it was on. Panther boy could sword fight and I was cut and bleeding in a dozen places where he touched me. With a quick move he flicked my left hand sword away and I was down to one sword. We were facing off when I heard a shot ring out and a sharp pain in my right thigh collapsed my leg. I fell and rolled, pulling my 9mm out of its shoulder harness and fired at the motion behind me. I fired three times and the first hit him in the forehead. The other two were superfluous! I swung around and emptied the other twelve shots right at Panther boy who wasn't injured, but was pushed back by the shots. That gave me enough time to pick up my sword and stand up.

That was about all I could do. I could feel wet blood all over my body and I was weak and tired. My arms were leaden and sore. I felt like Daniel-San in the Karate Kid only I didn't have any swan move. Panther boy moved in. I took in a deep breath, gritted my teeth and then dug as deep as I could for the strength for what was to come. The next few minutes of my life were a blur. I remember it as if it was in slow motion but he came after me time and time again. I parried and ducked, stabbed and swept as the battle raged on. Every move I made was a desperate one to save my own life. I knew if I yielded for a second I would be dead. Tears stung the corners of my eyes and my shoes were sloshing in my own blood. But Panther boy was getting tired and sloppy, so I waited for my chance. It was a long time in coming. My throat was parched and we were alone as sparks flew off of our swords. I reached as deep as I could and swung as he lunged. I realized the tip of my sword would be just short of his throat so I leaned forward and felt the tip of his blade enter my upper left arm. He smiled just as his head rolled off. He fell back and the sword in my shoulder twisted out. I screamed in pain and fell to the ground.

I lay there for a minute and listened to the sounds of the forest I had become so accustomed to. The chirping of the crickets, the deep calls of the owls, and wind in the trees were all music to my ears. But I was dying and when I looked around, I was alone. It didn't bother me, I had been alone most of my life. But having been alone so often I had also learned how to do for myself, so I untied my swami belt and cinched it tight over my leg wound and tied it. The blood seemed to slow down. I cut a sleeve off my shirt, wadded it up and stuffed it into my shoulder wound. It hurt like hell but slowed the flow of blood. Slowly I rolled to my knees and after a few seconds and leaning on my sword, I stood up. I looked around and all of the creatures were gone and it was just me and a burning car. I slowly limped toward the gate.

A pickup came barreling out of the gate and came to a stop next to me. I felt hands catching me and handing me into the truck. I looked up and could see the stars as the truck sped up the road. I like stars I thought and felt really happy. I had done my job and could die in peace! I heard someone shout out, "Hurry, we're losing him!" and felt the pickup fishtail as they gunned it. 'Don't worry, dying's not so hard,' I wanted to say but nothing came out. I was very calm and although in some pain it was fading quickly. I thought of Sharon and smiled and wondered why she didn't come to say goodbye. Well, I thought, I hope her next protector will last a little longer. But I felt pretty good about taking the creatures down with me. Someone jabbed a needle in my arm and I almost laughed. They weren't really trying to save my life were they? Why?

"Stay with me, man!" the guy who jabbed me. I did laugh at that.

"Christ, did he just laugh?" I heard a woman ask.

"Yeah, I think he did!" The arm jabber said.

"Unbelievable!" she said as I smiled, closed my eyes and died.

3

Okay, I didn't say I died completely, just a little bit, really. One moment I'm heading for the white light, the next thing you know old arm jabber is pounding on my chest and everyone's shouting and I'm in a room with bright lights. I was confused but glad that arm jabber stopped pounding on me.

The Hermit lived on private property adjacent to a national forest. The place was one of the most bizarre places I'd ever been to. It was a cross between an armed militia, a historical preservation society, and a hippie commune. Luckily for me one of their members was a retired surgeon and he and another member, who was also a doctor, stitched me up. I had mentioned jokingly to Sharon on the night we met that my blood type was O positive and I would have died if I hadn't as they had no way to type the blood. But they knew their member's blood types and had numerous volunteers for donors. Later they told me I took two and a half pints before I stabilized and that if I hadn't put the belt on my leg I would have bled out before they could've save me. It took them two hours to stitch me up and get my blood pressure steady. Somewhere around the second pint I came to as they were sewing my shoulder. They were using local anesthetic and to be honest it hurt like hell.

It took almost a hundred stitches to sew me up. As soon as the doctors finished, the healers arrived. There were three of them, two women and a man, and they dressed the wounds in herbs, pastes, and mosses. They gave me some tea which I drank and fell right asleep.

I dreamt of Sharon and this time she looked me right in the eye and thanked me. Then she hugged me and I felt electricity pass between us. I wondered if this was my dream or was she visiting me and looked down. She was wearing lingerie so it must have been my dream I said out loud. I was surprised when she whispered, 'Why can't it be both our dreams'. I contemplated that when I distinctly heard 'shut up and just enjoy it' as Rikki called out from the corner.

I awoke from the dream confused and groggy. The healers were gone and I lay in a comfortable bed with white sheets. It looked like a hospital room. Without moving I used my eyes to take inventory. I could see two arms, legs, hands, and feet so I was off to a good start. All of my weapons were gone. The room was quiet and dark and soft forest sounds could be heard coming out of small speakers. I also had an IV running into my hand and noticed a few monitors recording my vital signs. It was true holistic medicine, mixing modern medical techniques with ancient healing ones. I flexed a few muscles and actually felt pretty good and a lot better than I thought I would feel. So I gripped the rails and tried to sit up. Two things happened, I got a little head rush and a young girl who had fallen asleep in a chair next to me almost peed her pants.

"Oh my god!" She said and stood up. "You're awake! You shouldn't be sitting up!" That seemed like a good idea, so

I lay back down. "Here, I'll adjust the bed for you." She pushed a button on the bed and the back of the bed elevated me. "Now just relax, I'll be right back!" Then she was gone.

Now that I was sitting up I looked around the room with a little bit of disappointment when I realized that Sharon wasn't around. I mean when a guy goes and gets himself killed for someone he'd like to know that at least she appreciated it. But then I reminded myself that she's on a mission for the Goddess and I'm just the escort service. I understood the score, but that didn't mean that it didn't sting.

I flexed my arms and my legs and although they were a little stiff, I could still move all right. I leaned forward and didn't get dizzy and realized I had to pee. There was a small bathroom near the door, so I carefully swung my legs around and sat up. So far so good, I thought. But I still had an IV in my hand and the thing was attached to a pole, which was plugged in. So I pulled the plug, grabbed the pole with my hand and dragged it with me into the bathroom. I was very careful not to put any weight on my injured leg and favored it considerably, so I made it to the john and relieved myself. I don't know how long I had been out, but it must have been a long time because I had to pee like a racehorse.

When the young girl returned to the room with one of the healers they were both shocked to find me gone. "Quentin?" one of them called out.

"In here!" I called out as I flushed the toilet. The door flew open and an older woman addressed me.

"You shouldn't be out of bed!"

"I had to pee!"

"Come!" she laughed and led me back to the bed. "Now be careful getting in. If you need to pee, use this." She handed me a plastic bottle.

"Cool, I could use one of these in my car!" They both laughed.

"Well you can't have it, it belongs here!"

"Okay."

"Now stay in bed!"

"Why? I feel pretty good."

"Well if you want to keep feeling good, stay in bed!"

"Okay, I got it, stay in bed. Um, what time is it?"

"Time is unimportant." The younger girl said and smiled. I looked at her incredulously.

"Okay, how long have I been here?"

"Just the right amount of time," she answered. Was she trying to fuck with my head?

"Um, can I ask how long I was asleep?"

"Yes." She smiled and the older woman seemed amused.

""Yes?"

"Yes, you can ask?" she giggled.

"How long was I asleep?" I was losing my patience.

"Just the right amount of time." She said proudly as the older woman agreed.

What the hell was going on I thought. I risked my life for this shit! I couldn't even get a straight answer out of these two. Maybe they were some religious cult that always gave evasive answers or something, but I was done with it. What the hell was I doing here in the first place? She said I had died and that they brought me back to life. I let myself be killed for what, a woman who doesn't even like me? This was a new low for me. And now these two were having fun with me! The hell with this! I sat up and swung my legs around again, grabbed the IV and yanked it out.

"What are you doing?" the older woman screamed.

"I'm leaving! Do you know where my clothes are?"

"You can't leave!"

"Watch me lady."

"But you're not strong enough." I stood up and she stood in front of the door. "Where are you going?" She asked.

"To find a clock, for one thing! Then I'm out of here!"

"But you can't leave!"

"Why, am I a prisoner?"

"No!"

"Good, then I'm leaving."

"It's eleven thirty in the morning and you came here last night." The young girl said and looked frightened. "You were pretty messed up and the doctors and healers worked on you most of the night. You slept about seven hours! Please get back into bed!"

"Too late, I'm up. Where's my car?"

"Why are you leaving?"

"Why am I here is the question? Jesus Christ lady, I almost died last night because I'm in love with a girl who doesn't even like me and I wake up and you two can't answer a simple question. I've got things that I don't know even know what they are trying to kill me and I'm a pacifist, or I was until two days ago. You know what sugar, time may not be important to you but right now, it's kind of important to me, especially since last night I ran out of it and, right now, I'm on borrowed time. And the last thing I have time to do is to play twenty questions!" She was crying.

"Now," I said facing the older woman. "Please get out of my way."

"You're really leaving?" The older woman was crying as well. Listening to two crying women was more than I could take.

"Why is everybody crying? Look, I am so grateful for you all saving my life. I will never forget that and if there is anything I can do to repay that, let me know."

"You could get back into bed, please, for your own good." The older woman said through tears. I wasn't going to win here and I knew it.

"Let's start over. First of all I'm Quentin. Do you have names, because you're not wearing nametags?"

"I'm Miranda and I'm one of the healers. This is Ariana and she's a novice. She didn't mean to offend you. She thought you were reciting the litany of time, it's one of our doctrines."

"One of you doctrines is to annoy people?"

"No, to understand time. She did not answer you incorrectly, only not in the way you expected."

"Yes, yes, there is no past, there is no future, be here now, I read Richard Alpert's book and he stole it from the Buddhists. It's an ancient idea. Can I give you some advice though? Don't use it when a patient awakes already disoriented!"

"I'm sorry!" Ariana said shyly. I walked back and crawled in bed.

"So am I. Look, I shouldn't have overreacted, but you have to understand, I've had a couple of bad days. Now Miranda, what's the program? Whom do I need to clear it with to move around?"

"I am a healer so I can make that decision."

"Yet you won't?"

"You were dead!" she said.

"I figured that, with the bright lights and tunnel and all that, but really, I'm feeling so much better now!" I said and smiled. "I'm just not used to sleeping in beds."

"Why not?" Ariana asked.

"I sleep outside usually, in a tent when it rains."

"Really? For how long?"

"I left about six months ago. A couple of nights in Vegas, last night in Humboldt and tonight are the only times I've slept inside since I left."

"Nice, Quentin. I almost always sleep outside." Ariana said and Miranda smiled.

"Cool!" I said and looked her over. She looked about eighteen but could have been fourteen or twenty-eight. Some girls look like that, but she definitely had a natural beauty about her. Maybe I would stick around, I thought lustily. "So I get it, Miranda, I was injured. So what's it going to take to get up and around? I got a feeling even if I stick it out we're not going to be around long."

"You do seem to be moving well, but you must let us check your wounds and then we can tell you more."

"Great, call in the consultants and get on it. Is Sharon around?"

"Who?"

"You know, the girl I came in with, the Goddess?"

"She is around but we do not know where."

"Find her! I need to talk to her."

"Yes Quentin, I will do as you ask."

"Miranda, I am charged with her care and need to see or receive word from her that she is all right or I am duty bound to find her. Do you understand?"

"Yes, Quentin. We will find her."

"Thank you Miranda." I said and smiled as she left.

"Now Ariana,"

"Yes, Quentin."

"Where are my things?"

"They had to cut your clothes off."

"I understand that, but what about my knives, swords, and guns?"

"They are in safe keeping!"

"They will not be safely kept until they are in my possession, so please find them for me. Do you know where my car is?" I asked.

"Yes, but no one is allowed to get near it according to the Goddess."

"My clothes are in the car!"

"I can get you clothes."

"Well get moving sugar. I want to be dressed when the party starts."

"Okay. Look I'm sorry; it was stupid of me to treat you that way after all you had been through. I was trying to show off and I'm so very sorry."

"No Ariana, it was my fault. You didn't deserve a terrible patient and maybe when you get back you can share some of your ideas with me."

"Okay!" she said and smiled widely. "Let me go find you some clothes and I'll check on those weapons."

"Thanks Ariana." She left and I leaned back in my bed.

"What is your problem?" Sharon said as she entered my room. "You've got this whole place in an uproar! Jesus,

Quentin." I looked at her completely shocked. God, she was beautiful. "Now what do you want?"

"My car keys!" I said calmly.

"Huh?"

"I want my car keys back, please."

"I came all the way over here because you want your car keys? What's wrong with you?"

"My backpack is in the car and my clothes are in my backpack. I would like to get dressed."

"I can get you some clothes."

"Great and fetch my keys when you do."

"Why, are you leaving?"

"That was kind of the plan!"

"That figures, just about the time you start to get interesting and you up and quit."

"You know what my problem is Sharon? Do you know what's wrong with me? Two days ago I met the girl of my dreams and she can't stand me. Last night I was shot, stabbed, cut, kicked and sliced, and for what? For your disdain, ridicule and sarcasm? Do you even know why I asked to see you? Huh?"

"You wanted your keys, so you could leave!"

"You know what, you don't even know me. I just wanted to see you to make sure you got here safely because I promised you I would! I'm so sorry that I disturbed your important and busy life Goddess but the last two days of my life have been pretty disturbing as well! I am glad you're safe!" When I looked up I saw Ariana in the doorway watching with wide eyes. "Hello Ariana, did you bring me some clothes!" She nodded. "Good, then bring them here. Forget about the keys, Sharon. I have a spare set. Just unlock the car and take your shit and I'll be on my way and out of your hair. Then you can go find a champion that you actually give a shit about!" I took the clothes and went into the bathroom.

They were more like pajamas than clothes, with long cotton leggings that tied at the waist and a pullover cotton shirt. I actually groaned as I pulled the shirt over my injured shoulder. I was angry and I didn't like to be angry. But I was hurt more than anything. I tried to breathe deep and relax and remember that it was my fault. It was my thinking that was wrong. I told myself that if I could change my perceptions, I could change the way I felt. I knew she didn't love me so why did I expect her to act that way. I shouldn't have gotten angry with her. I walked back into the room.

"Sharon, I'm sorry, it's not your fault. I have the terrible habit of expecting more from people than they have to give. I'm sorry." She burst into tears and ran out and Ariana looked at me with confusion. Just then Miranda returned with one of the doctors. He looked livid! "Doctor, I'd like to leave." I smiled.

"You're bleeding!" he said with disgust! My shoulder was getting redder by the minute. "Now get in bed, dammit."

"I'd like to leave please."

"Why? What have we done except save your life?" He was right.

"I'm sorry. You're right. It's not your fault I ended up here and you did save my life, although at this moment I don't know why you bothered. But I'm sorry. Miranda, Ariana please forgive me." I climbed back into bed. "Doctor, I promise not to be a pain in the ass anymore. Please let me know as soon as I am cleared to go."

"Why are you in such a hurry to go?" He asked.

I looked out the door where Sharon had left, sighed deeply and said, "Because, I can't think of a reason to stay." Then I closed my eyes and the only time I spoke was to answer questions with a yes or a no. But inside I was empty and sad and all I really wanted to do was cry. Later, when everyone left me alone, I did cry into my pillow.

Ariana refused to leave and spent all evening trying to get me to open up, but I was morose so she just stayed with me no matter how many times I said she could leave. She slept there and around midnight I woke up and as I lay there in the dark watching her sleep I noticed a shadow in the doorway. The light behind the shadow showed in the silhouette that it was a woman. I turned my head to look at her better and she slipped away quickly.

Sharon left the clinic trying to hide her tears and then after a short walk into the woods let her tears flow. It wasn't fair and it wasn't right. Despite Quentin's assertion she did care for him and last night had been a nightmare! She had never been so frightened in her life but the Goddess reassured her that she should trust the Champion and so she focused on driving as best she could. But she was kind of impressed when this scrawny kid from Detroit leaned out of the car shooting an Uzi. When the car exploded and lurched out of their way she was kind of thrilled. But when he jumped out to do battle she was convinced he was crazy. Her first instinct was to stop and help but both Quentin and the Goddess were screaming for her to continue on so she gunned it while watching in her rear view mirror as the boy faced the enemy.

She didn't get to see the battle as she drove up the hill in a panic and learned that help was on the way for the boy. She was worried, as was the Goddess, as this apparently was a life or death test. She felt guilty for bringing Quentin into this when she realized he might not survive. She was there in the clinic waiting for him and had roused the medical staff that was waiting when the injured hero was brought in. Jesus, he was a mess! She was mortified to find out that he had been dead and revived and as they prepped him for surgery the Goddess had her sing a healing blessing that seemed to help. Then she waited in the waiting room for hours as they worked on him. Only after she found out that he'd live did she go to her apartment and sleep.

The next morning she was busy doing her duties as the Goddess when the request to come to Quentin was given to her. She was in a panic as she initially thought that meant that he was dying. Still she was glad to hear he was awake but the Goddess seemed perturbed by the whole interruption. Her panic only deepened when he announced that he was leaving and she realized he might be serious. Despite the Goddess' obvious displeasure she was glad he was alive and she was touched inside when he said that the reason he called for her was to make sure she was all right. But what made her cry was when he said that he expected more from her than she had to give.

It wasn't the first time she'd heard that and it hurt to hear it again. It was something her daddy often said and it was at the core of her being. She loved Daddy with all her heart but nothing she ever did was quite good enough for him. Oh he was loving and caring; only he was also cruel in an unthinking way. He was always there to congratulate and encourage her but was poor at hiding his disappointment by saying things like, "don't worry honey, the four-forty really isn't your race. To him it was the top of the podium or the lead in the play or else there was no reason to bother even trying. It was only after his death that she realized that what he expected didn't matter; it was about what she wanted. When Quentin said what he said it triggered all her emotions because despite how much she hated it when her Daddy said thing like that she missed him terribly!

The next morning I was in a little better mood, but still in a hurry to leave. Ariana left briefly to clean up and returned with a nice hot breakfast. I was starved but was polite enough to share with her.

"Quentin, you said you did it all for the love of a woman. Is Sharon the woman?" I nodded. "You were very harsh on her. She is the Goddess and is under great pressure."

"I understand, you're right, that's why I should leave. This is all a big mistake. I have no business here." I shut up.

"Please don't be that way Quentin! I'm trying to help. You can't leave until you're healed and most of your hurt is on the inside."

"Honey, only time and distance can heal that kind of hurt."

"Or love."

"Yeah, but that's what caused it in the first place!"

"You are very cynical!"

"Some would call me a realist. The difference is in your life experience. My whole life I've been the butt of one long practical joke and last night was the punch line, 'and then he died'!"

"So you're cynical because life has been harsh to you."

"I'm cynical because life is harsh! Because life will make a pretty girl like Sharon become a damn goddess that needs protecting. Because life will make a schmuck like me, who is so pathetic that I'd follow that goddess around and protect her out of my infatuation with her and she doesn't even like me. Really, Ariana, everybody would have been better off if you'd just let me die."

"Self pity as well."

"What is this psychoanalysis?"

"Not really, just two friends talking."

"Okay then; I'm sorry. So why was I harsh on the Goddess?"

"I don't know, but I don't think she's the person you think she is."

"Since I don't know her I can only judge her by her actions."

"But they are not always her actions."

"Huh?"

"Sometimes she's the goddess."

"I get that."

"Well the Goddess is a Goddess, Quentin, she expects more."

"So what are you saying, Ariana? That when Sharon came in and screamed at me it was the Goddess and not Sharon? That the Goddess didn't come to check on me but Sharon really wanted to?"

"Something like that, Quentin."

"So how would I know the difference?"

"You will learn. You are the Goddess' Champion and well chosen in my book. I can't promise that it's true, but it seems that how the Goddess feels about you and how Sharon feels about you don't have to be the same, do they?"

That got me thinking. The Goddess could easily have been perturbed by my little hissy fit. I was her Champion. The

Goddess expected me to fight and die for her. Since I wasn't fit to fight or travel I was wasting her time and until I was ready to go, she had no use for me. "So it was Sharon crying when she left and not the goddess, right?" She nodded. "Shit!"

"So tell me about your favorite camping places?" she said changing the subject. So I did.

After lunch Ariana walked me outside. The small infirmary where I was kept had a half dozen rooms and a large sun porch overlooking the forest. The sun felt good, but all I could see was the tree line a short distance away. But that was better than a small room with four walls. As the sun warmed my body I stretched and flexed what little muscles I had. Considering that I had been dead only about thirty-six hours ago, I felt pretty damn good. But I was restless. I had been sitting around for a day and a half and for me that was next to impossible.

"Where did you learn to fight? Were you in the military?" she asked.

"Me, are you kidding? No, I wasn't in the military!"

Then where did you learn to fight?"

"I didn't."

"I don't understand?"

"I never learned how to fight. Up until a few days ago, the only time I ever shot a gun was when I was eleven in Boy

Scout camp. And the closest I've come to sword fighting was using cardboard wrapping paper tubes with my brother."

"Then how did you do it?"

"Maybe I have anger management issues!" We both laughed at that. "Say, Ariana, where's my stuff?"

"I'll get it." She left and returned a few minutes later with a heavy bag. I took it from her and laid it out and started to remove my stuff. I was glad to see that everything was there, but it needed work. The battle with the three Demons had left nicks in my blades. And the guns that I had used were going to need to be cleaned and oiled.

"Ariana, could you please find Sharon and ask her to come see me when the Goddess is done with her today. I really need some of my own clothes and I also need to hone these blades, so I need my file and stone. Since I am apparently unable to leave this area I was wondering if she could retrieve the rest of my weapons so that I can clean them. You never know when you're going to need them."

"So you are staying?"

"I don't know, Ariana. If you're right and the goddess is in control, I kind of feel like maybe I should stay around if only to protect Sharon from where the Goddess will take her. I get the feeling that she may be just as trapped as I feel."

"I will tell her, Quentin!" she smiled happily and left.

As soon as she went I carefully removed my swords and held them in my hands. They were just heavy enough to give my arms a little workout and I stood up, and walked away from the building so I was clear of obstruction. I removed my shirt so that I could feel the sun, closed my eyes, and slowly began to swing the swords. My left shoulder was still pretty stiff, but my right felt great. For fun I conceived of myself in a large globe and that each of my swords was a paintbrush. Slowly I tried to paint every inch of the inside of the globe with the tip of my swords. It was good exercise and I loosened up quickly. My right leg was still tight, but working the muscles loosened it considerably. I felt very good as the fresh air and exercise invigorated me. So I picked up speed and continued to quicken the pace as I painted my sphere and spun in circles. My swords made noises in the wind as I went faster and faster, crossing the blades, jabbing, thrusting, spinning, turning, and squatting. The beaded sweat flew off of me as the blades moved in a blur. Then I started slowing them down until they were hardly moving. Finally, sweaty and winded, but feeling exhilarated, I ended my workout. Damn, I had no idea if that was any good for me, or for that matter how I did it, but it felt great.

When I turned around, Ariana and Sharon were standing there with wide eyes. I nodded to them, walked to the porch, put my swords down and took a long drink of ice water. There was a towel on the table that I used to dry myself off.

"How did you do that?" Sharon asked.

"Do what?" I asked confused.

"That thing with the swords. That was amazing." She said.

"I don't know. I just felt like loosening up and closed my eyes and moved." I wiped the back of my neck and took another drink of water.

"Let me look at you," Ariana said as she came over and removed the bandage over my shoulder wound.

"What the hell?" She said.

"What?" I said and looked down. There was a big nasty scar, but no bleeding. "I didn't make it bleed again, did I?"

"No, it's healed! I mean it's a lot better than it should be."

"I guess you healers know your job!"

"Yes, but, I've never seen a wound heal this quickly. Let me see your leg." I turned around and she removed the bandage. "Damn! Stay here. I want to show the doctor this." She ran inside.

"I can't even heal right!" I said as I plopped in a chair.

"I'm just glad you're all right. So I guess that means you're leaving then." Sharon asked hesitantly.

"Sharon, am I talking to you or the Goddess."

"Both, in a sense."

"Okay. Look. I'm sorry. I guess I overreacted. The thing is it occurs to me that you may be just as trapped as I am in all this. I was going to leave. Because between you and me, the goddess treats me like shit. I understand that she's a goddess and has a lot on her mind, but I thought, maybe Sharon isn't any happier about this than I am. That's when I realized that I couldn't leave you. You Sharon, not the Goddess! I'll put up with the Goddesses crap, but I'm staying for you, mostly because I'm afraid of where the Goddess might take you. So I'll stand by your side, Sharon, if you'll still have me!"

She threw her arms around me and held me close. "Yes! She whispered. "And thank you for saving my life, twice!" She kissed my cheek. Man I was on fire. Her touch was like a jolt of electricity and her kiss burned my cheek with its touch. But I released her and smiled.

"You're welcome, Sharon." Then I sat down, embarrassed and blushing.

Ariana returned with the doctor who seemed perturbed until he carefully examined the wounds. He shook his head and frequently looked up at me. He prodded the wounds with his fingers and looked confused.

"Well Quentin, you are a remarkable man. Although quite impossible, your wounds have closed completely and I can see no reason to keep you around here. If you'll come in, I'll remove the stitches and you can go. Damnedest thing I've ever seen!" So I went in and had my stitches removed. My wounds had healed so well it actually hurt to remove them. After they were out, I hugged Ariana and thanked all of the doctors. Then Sharon took me to the car. She had things to do so she gave me the keys and left.

Sharon was glad when Ariana came for her as she was unhappy with the way she and Quentin had left things. She had trouble sleeping as his words still stung and the memories of her father haunted her throughout the night. She wandered over to the clinic during a restless period and stood in the door staring at Quentin. She hated that she had disappointed him and wanted to be free to speak the truth so that he wouldn't think bad of her. She assumed he was saying goodbye and she wasn't looking forward to it.

Okay, what the hell, she thought as she watched the young man handle the twin swords. Who is this guy? Glancing at Ariana she noticed the desire in the young girl's eyes and saw enough to wonder if maybe she had some competition for his attention. All in all it was an impressive display. But when the boy expressed his loyalty to her and not to the Goddess she felt like she'd won a prize! She only wished she could find the words to thank him on their long silent walk to his car. But she couldn't.

The car was a mess! Shell casings and spent clips lined the floor and the remains of the slings from the harness were still clipped around the door post. I got in the car, started it, pulled the car into the shade, and popped a CD into the player. It was Pearl Jam, and I turned it up as I went to work. First I took off my cotton clothes Ariana had got for me and slipped on a pair of jeans and a tee shirt. I strapped a blade to my right calf, just in case. I gathered all of the weapons strewn about the car and placed them on a tarp, along with both weapons bags, next to the car. Then I cleaned the car. I looked in the cooler only to find warm beer, but it was better than nothing, so I drank one as I worked. It took a long time to pick up all the shell casings lying around the car, but I worked steadily as I piled them into a garbage bag. I removed the slings and carabineers and inspected them for damage, tossing anything that looked bad. Finally the car started to look normal again.

So I started on the weapons. One by one I carefully stripped, cleaned, oiled, reassembled and reloaded each of the weapons. Once all of the guns were cleaned, loaded and the safeties engaged, I reloaded all of the empty clips and then carefully repacked the bag. When finished with the guns I removed the file and wet stone from the bag and carefully cleaned and sharpened my blades. Despite what they had been through, both blades were still in good shape and in no time I had the nicks removed and they each had a keen edge on them. I put them in their sheaths and stored them in their bags. The sun started going behind the hills and I changed into a long sleeve shirt and jacket as the shadows grew. Then I strapped blades to each of my arms, and jammed a gun and holster into the back of my pants. No sense in not being prepared.

I started up the car and returned it to it's the parking spot I had first found it in. With my house now in order I realized that I was hungry. Only I didn't know where any food was. So I did the next best thing and went into the trunk and ate a granola bar. At least it was food.

To be honest with I felt like a fish out of water. There were other people around, but most of them avoided me as if I was a leper. They were polite, just not particularly helpful. I truly felt alien there and I couldn't figure out why. I had connected with Ariana, but she was a bit evasive when speaking about the commune. I hadn't really met anybody except for a couple of the healers, so I couldn't tell you much about where I was. I saw a number of different people but had no idea how many lived in the community. All I knew is that the white building away from the others was their clinic where I had healed. My car was parked in a small lot where a couple dozen old vans, cars and pickups were kept along with a purple school bus. There were a number of buildings clustered between the clinic and the lot, but I had no idea what any of them were used for. Behind the buildings was a very large garden and beyond the parking lot was a series of barns. I could see a few horses and cows in corrals between them.

Most of the people were wearing the same cotton clothes that Ariana had given me and I felt like I was on an ashram in India or something. Nobody moved too quickly and everybody seemed overly calm considering what had happened on their doorstep just two nights ago. That was a bit worrisome to me. But truthfully, I really knew nothing about them. After Ariana's little 'Time' snafu she was very careful about discussing anything about their doctrine with me, no matter how much I prodded. So I guess I felt like an uninvited guest. I could smell food cooking and it was making my mouth water, but as of yet, no one had invited me or for that matter, told me where dinner would be served.

So I went to my glove compartment, removed the baggie Rikki had given me and rolled a nice fat joint. Lying on the hood of my car with my back against the windshield I took my time smoking the pot. The effect was not as dramatic as the first time I smoked it, but I relaxed considerably.

"Mind if I hit that?" I looked over and a large very tan man with long hair and a scraggly beard wearing army fatigues reached over. I handed it to him and he hit it long and hard. I waved it off when he tried to hand it back. He took a couple hits before stubbing the roach out on his watch.

"I'm Jake Robbins, head of security around here. That was some damn good fighting the other night sir!"

"Thanks! Call me Quentin."

"I heard it was only the second time you ever fought Demons!"

"Yeah, I'm kind of new to the trade."

"Where you train?"

"I didn't."

"Impressive!"

"Thanks!"

"If there's anything you need, let me know."

"Um, is there a diner or a grocery store or something? I could use a good meal."

"No sweat partner, it's almost dinnertime. C'mon Quentin, follow me."

"Thanks Jake!" I happened to notice that Jake was armed as well. "So you fight Demons often?"

"Me, nah, not really. Truth is, Quentin, the real bad stuff can't get in this place. So they pile up out front and try to pick us off when we come or go. But they're only really effective at night so we mostly travel by day. We keep sentries posted, but can't shoot beyond the fence line or we risk breaking the protection wards. So we watch them and they watch us. Every once in a while one of them forgets and tests the boundaries and gets fried like a fly in a bug zapper, but for the most part it's a standoff. Or was! That part changed after you came through! Nice work by the way!"

"You saw it?"

"Everybody saw it! Our surveillance cameras caught most of it on tape, but most of the camp was either watching the monitors as it happened or were with us down by the fence!"

"You were there?" I asked incredulously.

"Sure, Quentin, we all were."

"Thanks for the help!" I said sarcastically.

"Sorry man, we couldn't help. First off, we couldn't shoot from the fence or we'd have destroyed the protective wards. Secondly, I wanted to lead a charge to help you, but the Hermit sent down word that this was your fight."

"The Hermit, eh?"

"Don't judge him too harshly, Quentin. He sees things that the rest of us don't. If he said it was your fight, it was your fight. Maybe you needed to fight to build your confidence or maybe you needed the practice. One thing I've learned about the Hermit is that anyone who thought he was wrong and confronted him came back sheepishly with an excellent reason! Besides, you were doing pretty well without any help!" He smiled and slapped my back. "So Quentin, what made you jump out of the car?" Jake asked.

"I didn't jump I fell!" I said confused.

"No, you jumped!"

"I beg your pardon!"

"Seriously Quentin, I've watched the tape a dozen times. You cut your sling and leapt out of the car and onto a beast."

"You're mistaken, Jake! I was grabbing my swords and as I removed one of them I must have raked the sling. The swords were very sharp and sliced the slings holding me in the car. When I leaned against them I fell out, swords and all. I was just lucky to hit the beast who cushioned my fall."

"Whatever you say Quentin, but I'll show you the tapes later. Hungry?" He said as she steered me into a large hall.

It reminded me of old Camp Ma-Ka-Ja-Wan that I attended years ago. The large lodge was dominated by a beautiful river stone fireplace, which was used for cooking and heating in the winter. The opposite wall was glass, floor to ceiling, and looked out over the bountiful gardens. To one side was a large kitchen and food line where people lined up. Men and women of varying ages dished up large bowls of food and each table sent a runner to get their tables food. I looked around the room and saw Sharon at a large table with no open chairs. I looked around and didn't see anyone else I knew, and noticed that a lot of people were staring at me and some seemed frightened. So I looked down and followed Jake to a table near the corner. It was full, but as we approached everything was rearranged to accommodate us.

Jake introduced me and I was surprised how many of them were honored to meet me. Jake explained that most of them were there for security and a little bit apart from the rest of the group. And they certainly seemed impressed with my feats from the other day. More than a few had been itching to fight those demons for months and were disappointed that they weren't let into the fight. I smiled a lot and nodded occasionally as I listened to them bitch. Maybe a lot of soldiers have the same complaint, that all they do is train and never get any real action, but from my perspective, they were lucky. The truth is that while I liked Jake, I'm not really a soldier guy. Okay, I did some amazing things, but that's not who I am. I'm the guy who lives in a tent and listens to the sounds of nature, not Rambo. So I was acting completely against my own nature. Or was I? I shook my head to shake off that thought, forced a smile, and tried to listen to the stories. I looked up and noticed Sharon looking away when I looked at her.

After dinner, I excused myself and went to the car. I knew what I needed and I decided to get it for myself. I grabbed my ground cloth, and sleeping bag and at the last moment I brought my swords and a few guns. I hiked a little way into the woods until I found a small reasonably flat open area to sleep in. I left my stuff, found the biggest tree I could and climbed to the top. The climbing stretched my muscles as I maneuvered around the branches and felt great. When I was near the top I could see things pretty well. In addition to the main compound, there were additional homes scattered on the hillside that rose up a few hundred feet above the fields. Near the top, the setting sun glistened off a glass dome set against a cliff face that rose to a peak. I guessed the Hermit lived in the dome. A dirt road snaked down the mountain through the compound and down to the gate at the bottom of the hill where it met the main road.

    I looked in the direction we had come from, now dark in shadow, and I saw in the far distance a series of dancing lights. I followed them with my eyes and realized that they were cars, with their headlights on, snaking down a distant hill.

    Suddenly I felt we were in terrible danger.

4

I fell down the tree as quickly as I can. It wasn't actually falling, just a controlled rapid descent. You dropped and swung and let gravity do the work. I usually did it in trees that I knew well, but the branches were wide enough apart to make hundred and fifty foot descent in less a minute. I don't know why I was panicking, except to say that deep in my gut I knew we were in trouble. As soon as I hit the ground I grabbed my stuff and headed to the car, strapping on guns as I went. Shit, I thought, where's Sharon? Where's Jake? I reached the car ditched my gear and grabbed my Uzi's and a bag of clips. I ran back to the mess hall. As I came near I recognized two of the security guys from dinner. They took one look at me and their eyes almost popped up.

"Soldiers! Notify forward command of an imminent attack. Tell them to prepare for a full frontal assault by superior forces!" Where did that come from, I thought.

"Why, nothing can get in here."

"I did and Sharon did!"

"So?'

"So it's not demons coming! Now move!" They snapped to and one grabbed their radio to alert the troops. Two seconds later Jake came bursting out of the mess hall.

"What the fuck is going", he started to say and then froze when he saw me.

I looked him square in the eye and said, "Its coming Jake and it will get through."

"What is it?"

"People, Jake, lots of bad people!"

"Shit, people can get through!"

"I think Sharon and I taught them something."

"Battle Stations, Plan Roger, I repeat, Battle Stations, Plan Roger!" He shouted into his microphone and men came running out of buildings followed by the frightened residents. Quentin, what did you mean they get through?"

"I don't know, but in my vision, I saw them right outside here!"

"Shit! How many?"

"It's going to be a long night! Look, you get down to the gate and rally your troops. Bring transport down so you can retreat. I'll organize our lines of defense."

"Lines?"

"Don't worry about that. Trust me, just engage them and fall back. We'll build barricades all the way up the mountain and fight them at each one if we have to. We may die, but we will make them pay the toll! So how many of the faithful will fight?"

"I don't know. Not many I'd guess, but you can try."

"Good Luck Jake!"

"Thanks Quentin. I'll see you at the first barricade. Johnson, stay with the Champion and assist him. Here are the keys to the armory!" He handed the young security guard the keys.

"I'll be there to provide cover fire for your retreat, buddy!" I called to him as he took off at a run.

I walked into the hall and it was filled with people chanting. Sharon stood at the front of the room chanting with the rest. I placed my fingers together, blew, and a loud whistle came out that almost toppled Sharon over and interrupted the mood. It was going to get worse. "Listen up!" I said in a loud stern voice. "In a few minutes a group of very bad people are going to storm the gate and they will be right outside our door in the next thirty minutes. Now anyone who is willing to fight to live, move over there." I pointed right. "If you can't fight, but are willing to help in the defense, move over here," I added as I pointed left. "If you can't do anything at all, move up front!" No one moved.

"Quentin, what are you doing?" Sharon asked.

"My job, Goddess! It's coming, look!" She closed her eyes

"Impossible," one of the people in ornate cotton clothes shouted. "Nothing can enter the grounds! We are completely safe! We have wards!"

"For spirits, not people!" Suddenly he didn't look so go good. Suddenly Sharon went rigid and her eyes popped open.

"Do as he says, we haven't a moment to spare." She shouted in a commanding voice and people actually jumped. Suddenly the groups began to form. I sent the fighters with Johnson to get arms from the armory. I instructed the helpers to load half of the vehicles with the children, elderly and pacifists and drive them up the hill with their lights off. Once they dumped their load they were supposed to turn around and drive back down the hill and park the cars in a series of vees blocking the road at points of limited access spaced out all the way to the top. The last cars should be blocking the dome's driveway and that was our final Alamo if we needed it. They immediately started loading cars.

Johnson returned with the new recruits and I put them to work using the remaining cars to build a barricade across the road where it came out of the woods. One of them fired up a bulldozer and began piling dirt against the cars, filling in the spaces between and beneath the cars. We left a gap near the center for Jake's men to retreat through and had the bulldozer to fill the gap after they had come through. Amazingly in a few minutes, we had a U-shaped barricade and Johnson positioned the men along it as he reviewed the weapons with them. I went back to the car and loaded for bear. In minutes I had more than a half-dozen loaded weapons strung on me, a bag full of ammunition, and a pocket full of hand grenades. Since the fighting hadn't started yet I leaned against my car for a moment and lit a cigarette. Sharon walked up behind me.

"Can you stop them?" She asked worried.

"We're going to find out. Now you need to get up the hill. Are you armed?"

"First thing I did. Look Quentin, be careful, okay." She touched my hand.

"You just be safe, okay Sharon. I'll see you when this is over. Now get to the top and help keep them from panicking. Maybe talk to the damn Hermit while you're there so that we can get out of here! Now go!" I patted her back lightly and she took off. I drove my car to the far side of the compound where the road started up the hill. If I needed a reload, this would be where I'd need it. I carefully arranged the remaining weapons and packed more ammunition into my daypack. Hopefully I could grab it on the go! I made my way to the barricade, stacked my weapons and ammunition and lit another cigarette. Everyone was looking at me but I just listened. I closed my eyes and could feel it building in the air. Soon all hell would break loose.

Johnson was listening closely to his radio and reporting to me. Outposts reported dozens of armed bad guys assembling outside the gate with more arriving every minute. Initial estimates suggested a minimum of a hundred men and they were heavily armed. I could hear Jake deploying his forces. Suddenly a loud screaming and yelling noise came from the bottom of the hill and with it a crash and then the roar of gunfire. The initial noise was deafening. Then Jake gave the order to fire and they all popped up out of their hidey-holes and opened fire. Their fire was more ordered and sustained and then the battle really began. I knew that Jake's scant forces would quickly be overrun and told the men and women on the barricade not to shoot at the first people they saw because they were probably going to be our people.

For the next twenty minutes we stood behind the barricade and listened as the sounds of the battle slowly climbed the hill. At first it was terrible near the gate, but then it stopped and for a few minutes you couldn't hear anything except for a few erratic gunshots. Then the night exploded again with gunfire, only it was a little closer to us. This happened over and over and each time the battle grew frightfully closer. Then we could hear a vehicle speeding up the road towards us as Johnson yelled to hold fire. He signaled the bulldozer who fired up the engine. The same pick-up truck that had picked me up came speeding through the gap loaded with armed men. "Close it!" Jake shouted and the bulldozer came forward into the gap. As soon as it did I swung behind it and shouldered my assault rifle and released the safety. Men jumped out of the pick-up and it sped off. Jake appeared at my side and hoisted his assault rifle and locked in a new magazine.

"Good position!" He said.

"Thanks!" I got a half dozen of em leading up the hill."

"We may need them! I sent the lightly wounded up the hill to the first barricade to provide us cover fire if we have to retreat."

"So how many?"

"Too many!" he said as he grimaced and looked forward.

The hoard burst through into the clearing behind a pick-up truck with a snowplow blade on the front of it. I reached down and grabbed one of the special guns Ricki had sold us and sighted the truck's engine. I squeezed the trigger four times until smoke and steam began to rise out of the pickup's hood as it ground to a halt. I aimed and shot the hydraulic pump for the plow and the plow dropped into the dirt. Ricki said the gun, loaded with armor-piercing shells could shoot through an engine block and she was right. The pick-up was now dead on the road right where it came out of the trees with its plow down. When they tried to push it from the back, the plow just dug deeper into the soft road. So they came pouring around the sides of the pick-up and entered our killing field.

Jake, firmly in control, had spread out his remaining men among the volunteer residents to keep anyone from firing too soon. I switched back over to the assault rifle and prepared for hell. Jake had everybody stay low as the bad guys advanced and shot randomly at us. Bullets bounced harmlessly off the blade of the bulldozer. Jake stared the enemy down and when he was satisfied, yelled fire and opened fire. I held the trigger down and emptied my clip as I swept across the field in an arc. Two dozen residents and security guards did the same and dozens of people went down in a grotesque dance as contorted bodies spun and fell on the blood-slicked ground. Our barricade was 'U" shaped and everyone behind it had a clear field of fire. Anything in that field dropped to the ground, either dead, wounded or scared to death. A few of the wounded or lucky continued to fire and another group gathered behind the pickup and shot at the barricade.

"Jake, what do we have out there?"

"Mostly city dregs, but there are a few mercenaries who are directing them." He replied.

"So, what would your next move be?"

"I'd try to flank us!"

"So would I. I'll take left, you take right!" I slung the loaded shotgun over my shoulder, grabbed a couple of Uzi's, stuffed extra clips in all my pockets, and headed left. Jake directed a couple of his men to take our places and headed right. The left flank was dominated by thick forest, but I made my way left and forward, looking for likely points of entry. Sure enough, after a short walk, the forest thinned out and as I headed toward the enemy flank I heard heavy footsteps walking in my direction. There was just enough moonlight to make out the silhouettes and there were a good dozen of them and they had guns. So I took up a firing position behind a large tree and emptied my gun in an arc across the field of fire. I dropped the first Uzi and swung the second one up. I could make out a few bodies in the moonlight and opened up on them. When the clip was empty, nothing was standing, but I was taking fire. I hunkered behind the tree and reloaded. The firing stopped and everything was silent.

There was a large rock on the ground by the base of the tree, so I picked it up and threw it as far to the left as I could. Then I quickly took up my firing position and waited. The rock landed with a thud and some rustling of leaves and I watched for the flash of their gun barrels as they shot at the noise. I shot at the places I'd seen the barrels flash and then the gunfire stopped. But it wasn't quiet. There were men groaning and calling for help. I felt terrible until I heard the barricade open up in gunfire again and realized that we were the ones being attacked. I reloaded and headed around the wounded men and towards the flank of the main force. I had two Uzis, a shotgun, four 9mm's, four knives, and a sword. I figured I could make a dent in their attack.

I could see the lights of their cars on the driveway and realized that the delay in their attack was caused by them taking the time to bring a large dump truck up the road. They had been backing cars down and pulling them aside to make room and it was almost to the pick-up. It was big enough to easily crash our barricade and my armor-piercing shells were back behind the wall. Time to improvise! I was glad I didn't forget to put a couple of the hand grenades in my pocket and realized that now was the time to use them.

I carefully looked over the area and tried to figure out how to get to the truck. The truck was almost behind the pickup and the area was crowded with men and most of them were carrying weapons of some sort. I was a little overdressed, but my handguns were hidden as were my knives. I cocked all my weapons and put the safeties on and then kept them covered with my jacket. I also hid the second Uzi under the jacket as well. I had the sword strapped to my back and the hood of my jacket covered it as well. So I took a deep breath and wandered into the enemy's camp.

The first thing I noticed was that their camp was in disarray. Apparently, nobody expected such resistance and everybody there was rabidly angry and wanted revenge. They hovered around the truck with hungry looks. I lit a cigarette and casually sauntered through their ranks. If somebody addressed me, I addressed them back.

"Hey, where you from?"

"I don't even know anymore, brother," I said. "Everyone I came with is fucking dead!" He looked at me with commiseration.

"I hear ya man, but payback time is coming!" he said with a crooked smile.

"Fuckin-A right!" I said and wandered on.

The thing about pulling together a big mercenary force is that since everybody is a mercenary, there are no uniforms and no familiarity with each other. So no one paid me any attention as I walked right over to the dump truck. I lit another cigarette as I watched them attach a chain to the pickup truck.

"Why don't they just push it out of the way?" I asked a guy standing next to me.

"Fucking plow is jammed in the dirt. They're gonna pull it back, remove the plow and then push the truck through the barricade. Shouldn't be long now!"

"About fucking time," I said as I fingered the grenades. I was right next to the truck and like most trucks, they had their gas tanks right beneath the cab. I saw a dark recess and waited until just about the time the truck started to back up. While everyone was focusing their attention on the pick-up, I pulled out the two grenades, pulled their pins, triggered their fuses and placed them in the dark recess. Then I casually walked away from the truck as I counted. When I got through the immediate crowd and back into the shadows I ran. At the count of eight, I dove to the ground behind a large tree and covered up. A few seconds later the ground shook with the explosion as the grenades blew up the half-full gas tank. The explosion actually lifted the truck into the air. Anyone standing on my side of the truck was down and their moans and screams were terrifying. A number of people came around the truck to inspect the carnage.

I popped up, swung my Uzi into place, took aim and sprayed the area. I quickly ran twenty feet to the left as they started to return fire to my original position. I reloaded the first and swung the other up and spread an arc of death at the rear of the truck. I slammed in a new clip, got up and ran towards their rear. I stopped behind a tree that gave me a good shot at the back of the truck where a number of people were cowering as they fired toward my last position. I unloaded a full clip on them and then grabbed my second weapon and unloaded that at them as I ran across the road past the back of the truck. I kept running until I found a couple of trees to dive behind and quickly reloaded the Uzi's. I opened fire on the entire left flank of the truck where a number of people were hiding when I felt a burning pain in my left shoulder and felt warm blood. I rolled over and sprayed the area behind me with bullets.

I could see a large group of people shooting at me from behind a car about twenty feet behind the dump truck and felt the sting of more than one bullet. They were silhouetted by the cars behind them but I was both blinded and illuminated by the car in front of them. I switched the gun over to single shot, carefully aimed and shot out the cars remaining headlight. The second it went out I rolled ten feet to the right behind another tree and reloaded as they shot where I had been. I rolled another ten feet, popped up and moved quietly in the dark until I had the car flanked. There were a dozen men hiding behind it and many of them were shooting right where I had been. I had one more grenade so I pulled it out, removed the pin and got set. I pulled the fuse and started counting. After six seconds I threw it behind the car and dropped it behind the tree.

The car exploded and the car behind caught on fire as well. I moved further down the road and opened fire on the large group of men behind the next car. I ran right at them with an Uzi in each arm. I kept running at them as I let go of the Uzi's and swung the shotgun around and fired at anything that moved. That gun had twelve shells and I used them all. I kept moving and pulled out the nine-millimeters. An Uzi is to a nine-millimeter like a paint roller is to a fine paintbrush. I had fifteen shots in each of the nine-millimeter's magazines and I used every one. I had no idea how I was running so fast and shooting so well except to say that I was in the zone. My guns swept right and left at the slightest sounds and motions and I coolly sighted and shot whatever moved. I felt another burn here and there where bullets were grazing me but kept going. When the first set of nine millimeters was empty I holstered them and pulled the other pair. I crossed the road and worked my way back up the other side.

Finally, I stopped behind a tree, reloaded everything but the shotgun, and caught my breath. I circled back towards the dump truck and almost to my original position. I was down to my last clips for the Uzi's, I was out of grenades, and was wounded, so I headed away from the chaos. I moved as quickly and quietly as I could and heard the still-moaning victims of my ambush. Circling around them I quickly returned to the barricade to reload. The barricade was silent as both sides hunkered down. I returned to the bulldozer where my ammo was stashed. I lit a cigarette, leaned against the barricade and drank from a water bottle. Johnson came up.

"Jesus Quentin, was that you out there?" I didn't answer him.

"Johnson, where's Jake."

"He's following in your footsteps and he and the boys are out harassing them down the road."

"He on the radio?"

"Yes." I reached for the radio and he handed it to me. "His code name is Valiant."

"Cute. Say, Johnson, do we have medics or something?"

"Are you hurt?"

"I need a few leaks plugged." He ran off. "Valiant, this is Q-bert do you copy."

"Ten-four. Kind of had you figured for a Cue-ball! By the way, nice show."

"Did it bring the curtain down?"

"Not quite, but it started the finale!"

"Roger that! I'm at Les Mis getting a bandaid and more toys. I'll meet you for the encore. In the meantime, I thought me and a few friends will sweep the front porch."

"Roger that, we'll be enjoying those California sunsets waiting for you."

"Ah Roger that, Valiant. Good hunting!"

"See you in Valhalla!" Johnson had returned and I told him to gather all the security people still on the barricade.

"It seems like I'm always patching you up!" Ariana smiled in the moonlight.

"Ariana, what are you doing here? It's dangerous!"

"I am a healer and there is healing needed here. Now shut up and let me heal you!" She carefully checked my wounds, cleaned them, packed them and bandaged them. "Quentin, you've been hurt pretty badly again. You really need a doctor."

"Can't Ariana, Jake's out there and the game isn't over. Just pack it with moss or something and say a prayer for me!" I reloaded my empty clips as I waited for Johnson to return.

There were five of the security people that hadn't been wounded or killed. Jake had another five with him. I knelt in the dirt and drew out the plan. Johnson and two of the men would work themselves around the enemy's right flank and I would take two around the left. When we were in position, the defenders that remained will open fire on the front, while we catch them in the cross-fire. They'll have no direction to go but retreat. We needed to push them back until we get to where Jake and his crew will be waiting in ambush on the West side of the road. Once it was clear that everybody understood, I grabbed my guns and ammo and headed out. Kranz and Burton were my back up and we headed out to the left flank. I headed towards the burning truck. The woods were full of men moaning and crying out and it was easy to slip through the lines. There was still a crowd of men behind the pickup and the dump truck behind them was smoldering as was the car behind it.

When we opened fire they went down in a heap and the few that didn't ran for their lives. Jake said they never stopped running. I moved down to the roadside and with Kranz and Burton spread out to my left, we started to sweep the woods by the road. Most of the traffic was within the first ten feet of the road, so I was busy. To conserve shells I used the Uzi in bursts as I worked my way slowly down the hill. Johnson was doing the same on the other flank and we cleared the road to just past the burning cars. But just past those burning cars was another group of thugs huddled behind a Hummer and they didn't look like they were planning on running.

"Johnson," I whispered into the mouthpiece he had given me. "Hold position until I let you know, roger?"

"Roger." He said. I told Kranz and Burton to wait for my signal and then slipped into the woods. In no time I worked my way behind them and came up on them through the trees. As soon as I opened up on the back of the car they naturally jumped to the side for cover where Johnson's boys gave them hell. The few that weren't shot started running and I took to the road and followed them.

"Move out, double time," I said into the mouthpiece as I headed down the road. I kept up a hail of bullets at the fleeing gunmen and more joined their ranks in running. Those that cut right or left into the trees found themselves fired on there as well by Johnson and the boys. We had them on the run by the time we'd passed the third car. The crowd of gunmen ahead of me grew as more joined the rout. Then I heard Jake's voice.

"That's far enough fella's, hold your positions." I headed into the trees with Franz and Burton and waited. Suddenly all hell broke loose as six automatic weapons opened in ambush. Those that were left standing ran for their lives. I had Johnson and his men join us and take our left flank and Jake's men took the right and Jake and I walked down the road. But it was over. Anybody still alive was running down the hill and we could hear cars leaving. It took us another twenty minutes to sweep the road to the gate and Jake was about to close it when I looked up. There, standing across the road was a very unhappy-looking Demon. I shed my guns and pulled my sword and walked into the road. I was tired and sore, but one sight of that Demon and all the carnage he had wrought angered me and I fed on the energy of my rage. I began to breathe slowly and deeply as I squinted my eyes and advanced.

The demon drew its own sword and we began to duel. At first, I was stiff, but as I swung the sword my muscles loosened up. I watched him carefully as he swung and sliced at me. He seemed to have unlimited energy. Yet I felt as if he was moving in slow motion and was having no trouble countering his moves. Once again I entered a near trance-like state and moved effortlessly. I picked up the pace of my own attacks and he was forced to defend himself. So I pressed him time after time. The faster I attacked the faster he countered and we kept fighting faster and faster. The demon was having a harder and harder time keeping up when suddenly he stood there with a strange look on his face. His eyes stared at me and blinked twice and then he collapsed into a heap as his head rolled away and started to steam. I looked up the road and all

I saw were taillights. I returned to the gate and Jake locked it behind me as I lit a cigarette.

Sharon had never been so frightened in her life. At first she was irritated at Quentin's interruption until the goddess showed her how he was right. While Quentin organized the defense she got busy as well as she sent runners to clear the buildings and cabins and organized sending everyone who wasn't going to fight up the mountain. The evacuation went quickly but not without the inherent chaos and a multitude of tears. Once the lower buildings had been cleared she saw Quentin who was dressed for battle. He looked more serious than she had ever seen him before and he had a grim determined look on his face. She headed up the hill with the last of the people who had stayed behind to help build up the defense and helped direct the additional roadblocks into strategic locations. She had just arrived at the top where Starshadow and the other leaders were directing people to the various homes in the compound. For an instance, the bedlam on top of the mountain grew quiet when the first shouts of battle cries and the erupting gunfire stopped everyone in their tracks. At that moment they all realized that it wasn't a game and the level of panic rose considerably.

Sharon was in the dark as much as everyone else but they all knew one thing, the sounds of battle were growing closer. The Goddess was on full battle alert and Sharon had never felt more alive. When the battle of the lower compound began the gunfire noise was deafening, but it was the screams and moans of the wounded that carried up the mountain. Sharon did her best to reassure the terrified residents, but regularly found herself checking her guns and ammunition. The Goddess was unwilling to check on Quentin as he was in the heat of the battle and a moment of distraction could cost him his life, so Sharon was in the dark as much as anyone else. As cool as it was to be the Goddess she was beginning to question her choice. It wasn't like her to risk her life for anything and only the Goddess' strength kept her going.

It was quiet except for a few bursts of gunfire when all of sudden the whole mountain shook as a fireball arose from the site of the battle. Everyone around her gasped and cried out as tears and sobs began flowing. The sounds of battle picked up again as it raged fiercely and then suddenly it was quiet again and stayed that way. She heard Quentin on the radio babbling about some musical and sweeping the porch and thought he was crazy until she heard Jake respond in a similar fashion and decided they were speaking in code. But she was glad Quentin was still alive. Soon the sounds of battle started again but this time it was clear the battle was moving down the mountain. There were two more upswells of gunfire and then it was quiet. The goddess was noticeably relieved.

Despite how tired I was I knew it was going to be a long night as the road was scattered with dead bodies and abandoned cars. After we had swept the hill looking for stragglers Jake opened the barricade and brought in their ancient but effective fire truck. They were able to quench the vehicles and surrounding vegetation, which was on fire as well. At the Hermit's bequest, the pacifists came down to help clean up and retrieve the bodies. I directed someone to the sight of my ambush where they located a few survivors and a lot of dead bodies. We had lost four security guards and two volunteers. In addition, we had another four guards and six volunteers that had been wounded. We found sixty-six dead thugs and another eighteen that were wounded. We collected dozens of assault rifles, shotguns and scores of handguns and knives as we swept the battle zone for the wounded. I helped until dawn when Sharon and Ariana dragged me to the infirmary. I didn't die this time but they kept me down and sedated for the next forty-eight hours while they patched me up.

Jesus, Quentin was a mess, Sharon thought as she stared down at the bandaged and unconscious Champion. The night had been horrible as the stack of bodies grew. The Hermit himself came down to direct activities and everyone had grim faces. Sharon was repulsed by the whole scene until the goddess pointed out that she could be one of the dead bodies they were collecting. Parents were told to take their children home and put them to bed and everyone else, pacifist or not, was instructed to help in the cleanup.

Sharon was appalled at the carnage and almost got sick a number of times as she aided the injured and passed the bloody dead. Tears ran down her cheeks as well as the cheeks of others around her and she could sense that everyone was in pain. Six of their friends were dead and another ten were in the clinic. She picked up enough from Jake to realize that Quentin had saved the day and his warning alone saved many lives. As she learned more of the details in the early morning briefing she tried to balance out her gratitude with her disgust for Quentin. If what Jake said was true then Quentin was responsible for more than half of the enemy's casualties. Clearly he was dangerous. Then as daylight broke she noticed how bloody Quentin's clothes were so she and Ariana dragged him to the clinic.

As she stood staring down at the sleeping patient she thought deeply about what the Goddess had warned her about. She could see what she had meant about the Champion but she never mentioned how scary it could be. Standing near him she felt both safe and frightened at the same time, trying to balance his protection against his carnage. The Goddess reassured her that if Quentin hadn't stepped up they would all be dead but it still threw Sharon for a loop. It wasn't a game anymore. People were dying and she wanted it to end even though she knew more would eventually die. Hopefully though, they wouldn't be her friends.

Two days later I was walking out of the hospital feeling pretty good physically and terribly mentally. Now that the lust of battle had left me, the reality of it set in. It was gruesome work and I hated the idea that I had killed someone. But I didn't just kill some, I killed a lot of men. Dozens, as in multiple! And it weighed on my soul. So when I left the infirmary I wasn't sure how I would react to the carnage that I would be seeing.

Shocked could be the only word I could use because there was no carnage. It was if nothing had happened. The barricade was gone as were the other vehicles and the road was clear. Only the blackened foliage where the truck had burned showed any sign of the struggle. There was no stinking mass of corpses and all of the enemies wounded were gone. A few of our people were still in the clinic, but otherwise there was no sign of the battle. I stood there and scratched my head, plopped down in the shade, and smoked a joint Jake had brought me. It was as if they had erased the entire battle but in my mind, as I looked across the open area, I remembered every inch of that area and what I had done there. Then I cried.

You see, no matter how much I could intellectualize the idea that if I hadn't killed them they would have killed us, it didn't really change how bad I felt about it. But what really made me cry was that I was so good at something that I hated I could do at all. One life was too many but twenty, thirty, maybe even forty? It was outrageous, grotesque and frightening. 'What had I become?' I thought as the tears fell.

Ariana came to my side and put her arm around me. I cried on her shoulder and she cried as well.

"You okay," she whispered when we both stopped crying.

"I don't know if I ever will be," I said hopelessly.

"I understand," she said as she took my hand.

Apparently the Hermit is either a wizard or has wicked connections because the battle never made the news. When I asked Jake where all the bodies and wounded were, he pulled me aside.

"Look Cueball, it never happened!"

"But I was there!"

"Yes you were and so was I and I lost four men, but as far as the world is concerned, it never happened and you don't want to know the details." That was it and nothing more but it didn't help my mood.

I skipped dinner and headed for the tree with my gear. I climbed the tree and felt the breeze in my face and opened my mind to clear my thoughts. But it was hard to do. I was having a terrible time understanding how I could be so good at something I hated. I tried to stop thinking about it, but my logical mind couldn't get around the idea. It made no sense. Only a week ago I knew nothing about weapons and now I was a killing machine. Once again my heart hurt in anguish so I tried to think of something else. I thought of Ariana and then suddenly something she had said suddenly made all kinds of sense.

I was the Champion. There was no way I would have ever done what I did the other day on my own. I was never really known for heroic acts or bravery. Yet I handled those nine millimeters like they were made for my hand and I fought with the sword like a musketeer and all without any training. But the other night convinced me that when trouble arose the Champion took over. Suddenly I knew weapons, tactics and felt no fear. Even my wounds healed quickly. No, it had to be the Champion! I climbed down the tree and had a good night's sleep.

The next morning I hunted down Sharon. There was an air of sadness around the compound as people mourned the death of their friends. But it was more than that. The peace had been shattered. Whether it was all of the death or if it was fear, the place had changed. I couldn't find Sharon, but I found Jake.

"Morning Cueball!"

"Morning Prince!" I joked back.

"How you feeling?"

"Physically I'm all right; mentally I was a wreck up until last night."

"What changed?"

"Epiphany!"

"Really, what?"

"Look Jake, I'm not Cueball. I'm not even the Champion. What I did will lay heavy on my heart for the rest of my life. But it wasn't me. Up until I became the Champion the closest I had been to combat was Rock, Paper, and Scissors. Before last week the only gun I had fired was a twenty-two in Boy Scout Camp when I was eleven. Twenty-four hours after I became the Champion I could take apart, re-assemble, clean, load and fire twelve different weapons. What I'm trying to say is that although it's me doing all these things, it's not me, it's the Champion. Does that make any sense?"

"So the Champion takes over your body?"

"Yes and no. Look, it's not like I check out and he takes over. But in situations like last night, I just know what to do and how to act. When the crash of battle is on me it's like everyone else is moving in slow motion."

"Yeah, I watched your sword fight and your sword moved so quickly that I could barely see it."

"Exactly! So what I'm saying is that guy is not the guy you're having breakfast with. The guy you're eating with cries like a baby when he thinks about what he's done!"

"So does the Champion come and go?"

"It's not like it's a separate mind but more like special abilities. When trouble arises something rises up in me and even my senses improve."

"Handy thing to have!" He said smiling.

"If you can live with the carnage. How many people did I kill, Jake? I'm ashamed to say that I don't know because I can't relive that fight. If I do, I risk going mad."

"Hang tough buddy."

"The Champion will drag me through, but when it's over, then what Jake? I didn't kill one person last night; I killed dozens, as in plural. When this is over, how do I live with the idea that I cut thirty, forty or how many more lives short?"

"You didn't walk into the Piggly-Wiggly and shoot people, Quentin. So when the future comes and you feel bad when you look back remember that you also saved a hundred innocent lives, not to mention my own not so innocent one. We were outnumbered and out-armed and if wasn't for you we would all be dead. And any one of those hoods you capped would have done you the same honor had you given them the chance. They didn't come here with flowers but with guns and some horrifying promises they had been made. You did more than save lives, Quentin, you may have saved the world. So ease off on yourself a bit."

"Look Quentin, although I would follow your commands anywhere, I believe you when you say you have no military training. You are not a soldier but you need to learn to act like one. Soldiers are taught not to question their decisions and to follow orders. If what you are saying is true, the Champion is giving the orders and you're just executing them. A soldier is taught that there is a world of difference between walking into a bar and killing someone because you want to and gutting an enemy with your bayonet before he guts you! It's war, my friend, and people die and it's our job to make sure that more of them die than we do. So do your job and protect the Goddess. Then, when it's all over, blame it all on the Champion and move on and let him carry the guilt."

"Thanks Jake."

"No problem Cueball, but just one more thing!"

"What?"

"I'll stand by you in any fight, if you need me. I owe you one! You're warning alone saved most of my men's lives and for that I'll always be grateful."

"Thank the Champion!" I said smiling. "If he's getting the blame, he should get the glory!" Jake laughed.

I was in a much better mood with that eight-hundred pound gorilla off my back and went out to enjoy the day. I hadn't been able to find Sharon and was sitting out front when this smiling young lady asked me to follow her, as the Hermit had granted me an audience. Apparently I was not sufficiently impressed enough for her standards, so she reminded me what an honor it was to meet him.

"Look Honey, anybody who can make eighty-some bodies disappear without a trace is definitely worth the price of admission. Is that his place on top of the hill?" She nodded. "Well I'll go put on my nicest shirt and comb my hair and then I'll drive up and see him! Okay?"

"I'm supposed to escort you there." She said firmly.

"Great, only I'll drive. The Goddess' car has been sitting around in the heat for a week and the drive will help clean out the cylinders. We can't have the goddess being chased by bad guys and have the car vapor lock on us, can we?"

"But he's expecting you!"

"He'll be fine. Now come on, the car is over here." I led her to the parking area where I started the car to warm up the engine. Then I stripped off my shirt and wetted a rag with a water bottle I had in the back seat. I washed up my face and upper body, rolled some fresh deodorant on and fished out a clean but wrinkled tee shirt and pair of jeans from my backpack. I dragged a brush and then a comb through my long blond hair and put it back into a ponytail. I had a knife still strapped to my leg and a small nine-millimeter in the back waistband of my jeans. I was travelling light. I brushed my teeth, put everything away and turned and smiled at the young lady who looked at me with disbelief.

"That's you're nicest shirt?" She asked.

"It's the nicest that doesn't have blood on it!" I smiled and got in the car. "Coming?" I called out as I opened the door for her. She reluctantly crawled in and fastened her seat belt.

"Sensible girl!" I smiled and headed out. "So what's your name?"

"Starshadow."

"Starshadow?"

"Yes, why is that a problem?"

"Hey, I'm Quentin, how would you like your parents giving you that name?"

"My parents didn't name me, the Hermit did. You have to earn your name!" she said proudly.

"Really? Congratulations then!" I said kind of sarcastically.

"Thanks! Turn here!"

"Gotcha Starshadow. So what did you have to do to get a name like Starshadow? Are you a bright star who causes shadows on men's hearts, because you're pretty enough for that." She didn't know what to make of that. At first she looked offended and then flattered and then, just confused. So I kept silent and concentrated on the narrow swerving road. As I climbed the hill I could see small houses through the trees. "So how many people live here?" I asked.

"Around a hundred, but a dozen or so are always off on some pilgrimage or another."

"Who lives in these houses?"

"We do. Only the security people, the newcomers and the neophytes live in the village. Most of the people live in the houses."

"Who owns them all?"

"No one owns anything, we just use them. The houses are assigned on the basis of service and spiritual progress. The higher we go, the larger and more prestigious the homes. Only the Hermits inner circle can live in the upper ring of homes."

"Where you live?"

"Of course!"

"So what's your husband do?"

"I'm not married, for spiritual reasons."

"You're spiritually opposed to marriage?"

"No, it's just not right for me now. The Hermit needs me and I have to be there for him. They'll be time for romance and babies later."

"All work and no play doesn't seemed very balanced to me!"

"I never said I didn't play!" She said seductively and I laughed. We were near the top and I could see a half-dozen houses on what appeared to be the last stretch of road.

"Which one is yours?" I asked playfully.

"That one!" She pointed to one of the last houses on the road. It was fairly large compared to the shacks at the bottom of the road.

"So maybe you could show me around it later?" I asked teasingly. She looked me over and smiled.

"Not likely!" She said she turned forward. Another rejection didn't put me in the best of moods. I pulled into the circular driveway and parked in front of a large geodesic dome. The morning sun was reflecting off the windows. We walked up to the huge house and Starshadow opened the door.

The foyer was small and led to the main room of the dome, which was fifty feet high in the center. A small forest grew inside the front of the dome complete with running water and a waterfall. A wooden deck ran through the forest and ended in a large seating area with couches, tables and chairs. The North half of the dome was partitioned into rooms going up three stories. Balconies ran in front of the rooms and there was a staircase running up either side. The first floor rooms included a kitchen and a sitting area with a large stone fireplace. Nice digs for a hermit! I guess I thought I'd be coming to a cave to meet some long-bearded wise man. So I was surprised to find the Hermit to be a nicely groomed gentleman in his early sixties standing by the edge of the dome wearing a silk shirt, khaki pants, and as he sipped an iced tea. But next to him was a vision of beauty. Sharon was wearing a long white sundress and as she stood next to the hermit the sun glistened off of her blond hair which hung in curls over her tan shoulders.

"Sharon, you look absolutely beautiful!" I said stunned. She looked at me and smiled for a second and then frowned.

"Quentin, we don't have time for such pleasantries!" she scolded.

"Nonsense, Sharon." The Hermit smiled. "Times such as these almost require pleasantries!" She blushed. "Welcome Quentin! I am the Hermit." He smiled.

"Nice to meet you. Nice digs!"

"I'm a hermit, not an Aesthetic."

"Makes sense to me! The Buddha himself believed that you could not transcend your body by punishing it!"

"Oh, a scholar." He said mildly impressed.

"In some things. So, are you the guy who's going to tell me what the hell is going on? The other night sure felt like a war to me."

"It was and it wasn't. What if I was to tell you that the world existed on two different but coexisting planes?"

"I guess my response would be, 'only two?"

"Why?"

"Simple logic. There is either only one plane of existence or there is more than one. If you accept that there is more than one plane of existence, then the number two is as arbitrary as the number twenty-seven or two million because if there is more than one plane, the possibilities of the number of planes of existence are infinite."

"Interesting," he laughed.

"Horseshit if you ask me," Sharon said.

"Probably both. Anyway, Mr. Hermit, what is this other plane that seems to be messing with ours?"

"Not the whole plane, my friend, just a few choice characters. Do you know why I am called the Hermit?"

"Nope."

"Because, Quentin, I stay on this plane by my own decision, alone and cut off from my brethren. I have one job, to watch the door, as they say. I look for signs that someone has crossed the planes and awaken the Goddess and the Champion to come back and keep the worlds separate. The spirits that currently are working through you, the Goddess and the Champion, who are sometimes called the Huntress and the

Hunter, have existed on this plane from the time the planes separated. They are ancient spirits from this plane sworn to its defense. So you can ascertain by the fact that you are both here that the plane has been breached again."

"How many came across?"

"Just one, but you don't understand. The first thing we learned when the plane was first breached was that most of you are defenseless against mind manipulation. One of the reasons that I've always been a Hermit was to resist temptation. But these who come do so to do great harm and they can be very dangerous and very hard to kill."

"Why?" I asked.

"Because Quentin, unfortunately on this plane we can read your minds and adjust them without you ever knowing we were there. If you located my brethren and tried to kill him, he would make you turn the gun on yourself or worse, make you into his slave."

"So were those slaves attacking us?'

"No, sadly, they were just dumb, greedy, hoodlums who were easily coerced. Thank you by the way. I was scared shitless they were going to break through! You were marvelous by the way, really saved the day!"

"Thank the Champion, not me."

"So you understand?"

"I think so. Either that or I'm just finding a way to blame somebody else for ending thirty or forty lives. That's just not who I am inside so I figured that it had to be the Champion."

"You are both astute and incorrect Quentin. The Champion will imbue you with the needed strengths, skills, and the will to use them but unlike the Goddess you wield the sword."

"But that's not me. I'm no Rambo. I was a card carrying pacifist although I think I lost my card last night. Really, despite the last couple of days, I'm not a killer."

"No you're not." He smiled. "Do you know why the Champion chose you?" He asked.

"He's got bad judgment?" I half-joked.

"No Quentin. He chose you for the same reason you fought last night."

"To save my ass?" I asked.

"No, to do that you could have fled. No, Quentin, you fought to save the innocents here. You are a natural protector and that is a very important trait in the Champion. You fought courageously not because you're a killer but because you were trying to protect the weak from people who would hurt them and I think if you ask yourself deep down you would do it again."

"Okay I see your point."

"Don't despair, Quentin. You have done a great job so far. You will be a great Champion."

"Great enough to kill the bad guy?"

"We can only hope."

"So how do I know he's not the good guy coming to take you back?"

"Suspicious?"

"No, just wary. If your buddy can manipulate my mind, so can you."

"True, but I am dedicated to protecting your free will."

"It sure doesn't feel free to me."

"I understand, but it is. You can walk away right now if you wish."

"Can Sharon?" I asked.

"I don't want to, Quentin!" She frowned at me. "And I trust the Hermit."

"Well, no offense sir, but I really don't trust him and neither should you Sharon!"

"Why?"

"Because he freely admits that he can manipulate our minds. I fear that his abilities make me start to doubt my own reality. Look Sharon, everything that has happened to me in the last week has been like one long bad acid trip, present company excluded of course. I keep expecting to wake up. Or, none of it really does exist except in our minds. It's easy to get rid of eighty bodies when the whole battle took place in my head."

"No Quentin," the hermit said quietly. "I'm afraid it's all very real. But it's your questioning of what is real that is probably why you were chosen."

"So are you prescient?"

"Not really, but the spirits of the Goddess and the Champion do know what they are doing. They each seek out someone who has the personality traits and needs that make it work. The champion has almost always been a good man, completely loyal and trustworthy, intelligent, compassionate and yet, is usually lost and without direction. Oh and they're usually hopelessly romantic!"

"So much for free will!" I joked.

"Not at all Quentin, free will has everything to do with it. You don't have to be the Champion, well didn't have to be. Now I think you're marked as him. The demons won't give a shit whether you've quit or not."

"Nice! So, now what oh great wise one?"

"Your cynicism and sarcasm are a welcome relief from the usual ass kissers I have to deal with."

"Yeah, so what is the set up here? All these people here under your control?"

"Yes and no, Quentin. While I refuse to directly influence any person's mind, that doesn't mean I don't understand what makes people tick. I cannot leave this property. It is protected for me and is the protection for the world from me. But I need agents to check on rumors and run errands for me. In exchange, they live here free and study my 'teachings'."

"Like that time bullshit!"

"I heard about that!" He laughed. "Sometimes they take it all so serious. Look, I need things done and I can give them all a little bit of what they're looking for. Most of these people want spiritual peace so I give them a little. No, I don't mess with their minds, but I do know a few techniques that can give them a boost up the spiritual ladder so to speak. So in exchange for taking care of some of my business for me they live in a peaceful and harmonic society dedicated to spiritual growth. We grow our own food, make our own power and live in harmony with the planet. It's a nice life for them."

"So how'd you make the dead people disappear?"

"Well, sometimes, I find I do need to use my powers and connections for the greater good. It happens that the local authorities are friends of ours and the easy way to lie is to tell most of the truth. All of their vehicles that remained behind were taken to a lot in Sacramento and wiped clean. The official story is that two large buses loaded with thugs were driving into the mountains to attend a gang conference when gunfire erupted between the two busses, which both crashed. Everyone but eighteen people died in the crash or from their wounds. Some were burned badly as well. The eighteen survivors were brought to me and that same story was implanted in their minds. Mostly the cops were happy to get these people off the streets."

"What about the ones that got away?"

"My friend the sheriff and his friends were waiting for them down the road. There weren't that many of them left and the fight was gone from them. While you were recovering, they were all brought here to meet with me and after they each had met with me they were sent home with memories of a horrific bus accident in which some of their friends had been killed. Frankly Quentin, I hated doing it, but it was easier than trying to explain seventy dead bodies."

"Very clever, but it does show that you are willing to use your powers when you have to."

"Only in regards to what happens to this land. Its part of the complicated protections set in place. I am allowed to use my powers, but only to keep this place hidden. Whether you choose to believe it or not, I cannot manipulate your mind other than to cloud your memory of what happens here. Oh, I may be also to compel you to fight for me if we were attacked, but you're a natural protector anyway."

"What about your followers?"

"I don't manipulate their minds either. The things I teach them are known techniques I borrowed from your own culture's masters, like yoga, meditation, absolution, and prayer. The only time I ever come close to using my powers is when we meet one on one and talk about what is holding them back."

"So you read their minds?"

"Not really, more like their auras or moods. All I do is ask questions and they find the answers."

"So how do you know what questions to ask?"

"Quentin, I have been observing this plane for thousands of years. Give me credit for developing a little insight into your people."

"Thousands of years?"

"Yes Quentin, a blessing or curse depending on your perspective. I have moved around from culture to culture, locked in this timeless struggle. I foresaw that this was where I needed to be this time and so moved during World War Two, after escaping from Germany when the Nazis tore Europe apart looking for me. The Japanese destroyed my back-up base in China and I had no place left to hide. The Nazi's wanted my ass bad and the Japs were just doing them a favor."

"So Hitler was an escapee from your plane?"

"No, his name was Klaus Reiner and you won't find a single picture or mention of him, but he was behind it all. I knew he had arrived and was in Germany, but couldn't find him. The time was ripe for him as Germany frothed with Nationalism. He met Hitler when the misguided youth was in jail and practically dictated 'Mein Kampf' to the young man. By the time Hitler got out, they had made a deal and Hitler went on to infamy, with Klaus whispering in his ear all the time. They would have won, but the Champion and the Goddess tracked Klaus down and killed him so the crazy Hitler was on his own."

"Wow, you just rewrote the history books."

"No, just made sure a few key facts were left out. To be honest with you, Quentin, Klaus was one of the craftiest I ever faced. By building on the fanaticism on the Nationalist movement in Germany, he was able to work behind the scenes unobserved. He was so efficient that you couldn't tell where the manipulation started or stopped. By controlling a few key people he was almost able to rule the world without ever declaring himself. Once he was gone Hitler started making all the decisions himself and that was the beginning of the end of the Third Reich."

"I guess it's plausible."

"And true, my friend. Most of the epic human struggles often involved an escapee of some kind."

"Let's hope not."

"Look Quentin, if you and Sharon fail to find the escapee that is exactly what will happen, in some way. Already beasts that have been summoned from the depths have attacked you. Luckily, this is more the normal way the escapee acts. They usually try to kill me, as well as the Goddess and the Champion, so that they will be free to rule the planet. They know we wait to catch them here before they can do any damage. That's what made Klaus so dangerous, he just blended in and let his puppets do the work. We had a hell of a time nailing him down."

"Why?"

"Because he really only used his powers to remain hidden. Although we know he was always around Hitler, he was never mentioned and never photographed. That's how we figured out who he was. The Champion infiltrated a rally and looked at each of the faces on the dais. A few days later he was reading the paper and saw a picture of the event and noticed that one of the faces was missing. After a few weeks of attending public appearances it became clear that Klaus never made it into the paper or any reports and that meant he was our guy, the voice behind the throne. The Champion and Goddess tracked him down and finally killed him and dragged his body back to the portal."

"After Klaus was dead the Goddess and Champion left and I fled, as without the Escapee's restraint, the crazy Hitler was in control. I made my way here, after the war, using money I had stashed in Switzerland, I bought this land while I waited for you. But I've lived through a couple dozen of these attempts in the last few millennia."

"So you're thousands of years old?"

"Let's just say I have led many lives. While my body doesn't physically age, I can appear as any age and usually let myself age naturally in the eyes of the world. When I get old, I move, rejuvenate on the trip, and start over. I came here in nineteen forty-seven and built this place and lived here alone until the sixties when I recruited the first helpers. Now, I just appear to be in great health for being in my sixties. As this plays out I will continue to age and when it is over I will leave and move to the next location."

"How will you know where to go next?"

"I can feel the tug of my plane. It takes a long time to create a portal from that side and it pulls on the energy of both worlds. It really is a tricky and dangerous maneuver and if handled wrong could destroy both worlds."

"So why come here."

"Our people are sworn to peace but in every society there are those that cannot accept it. Normally they are controlled, but sometimes they are clever enough to escape here."

"Why here?"

"For many reasons, the biggest being that they know your people are here. They also know I'm here. Our legends and religions are based on the fact that one day, the Dark One will open a huge portal between the worlds and come through the portal with an army of death that will be the end of our people. I was terrified that Klaus was the one. Just one panzer division would have been enough. But luckily he wasn't the one. Some escapees who come through, like Klaus, are a real threat. Others just come to play havoc with the world. Hard to say what the current one is planning but the army that attacked here suggests he has big plans."

"Will he make another attempt here?" I asked.

"Not that will be as successful. The demons cannot enter this property. As for humans, Rikki sent some friends who helped Jake upgrade some of our defenses so it won't be as easy the next time. Oh, by the way, he speaks very highly of you."

"Give the medal to the Champion, not me!" I answered. "He did all the work. Apparently I'm just in it for the ride."

"Sorry Quentin, but it isn't entirely the Champion. He can only aid you. No, it is your own noble spirit and protective compassionate heart that the Champion can inspire to do what is necessary. In the end, Quentin, it is your mind and decisions that will really matter. The Champion will give you the skills of a hunter, but it is your ability to use those skills that will make the difference. The same holds true for Sharon except that the Goddess can take control when needed."

"Good to know. So I guess what's really on my mind is what's next? I mean how do I end this freak show and get on with my life."

"A reluctant hero, I see." He said smugly. I guess if he was thousands of years old he would have probably seen everything.

"Reluctant? I'd be a fool not to be. Since this thing started people have been saying things like, 'if I survive' and enough has happened in the last week to make me understand why. All I wanted to do was to meet the girl of my dreams and now look at me. I've got a higher kill count than a 'B' movie!"

"And a romantic hero, which always makes it more interesting."

"Painful would be a better word for it." I said and Sharon winced.

"Patience, my boy. Give her time." Now she blushed and so did I.

After an uncomfortable silent moment I blurted out, "Anyway, what's next?"

"You and Sharon will leave in search of the escapee."

"Are we going anywhere in particular?"

"I'm working on that. We've been trailing a few thugs who think they got away. We're hoping to figure out who was paying for the attack and who was calling the shots. My agents are due back soon and then we should have an idea of where he's been working out of. In the meantime, I need you two to do me a favor and find a friend of mine who was following a lead. He sent word from Tahoe that he'd met somebody who knew what was going on and was following them to Virginia City. That's the last I've heard of him. I need you guys to find him."

"Right, just go to Virginia City and find him. Sounds easy," I said sarcastically.

"Just trust your instincts and listen to each other and you will do fine. Whether you like it or not, you two are a team for now and need to act and think together if you want to survive. There is no doubt that our adversary knows that you two are out there and will stop at nothing to kill you if he can. But together you two are quite formidable, so work together. Find Shorty and bring him back to me." He handed us a picture.

"So when I do meet this escapee, how do I keep from becoming his slave?"

"You have to act quickly and resolutely. But most of all you must learn to shadow your thoughts. If you can you can act without the escapee knowing what you're going to do. But the escapee will be wary because few humans can shield their thoughts from us."

"Great, so how do we shield our thoughts?"

"I've taught Sharon the technique, but basically it involves jamming the channels."

"How?"

"You can shield your thoughts through meditation, but that's not a very effective way to act. Instead you focus your thoughts onto the mundane. You'll have to find out what works best for you, but if you can count to a hundred and still be able to act, the escapee may only hear the counting. Sharon uses children's songs she learned as a child jumping rope."

"Blocking your mind is easy!" Sharon said. "It's being able to think and act that's nearly impossible."

"Yes," the hermit added, "the technique is difficult because you have to be able to focus on one thing and do another. But Sharon is getting the hang of it and she can teach you a few tricks."

"Let me try it!" I said. "All I have to do is focus on something and then do something else without you knowing I'm going to do it. Right?"

"Essentially that is it. Okay Quentin, now don't worry if you don't succeed the first time as it is a difficult technique."

"Actually, it kind of sounds fun."

'So shall we start?"

"Give me a minute and no fair peeking." Okay, I thought, I know what to focus on. When I was a kid I used to do the multipli- cation tables in my head at night before I went to sleep instead of counting sheep. While everybody had mastered the numbers one through ten, I had also memorized the tables up to the number twenty, which meant that I had learned four hundred equations. So I started. "Twenty times twenty is four hundred. Twenty times nineteen is three-eighty; twenty times eighteen is three-sixty.' It was easy for me to focus on the numbers as I had run them in my head for years. 'Nineteen times nineteen is three hundred and sixty-one; nineteen times eighteen is three hundred and forty-two.' I had thought about what I was going to do before I started and then focused only on the numbers.

When I was in the eighteens I leaned forward to kiss Sharon. I could see the smile on the hermit's face as he watched us. The smile turned to fear when he realized that my knife was at his throat. I sat back down and smiled, "So how'd I do?"

"Very well, Quentin, I'm impressed. I didn't realize the knife was coming until it was already moving toward my throat. I really thought you were going to kiss Sharon right up until you struck."

"So did I," Sharon said quietly.

"Sorry Sharon, I figured a little subterfuge might distract him."

"And it did! Really I'm impressed on all accounts. Math tables, huh?"

"You recite math tables?" Sharon laughed.

"Not only math tables Sharon," the hermit said. "He's starts at twenty and works his way down."

"Really? Quentin, what are seventeen times thirteen?"

"Two hundred and twenty-one," I said quickly and calmly.

"Is it?" She laughed when she realized that she didn't know the answer.

"It is." The hermit smiled. Suddenly I was a little embarrassed for both of us.

"It's no big deal. I use to memorize math tables to help me go to sleep."

"You memorized math tables to go to sleep? They used to give me headaches!"

"Well I tried counting sheep but all that bleating was keeping me awake." We all laughed at that.

"You are one strange guy Quentin," Sharon said. I winced inside.

"Thanks," I said sarcastically.

"I mean you're full of surprises!"

"Thanks!" I said but left out the sarcasm.

"You two should pack up and get moving. If you hustle you can be in Virginia City before dark."

"The car is right outside. Got any gas?"

"Down at the barn. See Gary and he'll hook you up."

"Great. Well, see you when we find Shorty."

"Let's hope it's soon."

"How soon?"

"A few days Quentin. By then we'll have a lead on the escapee and he's the priority. For all we know Shorty is shacked up with some barmaid."

"Might be hard to find him if he is."

"Everybody has to come up for air."

"So, you actually have a name other than hermit?"

"It's long so I go by Zach. I've had many names but I always came back to Zach."

"Nice, well Zach, I'll make you a deal. We'll go find Shorty and then we'll find the escapee to clean up your mess but on one condition."

"What's that Quentin?"

"When this is over, you and I sit up here and smoke a joint of Rikki's finest and then you tell me about your world. I love science fiction, mythology, history, religion and a whole lot of other things and so I would love to hear some of your world's stories. Forget all the mystical and spiritual bullshit and tell me about your homes, your family units and what you do to keep from getting bored."

"I can do that, to an extent. But I am limited in what I can tell you."

"Why Zach?"

"Let's just say it's an attempt to keep you from falling into some of the same traps we did. We have learned that there are some doors better left unopened and believe it or not, as screwed up as this world is, there are worse places. But enough of this, you must get going." He said and he waved us off. I headed to the door while Sharon stood hugging and whispering with the Zach.

Sharon listened to Quentin and the hermit talk and was amused by his relaxed manner. Most people treated the Hermit like some ancient priest or beloved father but Quentin didn't treat him special at all. As she listened she could never tell if Quentin was serious or kidding but she had already figured out that Quentin was pretty smart. She didn't quite understand it but from what Zach said the Champion and the Goddess didn't function exactly the same way. She was surprised that he didn't trust the Hermit as she had trusted him from the beginning. But Quentin's logic was flawless. She was surprised to discover when she asked the goddess that, even though they had been associates for six thousand years, a part of her didn't trust him as well.

'I am charged with watching this world. He does not belong here. His mission is noble and so may he be but he is not of this world.'

Before she had time to absorb that Quentin was inches away from kissing her while he held a knife to the Hermit's throat. The display had been impressive but she was surprised to find herself a little disappointed that he hadn't followed through on the kiss. But she had no time to ponder what had happened as in minutes they were loading up to find a guy named Shorty.

I headed to the car and warmed up the engine. I checked my gear and had everything, but Sharon's stuff wasn't in the car yet. I waited out there for about five minutes before she came out and when she did she was very quiet. We drove down the hill in silence and she directed me to her room. While she changed and packed her clothes, I got some gas and then went to seek out a few people. I went to the clinic and thanked the doctors and healers and hugged Miranda and Ariana. Finally I found Jake.

"We're headed out old buddy."

"Dangerous mission?" he asked quietly.

"Brother, I got a feeling that they're all gonna be dangerous!"

"I know. Need any back-up?"

"Not this time, prince. It's search and rescue."

"Shorty gone missing again?"

"As a matter of fact, yes he has. Regular occurrence?"

"Regular enough. You never know if he's in trouble or on a bender. Likes whiskey, women, and trouble all equally and he likes them a lot. That tends to get him sidetracked, once in a while. Still, he's a good agent."

"Agent?"

"The hermits got a few of them. Crafty guys like Shorty. You know, people who are good at digging into the dirty corners of life and sniffing things out."

"Thanks Jake."

"No problem, Quentin. Be careful. Nine out of ten times Shorty is shacked up with some blond, but every once in a while he gets himself into a real jam."

"How does he survive?"

"He's slippery. Look, Shorty is a good man and you can trust him if he knows that you're with the hermit and can prove it. But the man is a natural born liar when he's on the job."

"Good to know."

"Good hunting!" He said and I headed back to the car. Sharon was waiting for me and I climbed into the car.

"Where were you?" she asked.

"Saying goodbye to some friends," he smiled. She was quiet after that.

The drive out was kind of emotional for me. For all their work, there were still signs of the battle and as I drove down the road I thought about my parts in it. I could see the burnt foliage and noticed the road was pockmarked where my grenades had exploded. When I pulled out of the gate I saw where I had slain the beast the night of the attack. A quarter mile down the road you could see the blackened foliage where only a week earlier I had almost died. There was noticeable tension in the car as we drove down the dirt roads that didn't begin to dissipate until we hit the highway. My first stop was a store where I emptied my cooler and filled it with beer, food and ice. When we got back on the road we each had a cold beer and all was right with the world.

Sharon had no idea why Quentin saying goodbye to friends put her into such a funk and as they drove in silence she gave it thought. She strongly suspected that Ariana was one of those people and couldn't understand why that bothered her. But upon deeper introspection, she realized she was also jealous of him. He had only been there a few days and somehow made enough friends to be able to say goodbye to them. She had been coming there on and off for a couple of months and knew everybody but had few if any friends. The truth was she packed her bag and walked to the car quickly because she didn't have anybody to say goodbye to. Being the Goddess garnered her great respect but didn't make her friends.

5

We cut across north of the lake and past the old Cal/Neva Casino that Sinatra was once the part owner of. We both started laughing when we passed the Ponderosa, where they filmed Bonanza, on our way to Virginia City, which always played a part in the television series. We headed east on fifty and stayed on it right through Carson City where we headed east. The shadows were growing longer when we turned north on the approach to Virginia City.

"So what's our cover going to be?" I asked.

"It makes sense that we should be a couple on vacation," she offered me nervously.

"Great. Then don't go flashing Shorty's picture around."

"Why?"

"First, it blows our cover. But more importantly, it will draw attention to us from the wrong people."

"So what do we do?"

"We try a more subtle approach."

"Like what?"

"Like mentioning his name in a more innocuous way and looking for reactions. Just hang tight and pay attention."

I stopped short of town and removed another two grand from the trunk. Then we slowly climbed the hill into town and you couldn't help but think that you were also climbing back in time. As the sun dipped behind the mountains in the West you didn't have to squint hard to believe that it was eighteen-eighty and the old west. Most of the buildings were over a hundred years old. I experienced a kind of Déjà Vu as if I had been a miner here in the past life. Of course back then the road was muddy and paved with rocks, but not much had changed. As we drove down the main street I knew I had been there before, but a long time ago.

I got out of the car and looked around and for an instant had a vision of the town in the old days. Virginia City was a mining town and was always full of hard-working and hard-drinking miners. It was home to the Comstock Lode, one of the largest silver mines in the world and the entire area was honeycombed with abandoned mines and shafts as everyone who could afford a pickaxe dug for silver and gold. The area produced quite a bit of both, but the real money was made by the bars, brothels, and merchant stores. As I looked down the street, just for an instant, all of that came back. The street was dusty and filled with horses, wagons, and mules. Piano music could be heard coming from the doors of a half dozen bars and whores in corsets and stockings sat in the second story windows fanning themselves in the late summer heat. I looked up the street and saw where the banks were and even a couple of mine entrances dangerously close to town. Then I saw the Bucket of Blood Saloon and remembered it as a special place.

The vision faded but as it did I realized that when the mines dried up the town died and all that was left was just the ghost of a once thriving place. What actually remained were a few gift shops, photo shops, saloons, souvenir stores, restaurants and a couple of bed and breakfasts. But I was surprised to see that the Bucket of Blood was still there and promised myself to have a beer there. It was kind of creepy walking around somewhere I had never been before as if I had lived there my whole life, but that's what it seemed like. Sharon insisted we get a room at a nearby inn, and by luck was able to get one with two double beds. We each carried a bag with us and went to the room to freshen up.

We had quite a discussion about what to wear. Weapons, I mean, not clothes! Sharon wanted to pack heavy and I suggested we travel light. It was reconnaissance, after all. So we each carried a nine-millimeter and two extra clips. Between us we had ninety shots and if we needed more than that we were probably screwed anyway. I also carried a couple of knives. Then we went out on the town. First we had a nice dinner at a fancy steak house where I devoured a T-bone. Then I dragged her right to the Bucket of Blood Saloon. Ever since my vision I had wanted to enter the Saloon. I was a little disappointed.

You could see the remnants of the old saloon but most of the floor, once filled with tables, chairs, and Faro tables was now covered with slot machines whose flashing lights and bells seemed incongruous to the ancient western décor. The saloon in the old days would have been packed but today only a busload of British tourists in western wear filled the bar. Even the beautiful wooden bar had quarter slot machines cut into it! We took two empty seats at the bar and or-dered cold beers from the bored bartender. His name was Kevin and he hated British tourists because they were a pain in the ass and shitty tippers. I made sure I tipped him five bucks and he stuck to us like glue. We chatted about the bar, his job, his gold claim, and the town. Finally he asked the question I had been waiting for.

"So what brings you folks to town?"

"Oh," I said watching his face, "Our friend Shorty told us about the place and made us promise to come up and see it. It's everything he said it was, like a step into the past."

"So you're friends of Shorty," he said warily. His eyes said trouble.

"Well, more like acquaintances." The bartender's eyes narrowed slightly.

"Tell him the truth, sweetie." Sharon took over. "We actually met him a few weeks ago in Reno and we partied together one night. He tried to teach us how to beat the blackjack table."

The bartender laughed and smiled. "Now that sounds like Shorty! He's a card, he is. He was here a couple of days ago."

"Really?"

"Yeah. He sat at the end of the bar drinking with this tall thin lady and went up to watch the show. I think he left when the tourists left."

"Do you know if he's still around? We'd love to see him again."

"Hasn't been back in since, but I did see the lady in town this morning. Tall woman, thin and kind of severe face, you know pointy chin, sharp cheekbones. She drives a black BMW, nice car!"

"Oh well, no big deal" I shrugged. "He's probably long gone by now. Can we have another round?"

We went back to talking about the town for awhile. At exactly eight PM the British tour guide announced that dinner was served upstairs. The casino emptied out as they scurried upstairs for the meal. A few minutes later a handful of scruffy looking cowboys came in and stood at the bar where the bartender had their drinks waiting for them. I thought it strange that they were all wearing guns on their hips. One of them sat next to me and introduced himself as Ted and he explained that they were the house entertainment for the tourists. In a few minutes they would go upstairs and holler at each other and then they'd fire off a bunch of blanks and pretend to fall dead and collect their pay. We all laughed about it. Turns out he was a stuntman who worked a lot in Hollywood but lived up here in gold country and like everybody else around here spent most of his time working his small claim. Things were going swell until the bartender mentioned we knew Shorty.

"So how do you know Shorty?" He asked suspiciously.

'We partied with him in the city!" Sharon bubbled over. "He was crazy fun to be with."

Ted laughed at that. "Yes, he can be crazy fun. Well it's been really nice meeting you folks, but its show time. Say you folks want to watch the show? Come on up I'll show you where you can stand." So we followed them up and stood in the back of the room as the hungry tourists shoveled in the peach cobbler ala mode. Suddenly loud cowboy voices started up as they began their show. A couple of drunken cowboys invaded the party and the sheriff and his deputies came to settle the boys down. It started with a fight between two of them and after they had landed on a table as a finale to the fight scene they rose, pulled their guns, and bullets blazed.

Sharon seemed engrossed by the show and it was entertaining, but I was nervous when I saw Ted and another of the cowboys fiddling with their guns and whispering. I kept a careful eye on the two and noted that both of them glanced regularly in our direction. When the guns came out I noticed that two of them were aimed in our direction and yanked Sharon to the ground as plaster dust and wood splinters from the wall and door frame behind us splattered on us. I crawled on my belly through the door pulling Sharon with me and slithered down the stairs on our bellies as bullets impacted on the railing and walls. Suddenly there was screaming and pandemonium in the room as the crowd panicked. I grabbed Sharon and we made a run for it. As we re-entered the bar, Kevin was standing there looking bored until we went running out. I kept my eye on him as I escorted Sharon out the door, but he never moved. As I was backing away from the door I saw one of the tourists come running into the bar splattered in blood.

"Run!" I said and we hightailed it around the corner. "Sharon, go pack everything up and load the car. Drive it up a few blocks and pick me up behind the saloon as soon as possible."

"Where are you going?"

"To see if Ted makes a run for it. If he does maybe we can follow him."

I stayed to the shadows and worked my way through the streets to a place where I could see the back of the saloon. Sure enough I could see two people exiting the fire escape and one of them was Ted. He looked frightened. Sirens were coming and in the dim light the two men looked around and looked scared. They slowly walked away from the building in my direction before turning left and heading down the street behind the saloon. I slowly moved from shadow to shadow as I trailed the two down the street. They turned right and headed up a steep path. I couldn't follow without giving myself away so I listened carefully as they scuffled up the hill in their cowboy boots. Finally about halfway up the hill they stopped and I heard a squeaking noise like an old hinge. I saw a flashlight go on and marked the spot and then the hinge squeaked and the light went out.

I reached in my pocket and pulled out a walkie-talkie, turned it on and called Sharon.

"Where are you, the place is crawling with cops." She asked.

"I'm on the street behind the saloon and six blocks south. I know where they went."

"Great, I'll be right there." A minute later she pulled up with the lights off. I went to the trunk and started digging through the gear. Sharon joined me. "So what's the plan Quentin?"

"The plan is for you to lay low. I'm going to follow our friends into the depths of hell and either find Shorty or find out why Ted tried to kill us."

"I'm going with you!"

"No you're not. It's way too dangerous, there is no reason for you to be there, and we need you alive." I slipped on black clothes and inked out my hands. I put the shoulder harnesses on and filled each holster with a set of nine-millimeters. I dug out a pair of night vision goggles and strapped the sword to my back. I slipped spare clips into my pockets and then slipped a black facemask on and covered everything with a hooded sweatshirt. I turned on the goggles, adjusted them and headed up the hill. I carefully walked up the hill practicing with the night vision goggles as I went. When I reached the area where they disappeared I discovered an old boarded up mine shaft. I removed my goggles and examined the boarded up entrance. I tested the door and it squeaked open. I put a gun in one hand and cocked it and removed the safety and replaced my goggles. I swallowed hard and stepped into the darkness as the door swung shut. I stopped and listened for a full minute for any sounds, but there were none. I moved forward.

There he goes again, Sharon thought as she watched him disappear into the side of the hill. How does he do it? He's fearless! As for herself, the Goddess had to calm her down to stop her from shaking after Quentin had sent her to get the car. Did that cowboy actually try to shoot me? He would have if Quentin hadn't saved her, again. Quentin called and she drove through the dark street to where he was waiting. She can't say she agreed with his plan but to be honest she had absolutely no interest or desire in going into an abandoned mine!

'That's his job!' the Goddess reminded her.

'Yes, but...'

'No, Sharon, you need to always remember that. It is his job to risk his life and save ours when necessary. He is expendable.'

'Expendable? Are you kidding?'

"No, my dear, I am not. Do not get me wrong, Quentin is a fine young man and makes a fine Champion. Personally I find him smart and funny and I like him, but if he dies in there a new Champion will be chosen and the quest will go on. If we die it takes time for me to integrate into a new host and that's time we don't have. That's why the Champion exists. I am fully capable of doing the job without him but he would have a really hard time without us.'

'Yes, Goddess.'

'Sharon, this is what I've been trying to tell you. When Quentin saved us tonight he was doing his job. Just like walking into that tunnel is his job. But he's right to ask us to stay. There is no reason to endanger ourselves.'

'But what if he needs our help?'

'Everything I've seen so far from that boy suggests he'll be fine. He's a lot tougher than he looks! That's the trap. We are the Goddess and we can fight, but healing and love are our greatest weapons. He is the Champion and he's made for these types of adventures.'

'So has a host ever fallen for the Champion?' Sharon asked hesitantly.

'Many times and it usually ended badly.'

'Do you have an example?'

'Ever hear of the Dark Ages?'

'Of course!'

'What you didn't know was that a silly girl named Imelda brought on the whole thing.'

'How?'

'She fell in love with the Champion and sacrificed our life to save his, which failed anyway as he got killed as well. By the time I integrated into a new host the bad guy had set up shop and had most of Europe under his control. We finally caught up to him and killed him. But releasing the nobles didn't release their greed and we were unable to repair the damage.'

'Did it ever work out between the Champion and the Goddess?'

'On the rare occasions when they are both special enough to realize that there is a job to do. But I wouldn't recommend the experience. Do you understand?'

'Yes, Goddess.'

Did I mention that I was claustrophobic? Because walking down that narrow, damp, dark tunnel in the dark was terrifying to me. As I went I could see where the old shaft had been reinforced here and there with modern materials. The shaft ended at a cave-in, but just before the shaft was blocked someone had cut a new shaft angling to the left of the old one. This shaft was even narrower and looked like it had been recently dug as most of the timbers were fairly new. About twenty feet down the shaft it opened into a larger shaft of what appeared to be a real mine. So they had cut access from the little shaft to the big one. But I had no idea where to go.

The shaft went both left and right and there was no light in either direction. I listened carefully for a few seconds when I heard a door close quite a ways down the shaft to the left. I headed in that direction and counted my steps as I went. When I had reached three hundred steps the night goggles picked up some light bleeding around a doorframe. I listened at the door and could hear voices. A woman was screaming and swearing and Ted's name got mentioned frequently. I heard two other male voices trying to calm her down. "You shot a tourist?" She screamed. "What were you thinking? Why didn't you wait until after the show, follow them, and then kill them?" I could hear Ted mumble something. "Shut up, you imbecile," she said. "Kill them!" I heard her say and I heard Ted shout out when two guns roared to life. I clearly heard two bodies hit the floor. "Now get Shorty and let's get out of this place!" I quickly backed away and removed my weapons. It was now or never.

The door opened and the shaft filled with light so I flipped up the goggles. I was tucked into a corner and still in shadow but I could clearly see the western dressed woman leading the way with a flashlight. Behind her two men led a short man wearing a hood. In the room I could see Ted and his accomplice's bodies. One of the men turned off the lights in the room and the shaft grew dark except for their flashlights. I flipped my goggles back on and followed them. I stealthily moved closer to them which wasn't that hard since they were clumsy and loud.

"After we get Shorty back to the van, you two will need to come back and get Ted and Andy's bodies and dump them deep in the shaft. We need the gold we're stealing here for the boss. Where's the damn door anyway?" I knew it was time to strike.

They had stopped as she fiddled with the door lock. I swiftly moved forward and hit the first man in the back of the head with my gun as hard as I could. I heard a cracking noise and he dropped like a rock.

"What the fuck?" the woman said as she spun around. Just as she spoke my gun butt crashed into the second man's startled face and he dropped as well. Her flashlight spun around just in time to see my gun pointing directly at her face. She dropped the flashlight. "Who are you?"

"The real question is who your boss is, but there is plenty of time for that!" I reached over and removed the hood from the man. "You Shorty?" He nodded because there was duct tape on his mouth. "So, what's your name?" I said to the woman.

"Monique." She said frightened. I ripped the duct tape off of Shorty's mouth.

"Ow," he said. "That hurt! You didn't have to be so rough."

"Shut up Shorty. Do we need her?"

"Who are you?" he asked confused.

"A wise mutual friend sent me. Do we need her?"

"Absolutely! She's the reason I'm here."

"Great. Monique darling, what's on the other side of the door?"

"The cellar of my home."

"Anybody else home?" She was silent. "Shorty, do we really need her?" I cocked my gun.

"No, nobody's home, just me and my cats." She said frightened.

"Let's hope you're not lying as you will be the first to die. Unlock the door." It took a while for her to unlock the door and open it. As she did I removed the goggles as the shaft was bathed in light. Shorty was in handcuffs and I had Monique unlock them and then had Shorty place them on Monique. As he marched her upstairs I called Sharon and had her bring the car to the house. Shorty, who knew the layout of the town better, gave her instructions as we were now half a mile away. A few minutes later she pulled up and we marched Monique to the car. I placed a hood on Monique's head and we lay her in the back seat with Shorty watching over her. As soon as we pulled out of town I pulled out one of the cell phones Frankie had included. Supposedly they were untraceable. I called the local authorities to report that I had seen two drunken cowboys with their guns out go into Monique's residence. I gave the address and hung up. We had left the doors open and the lights on so that eventually they'd find the two unconscious bodyguards and the dead cowboys.

We drove west in the dark and Sharon was nervous. Monique wanted to know where she was going so Shorty placed duct tape across her mouth. Once we passed Carson City and headed into the mountains I started to relax and grabbed a beer. Shorty had one as well but Sharon declined. We didn't bother to offer one to Monique who was softly whimpering. I drove around the lake twice as we killed time and to help disorient our guest. An hour before dawn we headed west and worked our way back to the Hermit's place. The sun was clear as we approached the gate and stopped. I smiled at the camera and the gate swung open. I drove straight to the top of the hill to the Hermit's house and banged on his door. I was as surprised to see Starshadow standing there in a silk robe as she was to see me.

"I need to see the Hermit!" I said as I walked in and brought the others with me. Starshadow was too shocked to be embarrassed until Sharon followed us all in and shook her head at her. Then again, we must have been quite a sight. I was still dressed in black and had smudges of black paint on my face and hands. Sharon was still dressed from the bar and looked nice, but wilted. Shorty's clothes were filthy as he had been in the shaft for a couple of days. Monique was dressed cowboy casual and wore handcuffs and a hood. We marched right into the garden gazebo where Zach was sipping coffee.

"Hey, Zach!" I said as we walked up. Starshadow almost peed herself when I called him by name. "You got any more coffee; it's been a long night?" He smiled.

"Starshadow sweetie, why don't you go make a big pot of coffee for our guests? While you're at it, darling, why don't you make us all a big breakfast?" She blushed and left to do as he asked. He rose and hugged Shorty. "Shorty my friend, I missed you. We were worried."

"Yeah, sorry boss, she caught me with my pants down. But she's the prize. You should be able to get the location of the bad guy from her as she was taking me there."

"Wonderful!" Zach said. "Who is she?"

"Monique Delabare, antique dealer, a spy for the enemy, and a claim jumper to boot! She runs an Antique Store in Carson City and lives in Virginia City. Her house sits on an old gold mine that snakes under the town. She accessed it with the help of a few others and they were squeezing gold out of the nooks and crannies. She was selling the gold and sending the money to her boss."

"So what happened?" he said as we all sat down. He led Monique to a hammock, laid her down and placed his hand on her head. She instantly fell asleep.

"What'd you do?" I asked.

"Gave her a little rest until I'm ready to talk to her. The more I know and the less she thinks I know the better. So what happened?"

Shorty explained that he had been tailing this woman after he ran into her in Tahoe. He had her under surveillance but spent a night in the bucket of Blood and woke up in the shaft. Apparently, he'd been invited upstairs for the show as well and then Ted and his buddy shanghaied him. Sharon told the hermit about our trip, the bar, and then getting shot at. Then I told him how I tracked them down and heard Monique order the two men shot. The hermit listened to all without questions or judgment. As we were finishing Starshadow brought the food and tried to be a good hostess. She was wearing her cotton clothes again but couldn't stop blushing, especially when our eyes met.

After breakfast, Shorty disappeared and reappeared twenty minutes later clean and dressed in the same type of cotton clothes Starshadow was wearing. I was exhausted and so was Sharon so the hermit had Starshadow take us to a room to rest. Before I left he handed me a joint and I smiled. Twenty minutes later I was clean, stoned, and sleeping.

Sharon was quiet on the ride home as the Goddess had upset her. But as she sat staring out the window she realized the truth in the Goddess' words. She certainly didn't want to be the one who brought about the next Dark Ages and tried to focus on keeping her head in the game. She was pretty surprised when Quentin showed up with Shorty and the woman Shorty had been tailing. As impressed as she was she had to remind herself that he was just doing his job.

At one point during the trip home, she glanced over at the strange young man and knew that he might die and that idea really seemed to upset her. If he died it would be on her and she would have to carry that burden for the rest of her life. She suddenly wished that she'd never written on his car as she felt terribly guilty.

'If not him then someone else would be sitting there,' the Goddess reminded her. 'And you would probably feel the same way about him.'

It was hard to argue with the Goddess and she was usually right. But that didn't make her feel any better. It was only when the sun started coming up that she realized how tired she was. She was surprised to see Starshadow in just a robe when they arrived and tried not to look upon her with too much disapproval. She thought something might be happening between those two, she smiled smugly. By the time she had taken a hot shower and crawled between the cool sheets she had forgotten her funk and slept peacefully.

I awoke in the early afternoon feeling groggy but rested. I slipped on some jeans and a tee shirt and splashed some water on my face and felt a whole lot better. I packed up the black skin-tight outfit and stuffed it in my backpack and lugged it and the rest of my stuff to the car. While I was there I grabbed a cold beer. I remembered to ice down the cooler before we came this time. I left most of the weapons but still carried a nine-millimeter and a couple of knives. The hermit was sitting with Starshadow in the atrium and there was no sign of the others so I joined them.

"Did you rest well?" Zach asked.

"Yes sir, I was beat. Where is everybody?"

"Sharon's still asleep and Shorty went down to see some friends."

"Where is Monique?"

"She is resting but she is no longer a threat."

"Did she tell you what you needed to know?"

"Mostly. She knows her master is in LA and goes by the name Marcus Aurelius, but she knows it's an alibi. She was down on a shopping trip last year when she went out one night to a bar and met him there. She's been sending him the ill-gotten gains from her mining operation ever since. Odds are it was her money that financed the attack on our place. She knew to look out for anything associated with us and Shorty got a little loose-lipped at the Bucket of Blood and let it slip to Ted that he was keeping an eye on Monique. That's why they snatched him."

"Speaking of the Bucket of Blood, have you heard anything?"

"State Police raided her house and found the two thugs groggy and locked up in the basement. They arrested them and then found the two dead cowboys. They're still doing ballistic tests but the cowboys' guns will match the bullets that killed the tourist at the bar and the thug's bullets will match the ones in the cowboys' bodies and we won't see any of them again. Police say the cowboys were drunk and accidentally loaded the wrong shells in their guns. They weren't sure why the cowboys were killed but suspected that it had to do with a fall out between partners as part of an illegal mining operation police had discovered while investigating the shooting. Nice work!"

"Don't look at me, I was winging it. They tipped their hand by trying to kill us and then got killed by their own partners. I just rode the wave and jumped in when the time was right. Frankly, I was scared to death."

"Nonetheless you succeeded remarkably well. Well hello, sleepy head."

Sharon looked refreshed, clean and content, not to mention beautiful. I smiled as she walked up and she smiled and winked at me.

"Would you like something to drink, my dear?" Zach asked and she asked for a coke. "Starshadow honey, would you get her a coke and Quentin and me a beer, please? Thank you, darling."

"So what's going to happen to Monique," I asked.

"It's already been done. I wiped away any memories of contact with the enemy and opened her heart. She will be staying with us for a while."

"Really?" I asked skeptically. "I thought you weren't allowed to manipulate minds."

"I am allowed to deal with certain threats in certain ways. She has not been harmed only neutralized. The contact with our enemy has been erased from her mind and I planted the seed of hope in her. She is safe here with us but if she does leave she will be wanted by the police for her connection to the murder of the two cowboys, so basically her life is ruined. I offered her another chance at life. Here she will be safe, can prosper, and can grow as a person."

"Maybe, but can you change human nature? I mean once a bitch always a bitch, right."

"We'll see. But I can do no less or no more. In a sense, she is a humanely treated prisoner of war."

"Fair enough. So what's next?"

"Relax for a couple of days and recover. I've got my people in LA checking out her information and I'll know where the escapee is in a couple of days. In the meantime relax."

"Thanks, Zach. I'm gonna get out of your hair and head down the hill. Send for me when you need me. Sharon, are you coming."

"Yes, just give me a minute." She said as she headed to her room to get her things.

I parked in my usual place after dropping Sharon off at her guest suite and tidied up the car. With nothing on the agenda, I rolled a nice joint and hunted down Jake. I found him and Shorty swapping stories behind the security office. I fired up the joint and the three of us sat back and smoked it.

"Thanks for saving my ass, Quentin! You seem to be amassing quite a record." Shorty smiled. I looked at him questioningly. "I saw the surveillance footage from the battle here and Jake filled me in. You're quite impressive."

"Not really Shorty, I just seem to be possessed by the spirit of some dead warrior."

"Well thank him then. Either way, thanks, you did a lot more than save my ass; you may have saved everybody's. She wanted me for the same reason I wanted her."

"But they already knew where we were." I wondered.

"True, but if the enemy had turned me I would have been a terrific spy for him. No, you did some good work there and shut down an operation that was supporting the enemy as well. Good show, sport."

"You're welcome."

"So those two dickheads really shot a tourist?" Shorty asked.

"Didn't see it myself, but saw another come down covered in blood. We were hightailing it by then as they were actually shooting at us."

"Crazy motherfuckers, for sure. Anyway, thanks Quentin, I owe you one."

"That's two of us owe you, Q!" Jake added with a smile.

Shorty sat back, took a long toke and looked out on the warm sunny afternoon. Looking at the joint, he smiled and said, "Make that two I owe you!"

At lunch, I noticed that people's attitudes toward me had changed dramatically. Before everyone had looked upon me with suspicion and fear but now people seemed to look upon me with honor and awe.

Jake explained it. "The old man came down and addressed us himself at the funerals for the fallen the day you and Sharon left. Afterward, we had a luncheon and he addressed us again and soothed our grief and answered our questions. He made it very clear that you were the reason we were all still alive and that the champion should be awarded the same respect and honor the goddess gets. And his word is law, as you might have figured."

Nonetheless, I found it almost disconcerting to go from being basically ignored if not avoided to being greeted with a smile by every resident. I probably still scared the shit out of them but they were too polite to show it. At dinner, I was offered a seat at the elder's table where Sharon and Shorty were seated and Jake talked me into eating there. Most of the eyes in the room were on me as I walked to the front and took a seat between Starshadow and Sharon. Shorty was on the other side of Sharon and the large round table had eight other people I didn't know but figured they were important because of the way they carried themselves. They all had silly names like Burning Candle, Golden Hands, Moonglow, Mariner, and Thunderbolt and I did my best not to laugh. By their names alone I knew I was sitting with the elite and I wasn't really feeling comfortable.

Did I mention they were all vegetarians, even Jake? Don't get me wrong, the food was great if you like brown rice and tofu. Me? I always figured God gave me canine teeth, designed for the tearing and rendering of flesh, for a reason. Besides, I love a good steak. But when in Rome! So I slathered everything in hot sauce and dug in.

"So Quentin or do you prefer being called the Champion?" Moonglow started.

"Quentin is just fine, if you please."

"Wonderful, well Quentin, on behalf of the community I would like to thank you for protecting us."

"I was protecting her, as I promised to do." I said nonchalantly gesturing to Sharon.

"Oh, well nonetheless, thank you." he said flustered.

"You're welcome." I mumbled.

"You really were quite amazing, from what I've heard." Burning Candle smiled.

"That's what all of the girl's say," I winked to her. Everyone laughed.

"He saved my ass!" Shorty dropped in.

"For which we are all grateful." Moonglow said, but not convincingly.

"Well," a pretty woman in her thirties called Running Brook said smugly, "as a pacifist I can't say I approve of your methods, but I appreciate the results." I laughed. "Is that funny Quentin?"

"No, but it reminds me of philosophy class. Pacifism can only truly exist in a tame world, not in the violent world we all live in."

"I'm a pacifist in this violent world!" She said proudly.

"Only at the expense of others." I smiled back. "As long as there are cops, soldiers, and 'Champions' in the world you are free to call yourself a pacifist. Only when you're under the knife will you know the truth."

"I am willing to die for my conviction." She said proudly.

"Look, Running Brook, if you place fifty pacifists in a room you have utopia, a totally safe environment. Now add one psychopath with a knife and you'll either have fifty dead pacifists or a few who have to compromise their views to survive and ensure the survival of the others. Pacifism is an intellectual position afforded by the luxury of civilization. But until the pacifist is tested in a life or death situation, it remains an intellectual exercise. In truth, the only real pacifists are dead." Shorty sprayed his drink laughing loudly at that.

"Interesting," Thunderbolt, a middle aged man, joined in. "So you ascertain that a belief is only real when it is tested."

"Otherwise it's just intellectual masturbation. You can call yourselves vegetarians because you have the wealth and comfort to live that lifestyle. Try having that same conviction while you are starving to death on the streets of Calcutta as you squat next to a sacred cow. Now that's spiritual commitment! How many of you have ever really been hungry?" A few raised their hands. "No I mean really hungry, as in I haven't eaten in two days, there's no food in the cupboard, the wallet's empty, and the dog is starting to look pretty good to me hungry? Then we'll see how you feel about meat."

"I see you're point," Running Brook said, "but you have to believe in something."

"You can believe whatever you want. All I'm saying is that until those convictions are tested you will never really know. Let me ask you a question, Running Brook, do you own a gun?"

"Of course not."

"A knife? Sword? Num-chuks?" At each she shook her head no.

"So if someone came to kill you, you would have no way to defend yourself?"

"True, but I'm a pacifist."

"Or just weak. If you have no way to defend yourself then you have no way to test yourself. You're a 'submissionist' or a victim, but not a pacifist. Now if you're sitting there waiting for your killer to arrive with a loaded shotgun in your hand, and then you choose not to use it, well then I would agree that you're a pacifist, at your funeral of course. Hence, the only real pacifist is the one who died choosing not to act when he had the means to do so."

"I could never take another human life!" She replied and most of the others agreed.

"Next time I'll let the bad guys through and we will test your theory." I said sarcastically.

"He's right," Sharon defended me. "You can't understand until you're in the position, but when it's kill or be killed, you'd be surprised at how quickly your convictions get tested. The question is not what would you be willing to die for, but what would you be willing to kill for? Your survival? Your children's survival? The Hermits survival?" She looked at different people as she mentioned the reasons. "If people are not willing to fight for what they believe in then their ideals will die when they meet those that are willing to die for what they believe in. Just a few days ago armed hoodlums made it right outside these very doors and if it wasn't for warriors like Quentin, you all would have had to face the ultimate test for a pacifist; to die without defending yourself and your loved ones!"

"However," I smiled, "if being a pacifist means that you would never willing or purposely hurt another human being, then I would say that I am one too."

"Really?" Running Brook asked skeptically.

"Sure. When I rescued Shorty I could have easily shot the two men who were holding him, except I only rendered them unconscious by hitting them with my gun and placing myself at great risk in the process."

"That's true!" Shorty added, enjoying this.

"It actually would have been easier and safer to shoot them, but I chose not to." I added.

"That's true as well," Shorty was grinning.

"So my choice to injure them, when killing them would have been to my own betterment, proves that I am a pacifist."

"Knocking someone unconscious does not make you a pacifist." Running Brook said smugly.

"When the easier choice is to kill them? My point is, we're not who we say we are but we are the choices that we make. My choice to not kill them and placing my own life at risk to do so makes me more of a pacifist than you, whose beliefs have never been tested in a life or death situation."

"The other night we faced possible death and we chose not to fight." She said proudly.

"No, you chose to let others fight for you. If we had failed and they had come to you, then you would have faced death and if you chose not to fight you would be dead."

"Perhaps we could have persuaded them not to kill us."

Shorty laughed and sprayed his drink again as he did. He wiped his face and smiled, "Let me know how that works out for you. Quentin's right. Pacifism is an invention of civilization. In a world where the barbarians are at the gate no one has the time or the luxury to be a pacifist. Well Running Brook, the barbarians are at the gate once again. Will you protect your own life and the lives of your children or will you die and let them kill and rape your children just to say you're a pacifist? All of you look deep into your hearts and ask yourself the question you've been avoiding your whole life. What are you willing to do to save your own ass and the asses of your friends and family? Will you let them die? Will you let the Hermit die? Because it almost came to that and it could come to that again. I understand the concepts and beliefs of a pacifist and I have to believe that every pacifist has his, or her, limits. What's the fucking point of spirituality if it ends up making you dead?"

"To make a better world?" Starshadow offered.

"By dying?" Shorty asked. "That's my point. You can't do shit when you're dead except rot and martyrdom is a lonely and sketchy path with little to no payoff. The margin between a martyr and a dumb ass is pretty thin, in my mind. And a martyr to what? Peace? Give me a break. Your enemies would piss on your smug grave! You're right, if everyone was like you it would be Utopia, but they're not and as a result you're at great risk. You hide up here where it's safe and pleasant and the hermit feeds your egos. Would you still be so pacifistic if you lived in East Oakland or in Compton? If things don't go right a shit storm is going to fall on this place as they go after the Hermit. Each of you will have to decide whether it is better to die for your ideals and have your ideals die with you or to try to live to carry them on. Those that survive can bury the true pacifists." He said and laughed again.

"But in the next life?" An older man asked.

"In the next life? They'll be pie in the sky when I die, huh?" Shorty laughed again. "Don't count on it, Oakstaff. I know the hermit isn't feeding you any of that shit! No the measure of a man is his time on earth and what he does with it. Checking out early just to make a point rarely works."

"It did all right for Jesus!" Running Brook said sarcastically.

"Did it?" Shorty smiled. "I mean did it really work out? Here he goes around preaching love and peace, gets his ass capped and now it's fuck you, I'm saved and going to heaven. No, I'll bet if Jesus was sitting here drinking a beer with us and you asked him if he'd do it all over he would probably have chosen to stay a carpenter. Better pay, better hours, and a much better retirement plan!"

"Better than heaven?" Running Brook asked.

"Heaven? I don't think Jesus ever mentioned heaven. The kingdom of god, maybe, but certainly not heaven the way most Christians fantasize about. Have you ever read the description of heaven in Revelations? The streets are paved with gold and the buildings encrusted with jewels! But is there any mention of a blade of grass, a tree or a bird? Nope. And if you think about it it's pretty ironic that the streets are paved with gold and the buildings are encrusted with jewels in a place where money isn't supposed to matter!"

"Why do you think Jesus would have chosen differently?" Mariner asked.

"I don't know," I added, "it could go either way. I mean Christianity has offered solace and refuge in hard times to billions of people, so it has had its positive effects. Marx would argue that religion keeps societies down by using its authority to keep the people working hard for the man. He believed that religion was the opium of the masses, but what he didn't say was that people needed opium to get through the day. But if I were Jesus and saw all the shit that had been done in my name by overzealous Popes, crusaders, conquistadors, missionaries, and let us not forget over four hundred years of inquisitors, I think he could make an excellent case for changing vocations. Odds are he wouldn't recognize Christianity anyway."

"Why?" Swallowtail asked.

"Cause Jesus was a Jew." I pointed out. "He would expect that anybody worshipping in his name would be following the original Jewish rituals of Passover, Hanukkah, Yom Kippur, and the other high holidays as well as the kosher laws as well. What did he say, 'I came not to abolish the law but to amend it.' The Last Supper was a Passover Seder Dinner. Communion as Christians know it came directly from that Seder dinner. Unleavened bread and wine are crucial aspects of the ceremony. We know what he said about the bread and wine but what he said about the salt water, lamb bones, roasted eggs, roots and the rest of the Seder Dinner got left on the cutting room floor. Jesus was a Rabbi and as such was expected to lead the Seder Dinner. He would expect all Christians to follow the traditions as well."

"That was the way it was when he walked and that's the way it was in the original church set up by Peter 'the rock'. In Peter's church Christianity was a sect of Judaism, which makes sense if you think about it. I mean Yahweh, Jesus' dad, was a mean god with a sick sense of humor and a very short fuse. Don't believe me? Well then ask the folks at Sodom and Gomorrah or Noah's neighbors what they think of God's compassion and forgiveness. But that's no surprise, wasn't that part of the Ten Commandments? Something like, 'I am a jealous and vengeful God.' Not the kind of God you'd want to mess with, you know what I mean. Could be Heaven's actually a trap and when we get there we'll find out how pissed off God really is at us for nailing his son to a cross."

"So you think heaven is a trap?" Swallowtail asked.

"I really don't know, but I wouldn't be surprised that if there is an afterlife it's not like anything any of us could imagine and as wonderful as it may be it will probably be equally terrifying."

"Why?" Sharon asked intrigued.

"Because it's god, the infinite, creator of the Universe and we are his perverse creation. My gut tells me that it will be more like getting dumped into the primordial soup than having lunch with George Burns and judgment day could really suck if Yahweh hasn't softened up. I mean we killed his kid! We better hope the Christian concept of forgiveness made its way back to the home office."

"So how come Christians don't follow the Jewish Holidays?" Swallowtail asked me.

"Oh, Paul fixed that one and he and Peter never really agreed about it, but eventually Peter came around to Paul's point of view. Paul had big plans and knew that he had to change everything around to make it a better sell to the Romans. But he also knew that if you sell it to the Romans and you sell it to the world. So he basically stole the best parts of Roman lore and created Christianity, changed what he saw fit, and added what was necessary to create the church as we know it. He knew the Romans would never convert to Judaism, as

Peter originally thought was necessary, so he changed the rules around to eliminate having to convert. He fine-tuned it in the provinces and finished it off with martyrdom and Christians love a good martyr. The Roman government tried to suppress it which made it even stronger and the church was born. Soon to follow was the idea of a Pope and then the church spent the next fifteen hundred years selling salvation at a premium and suppressing anybody who didn't agree with their dogma. No one would even know that there were other versions of Christianity if some kid hadn't stumbled upon the Dead Sea Scrolls which ended up containing the Gnostic Gospels."

"The Gnostic Gospels?" Sharon asked.

"Yeah, the other versions of the Christ story that didn't quite make prime time. Some of them were dubious but some of them had better pedigrees than the four gospels, none of which had authors who had actually ever met Jesus. One of the Gnostic Gospels was allegedly written by or at least is the version attributed to 'Doubting Thomas', one of the actual twelve disciples and he certainly has a different perspective on things. And most of them have one thing in common; Mary Magdalene was Jesus' wife! Until around 300 AD, when Constantine on his deathbed made Christianity officially legitimate there were scores of different versions of Christianity out there. Shortly thereafter there was one and all other versions were branded heresy. After that Mary became a whore, Jesus divine, and salvation attainable for a price."

"That's a pretty cynical view, young man!" Oakstaff said disapprovingly.

"I'm sorry if I offended you, I was speaking historically. Religion and history do not make very good bedfellows. Sadly too many people confuse the two."

"What do you mean?" Starshadow asked.

"Religion is based on faith and history on fact and both can be right even when they're in conflict."

"How Quentin?" Mariner asked.

"By understanding the purpose of religion. Once you realize that it isn't the facts that are important but the message then you can begin to understand that you don't have to defend every little story. The Hebraic tradition is one of storytelling with a purpose. One of the funniest memories I have from college was sitting in a bar listening to a fundamental Christian argue to a Jew that Jonah and the whale was true. The Jew simply laughed and said the point of the story was about faith in god and the story didn't have to be true as long as it illustrated the point. He was exactly right. But to the fundamentalist, everything had to be true or none of it was and that's a hard place to put yourself."

"So I take it you aren't a Christian?" Swallowtail asked.

"Certainly not as most people would define it. But Jesus was amazing and if people lived the way he instructed us to we'd live in a better world, maybe."

"Maybe?" she asked confused.

"Yeah, maybe. Truth is it didn't even work out for him, did it? Turn the other cheek only works if they stop slapping! The thing is that Jesus' message was awesome but like a roomful of pacifists it can only truly work if everyone is on the same page. Of course you could make the same argument for socialism, communism, and just about every ism or religion. It all works if everyone agrees to the rules, but how they deal with the rule breakers and the natural greed of humans is where it all falls apart. Jesus gave us a set of rules to live by so we weren't overcome by our natural instincts of greed and lust. But his turn-the-other-cheek idea, while good for your spiritual growth doesn't aid you in a world that can create Romans or Nazis!"

"He sacrificed his life so we could live forever!" Golden Hands pointed out.

"Actually, I doubt that was something he actually ever said or even meant to do."

"You don't believe in the Resurrection?" he asked.

"Don't have to! In fact, for me, it ruins the whole thing."

"Why?"

"If Jesus is the son of man who attained perfect union with God, then there is hope for us all. If Jesus is the divine Son of God, had a virgin birth, and miraculous resurrection, then what assurance do we have that we can attain the same level of consciousness since we're not any of those things. If Jesus was a man then the path to salvation is through meditation, prayer, and acts. If he's divine from birth then salvation can only come through him. It's Jesus' humanity that opens the path to enlightenment for all of us and allows us each to return to the garden on our own. If the only salvation comes through belief in him then it's just a club that you can join to go to heaven. At least the Buddhists were smart enough to recognize that Buddha's divinity started with his enlightenment after walking a long and arduous human path. Yet even they have two different versions of the Way."

"So are you a Buddhist?" Moonglow asked

"No, I'm a Philosophia Perenis kind of guy?"

"What's that," Sharon asked.

"It's Latin. It means the ideas that seem constant throughout all religions. If you study carefully most of the world's major religions, threads of ideas that are present in all of them become clear. Ideas like 'Do unto others' and Judge not lest ye be judged' can be found in most of the major religions religious teachings. These are the tenets of faith that I hold in my heart. It's essentially a personal moral code culled from a dozen religions. But unlike other religions I don't feel a need to impose my beliefs on anyone else nor do I need their approval or agreement in what I believe."

"And yet you can kill dozens?" Running Brook challenged me.

"Yeah, I did, so you didn't have to. Spiritually it was a bummer, but I'm alive and so are you, so what the hell. I'll never forget what I did, but I can't afford to worry about it as I am sworn to protect the Goddess by any means. But if I go to hell for that, so be it! Frankly, the very concept of eternity is hellish in itself?"

"Why?" Starshadow asked.

"Tell me, is there anything you want to do forever?"

"Sure! I love ice cream." She said.

"So you go to heaven and can eat all the ice cream you want! Let me know how you feel about ice cream in a couple million years! The fact is there is nothing I want to do for an eternity. There's nothing I want to do for a ten thousand years let alone a million unless it's endless sleep with endless wonderful dreams. Who knows, maybe all of this is just one of those dreams. Doesn't matter, I'm along for the ride!"

"What if there are fun things to do in heaven?"

"I love roller coasters but don't want to ride one every day for a thousand years. My great uncle was only eighty when he said he was bored because he'd already done everything. No," I ended, "I'll settle for the long sleep, thank you, eternal rest!"

"So you want to just fade into the black when you die?"

"Dreams would be nice, but I'd be all right with that, but whatever happens when I die is what's going to happen despite what I believe. No, I'll just go along for the ride. Besides, I doubt religion is any more correct about the afterlife than it was with Zeus being the cause of lightning. Religion has always tried to explain the unexplain-able and the only real mystery left is what happens when you die, hence the resurrection and salvation focus of modern Christianity as well as Islam, not to mention the reincarnation of the Buddhists and Hindus. Only the Jews seem to be happy with the lives they have been given."

"Goddess?" Burning Candle asked.

Up until now, Sharon had remained quiet throughout the conversation as she studied Quentin. At first, she was amazed at his knowledge of religion and then amused by his playful disregard of it. She hated to enter conversations like this. "Yes?"

"What is the truth?"

"The truth is in your hearts and the truth can be different for all of you. What happens after you die is what happens and no matter how wise or foolish you live your life, you will all face that moment of death the same way. I am the goddess of Earth and as such am concerned about what happens here as you should be as well. If you are living in peace and harmony with the world around you then it's working. But as Quentin points out the world is not filled with nice people. You must all work to make the world a place you want your children to grow up in."

"But is there a heaven?" Swallowtail asked.

"That is not my concern. This is my home and where I awaken when called. My work is here and for now, so is yours. Heaven can wait." She smiled.

"Frankly, I believe if there is any afterlife it isn't going to look like anything you may think it does." I took back over sensing the Goddess was uncomfortable with the line of questioning. She's probably right. God knows what might happen if it turned out that all of the religions were just a manifestation of society's collective insecurity.

"How so?" Starshadow asked.

"Just a hunch based on the fact that most people believe that when they get to heaven that all of their ancestors will be waiting there with smiles on their faces and then they can all be together!" I shrugged. "Sadly though, the fact is that we don't know what happens after you die. Well, actually we do know that the body decays, dust to dust as they say. But the consciousness is a whole different story. The thing is who we are, our self-awareness in the universe is a construct of our mind. It's a mishmash of self-perception, behaviorism, life experience, and ego, and for thousands of years, the world's philosophers and psychologists have been trying to understand what it is. But each of us despite being unable to define it knows exactly what it is; it's that inner voice that says 'I am right here, right now!" But if we leave our bodies to rot and decay, then isn't that all there is left of us; our self-awarenes or our souls? And I can't imagine a future with me being a floating consciousness or what I would do as one unless we simply blend back into our creator's consciousness. Better that than being consumed by God, as no one likes to be thought of as food, but in the end, the result is the same. No matter what happens I'm pretty sure Granny and Uncle Bob won't be hanging at the pearly gates waiting for me in corporeal form with a deck of cards to play Pinochle. Personally, I think Valhalla sounds more interesting."

"But terribly violent!" Starshadow pointed out.

"Not anymore than the world it was created in and not any more than most other religions. Vikings were promised the exact same thing that the crusaders were, weren't they? A place in heaven for their glorious deaths in battle! And when the so-called Christian crusaders finally took Jerusalem they killed every living person in the city whether they were Arab, Jew, man, woman, or child as they 'cleansed' the city in blood. Valhalla was the perfect heaven for a hard-fighting people who had to plunder the coastlines to get what they needed in order to survive in their barren homeland. A hearty people like that needed a hearty god and hearty heaven. Fighting all day, drinking and feasting all night, a permanent hunting lodge; isn't that what all heavens offer, a way out of the daily toil and drudgery of our lives? Even Hinduism and Buddhism tell you if you're good you can come back to a better life, you can come back as one of 'them'! You know, the guys whose life looks better from where you're standing. You know, the way the people who live down here look at the people who live up near the hermit!"

"Envy is a result of desire." Golden Hands said quietly.

"Nonsense! Envy is the natural result of social order. The poor worship the rich not out of envy but because they sit at the bottom of the social order and dream of rising, just like those who live down here hope someday they can move up the hill. Your elite living up at the top of the hill, having the best views and direct access to one of the most brilliant men on the planet, are no different than the elite of any society whether capitalist, socialist, communist, or any other 'ist'! The cream of the crop always rises to the top and cut themselves the biggest piece of the pie."

"Isn't that the way of life? Haven't they earned their place?" Burning Candle asked.

"Have you?" I baited.

"What do you mean?" Running Brook asked agitated.

"I'm guessing that this is the special table and that you are the top dogs around here. Am I right?"

"We are the spiritual leaders, if that's what you mean." Oakstaff answered.

"Exactly! So if I get this right you, the spiritual elite, are entitled to a few extra perks, like the best houses and direct access to the boss. Don't be ashamed, it's the natural order of things. In a capitalistic society it's the rich at the top, in a spiritual society it's you, but it's still elitism and I don't buy into it."

"Why?" Thunderbolt asked.

"Because I don't buy into your value system. You value spiritual growth and so do I, the difference being that for me it's a personal thing, not a social status. Personally I value the healers who saved me, the officers who fought with me, and even the people who cooked this food for us as much as I value your spiritual wisdom."

"So cynical," Starshadow commented.

"Maybe, or maybe just realistic. But the truth is it doesn't matter because you all buy into the false hierarchy, so who am I to judge."

"So what would you do differently?" Star shadow asked.

"Me? Hell, I don't know. Let me ask you this? In the Christ story, do you see yourselves as Christ or as the Sadducees and Pharisees he railed against?" I was silent and so were they. For that matter so was most of the room. Apparently everyone was listening.

"You make a point," Running Brook said quietly.

"Oh, don't get your panties in a twist, we're just talking!"

"No," Thunderbutt or whatever his name was said, "You are the Champion and what you say matters!"

"Nonsense! A few days ago you wouldn't even talk to me! Only after the old man came down and chastised you did you did you ask me to dine with you! No, don't let me upset your apple cart. You have it pretty nice and I can see no reason why you may want to reorganize the social order around here. They might," I gestured around to the silent faces watching us, "but that's your problem."

"One you seem to have created," Sharon teased. "So, Quentin, how would you reorganize things?"

"Me? Okay, first if you really are the spiritual leaders of the community then you should spread yourselves out amongst the people instead of dining alone. Of course you risk having to hear of other people's opinions and problems, but you'll also have the opportunity to explain why you make the decisions you have to make as administrators. You know, create a feedback loop." I looked around and saw a family at a nearby table. "Excuse me sir, how many members are in your family?" The heavily tanned worker smiled.

"I'm George Briggs." He said proudly, "There are five of us; me, my wife and three kids."

"And how many bedrooms in your house?"

"Two."

"And how long have you lived there?"

"Five years sir."

"Thank you! Starshadow, how many bedrooms are in your house?" She was silent for a minute but I knew the answer was a lot as I had seen the house.

"Four." She answered quietly.

"I'll say no more." I sipped the wine in my cup.

"Are you suggesting that we should give up our homes?" Thunderbolt asked angrily.

"I ain't suggesting anything! Personally I prefer to sleep under the stars. Where you sleep is not my concern."

"I am humbled by the truth of your observations," Burning Candle said quietly and maybe a bit sadly. "Perhaps you are right and I was blinded by a sense of entitlement. Too often we, the elite as you call us, huddle amongst ourselves and

I for one vow to reach out. Thank you Quentin, for your wisdom."

"No charge!" I laughed. "God, you people need to lighten up a little. You know, make a joyful noise unto the lord and all! I've never understood spiritual growth that prohibits you from celebrating the fact that you're still alive and kicking!"

"Cheers to that Quentin!" Shorty smiled and raised his glass.

Running Brook stood up and raised her glass, "To you, Champion, and to all of you who stand between us being pacifists and victims! Thank you!" Everyone in the room stood and raised their glasses.

After that dinner broke up and a few of the elite stormed away.

"You sure put a bee in their bonnet!" Shorty laughed behind me. "Twenty bucks says a few of them are on their way to see the old man and complain!"

"Come on Shorty, let's go blow a joint!" I laughed back.

"Lead on McDuff!" We made our way out of the crowded dining room and headed to my car.

"I hope I didn't piss off too many people."

"Fuck em!" Shorty laughed. "They're all a bunch of stuffed shirts anyway."

We arrived at my car and I removed a couple of joints from the glove box. I lit one and handed it to Shorty who took a long toke. I hopped up on the hood and lay against the windshield and Shorty joined me. He handed the joint back to me.

"Rikki's shit," he asked after exhaling a cloud of smoke. I nodded. "Thought so. Crazy woman grows some good smoke!" We sat and smoked in silence as we watched the stars. When the joint was spent, Shorty slid off the car and said, "Thanks for the buzz, buddy. Now I have to meet a young kitchen wench that fancies me! Have a good night."

"You too, Shorty." He left and I was left alone to contemplate the universe.

Sharon watched Quentin carefully and was amused at the way he handled himself with the Hermit's inner council. It wasn't much different than the way he treated the hermit. He wasn't disrespectful, but he didn't seem to think much of status. They were a brilliant group of people with a variety of skill sets. Goldenhands was the Doctor who saved Quentin's life. She had gotten to know them the last few months and found them all pleasant, intelligent, articulate people whose company she had grown to enjoy. But when Quentin confronted them with their own hypocrisy she herself found herself feeling guilty as well. She always ate with the elite and not with the 'people'. No one likes to be forced to look into a mirror or their own soul but Quentin had a way of winnowing his way in and challenging your basic values. She had always trusted the hermit until Quentin said she shouldn't mostly because he was usually right no matter how annoying it could be.

Before the Goddess came she had never really thought much about religion. As a young girl, she had gone to Sunday school but by the time she was in high school, she started working weekends and fell out of the habit of attending. Like most people she blindly accepted what she had been told without giving it much thought. But being the goddess gave her a completely different look at religion. Early in their relationship Sharon had asked the Goddess about life, the universe and everything. 'What is the truth?' she asked her.

"The truth is you are right here, right now.' She answered coyly.

"Obviously, but what else?' Sharon asked frustrated.

"Why does there need to be more? This is life, Sharon. This moment! The next moment will be life when it comes but until then it is the future. The moment we are having has already begun to become the past. All you have is this moment to do, think, act, love, and feel.'

'But what happens when I die?' She asked the ultimate question.

'Why do you care, you'll be dead? This is my world and when I am called I am and when I'm gone I'm not until I am again. I am not concerned with what happens after you leave my world and nor should you be. We have too much work to do in this world!' It was all she would say on the subject.

So when Burning Candle brought her into the conversation Sharon knew they were not going to get the answer they wanted. She was surprised to find out that Quentin also felt that what happened after you died didn't matter, even if he had a strange way of expressing it. Valhalla? The expressions on some of their smug faces were worth it, she thought! If Quentin was nothing else he was smart and funny and she suspected that neither of these traits had anything to do with the Champion.

6

Shorty was gone the next day and rumor was he was back on the job. For the first time I had some time to relax and check things out. What a whirlwind of craziness it had been recently and I looked forward to exploring the neighborhood. Actually, it was a pretty good set-up. Using wind, solar, and water power they actually created enough power for the commune so that they sold the excess to the power company. They had huge fields for both food for the people and hay for the animals and had enough dairy cows to provide milk and cheese, which they made themselves. Each person contributed their labor where they were most effective. They had their own nursery, day care and school and the jobs to run them were shared. Each according to their abilities seemed to be in place here as Jake explained it to me as everyone eventually settles into what they do best to contribute. Shorty is a spy, his girlfriend works in the kitchen, Ariana is a healer and Jake handled security. Everyone liked their jobs and was happy. I had to hand it to the hermit; he had created a mini utopia. It was easy to get used to.

The place was beautiful but Sharon was even more so. Watching her lead the people and do her duties as the Goddess made her even more attractive to me as I learned she was compassionate and her heart was full of love. I watched her play with children and sit with the old. She went about her duties with both grace and style as I began to realize that her inner beauty was even greater than her outer beauty. I also noticed that she treated me differently than she did everyone else. While she was calm and reassuring to all of the people there she was stern and less forgiving towards me. I gathered that Sharon had a problem with me and I guessed it had to do a lot about how I expressed how I felt about her. But I had yet to even pin that down. The thing that confused me the most is that despite our communication problems I felt deep in my heart that we had a connection that I couldn't put my finger on. Maybe it was the whole Goddess/Champion thing but I felt as if our destinies were tied together.

I never felt more like the Goddess than when I was at the commune where I had a lot of things to do and none of them were normal. I always seemed to be blessing or teaching something as the Goddess. Obviously, the Goddess was very good with plants, which is a good thing because I was never any good at growing anything but mold on old cheese! I was learning and that was the best part of my job. The Goddess in me flourished in this environment and I suspected that the Goddess, secretly enjoyed the adoration she received here. I'll admit it. I enjoyed it as well. I had never had that before in my life and it was nice to be respected. But damn, I was busy. I was up early every morning and moving all day long. Truthfully, I really didn't have much time to think about anything other than what I was doing at the moment.

I think I misjudged Quentin in my initial assessment of him and his performance to date has been exemplary. Even the Goddess seemed somewhat impressed, but she was always so fatalistic about him. Then again, she's probably seen enough of them die to be wary.

Above the dome, I discovered the mountain continued up behind it but the cliffs were sheer and worthy of a good climb. I had learned the basics of climbing from a guy name Gene I met in the backcountry of Yosemite who hung out with me for a week. He taught me how to tie the knots, and the basics of climbing like how to belay a partner. Since I was alone and three days from the nearest road he figured me to be a loner so he also taught me how to self-belay when climbing alone. Free climbing without protection allows you to move light and quickly but without any safety net. One mistake and you're dead or seriously injured. While I was there I bought a rope, a harness, and a variety of climbing protection from the mountain shop and loaded it into the trunk of my car. One day when I was bored I climbed the peak behind the dome.

It was a pretty straightforward climb for most of the climb with only a couple of hairy stretches that had me tie in to the rock and self-belay. It slowed me down having to go back down and clean the pitch but better safe than dead I reckoned! Honestly, it was a delightful climb! The sun was hot as I cleared the trees and warmed my bones from the cool morning mountain air. There were two really nice pitches and a variety of crack sizes and narrow chimneys. It was challenging but not overly terrifying with just enough scary parts to keep the adrenaline pumping. Near the top I found a large ledge where I could sit and relax and so I did. For most of the afternoon!

The view was stunning. Looking down the entire complex lay out before me. It lie in a sea of trees stretching out as far as I could see interrupted only by a few scattered homes and roads which looked like long scars in the green carpet. I could make out people leaving the dining room and working in the fields but they were like ants. Up here I was away from the stress and the pressure of being the Champion and for just a minute could breathe.

Perspective! Clearly, some was needed here as I tried to get my head around what was happening to me. It took me a long while to realize that there was no way to really understand what the hell was going on. It didn't really matter since I realized I was on this roller coaster until it crashed or got to the end of the ride. So I focused on Sharon.

In many ways, my feelings toward her made even less sense than the whole champion thing. I had loved Cheyenne but this was different. Cheyenne and I had no future and we both knew it but I could actually see myself with Sharon growing old and that had never happened to me before. It seemed after each thing I accomplished her opinion of me grew and her words grew warmer which gave me hope and had me secretly wishing for additional opportunities to prove myself to her. As I watched her do her Goddess thing around the people I began to respect her more as a person.

I had been so busy whining about getting sucked into this whole thing that I forgot about how much she had sacrificed as well. Hell, I'd been the champion a couple weeks but she was chosen over a year ago and had been in training ever since. Being the Goddess was a full-time job for her and to be honest she was pretty good at it. I watched her one day talking to a child who had been crying and saw in her eyes and words the reason the goddess had chosen her and in some ways the reason my own heart did as well.

I was startled and surprised when an old white owl flew up and perched on the branch of a small tree that stuck out from the rock. The bird settled and stared at me and I stared right back. For hours! My mind was clear as I just stared into the owl's eyes and it stared right back. I had seen owls before but never one like this. In these eyes, there was both age and wisdom more human than any bird I've ever seen. I once stared down a German shepherd for an hour and saw a depth in those deep sad eyes. In the owl, I saw that same depth as those eyes seemed to sink into my very soul. Remembering my Native American studies I realized the owl could be a spirit guide. Only the damn thing didn't deliver any grand vision to me. Instead it just sat there and stared at me as if it wasn't there to impart wisdom as much as it was there to assess and study me. So we sat and studied each other.

I'm not sure who flinched first but after a couple hours it simply disappeared. I closed my eyes for just a second and when I opened them it was gone. But I didn't see it flying anywhere and figured it probably dropped lower and found a new perch against the cliff. So I set up my first rappel and headed down. I descended what took me four hours to climb in about fifty minutes. I had enjoyed the climb but was perplexed about the owl. Was it an omen, a spy from the goddess, or just another strange unexplainable experience for me and in the end I realized it didn't really matter which it was.

The next night I was getting my sleeping bag and tarp out when I heard a sound behind me. I turned to see Ariana standing there with a smile and a blanket. "Mind if I join you tonight?"

"Sure!" I smiled and headed for my camping spot.

"Nice spot!" she smiled as I laid out the tarp and placed the sleeping bag on it. We sat down, I lit a joint and we talked late into the night.

I told her my story and she told me hers.

"Mother arrived here alone, pregnant, and scared. I was born in the clinic that you were at and was raised here by Mom and a whole lot of people. She was always disappearing for a week or even a month at a time. I stayed with Jake or one of my friend's families as the adults kind of watch all the kids anyway. I have a lot of good memories from when I was growing up. Mom and I shared a hut near the bottom of the hill."

"She was just as beautiful as her name was, Briana. Jake says I look just like her. She worked in the gardens and I sometimes worked with her. God I loved her and then she was gone," she trailed off slowly.

"What happened," I asked gently.

"I don't know. It's life's great mystery, I guess. She went away and never came back. She might be dead or she might have just disappeared. At first no one noticed. She had disappeared many times before. She was an agent for the Hermit, like Shorty, and she loved the adventure. Every time she returned she wouldn't tell me where she'd been but she always seemed more alive and our time right after she returned was special. Only she didn't return this time, ever. I saw the truth in Jake's face first, the worry in his eyes. One day he went to see the old man and then he disappeared for a while. When he came back he was so sad and I knew the truth. Mom was never coming back. I was eight." She was silent and I let her be so.

"I cried a lot and raged when I could but in the end things were only a little different. I stayed with Jake until I was twelve when I moved in with Miranda and her husband. Jake felt I needed her touch to help me through puberty and he was probably right."

"Is that why you became a healer?" I asked.

"It didn't hurt, but I was always interested in herbs and what they could do. Mom taught me about plants as we worked in the garden so I was on my way when I got to Miranda's house. But she did help me train and she's pretty good at what she does."

"So will you stay here or move on?" I asked as I stared at the starry night.

"Good question. When I was younger I refused to ever leave the property in fear that Mom would come home and I wouldn't be here." She leaned on one elbow and looked right at me. "But now, if I had a good reason to leave, like I was in love with someone who didn't want to stay," she paused, "I might leave. But I would want to come back and visit the people here. Jake was like a dad to me and these people, who you saved, are my family. So if there is anything you want from me," she paused again as she looked at me, "then just ask!" she smiled.

What the hell, I thought? I was pretty sure what she was offering and the offer was actually quite tempting as she was a very pretty girl, but all I could do was think of Sharon. So I changed the subject. "Do you want to go look for your mother," I asked gently.

She rolled onto her back and said, "Why? Where? How?"

"Good point."

"Jake said he did everything he could. He checked hospitals, death records, and even viewed a number of Jane Doe corpses but she vanished without a trace. Not even the hermit knows where she went. Personally I think she's dead because if she's not then she left me by choice and I can't live with that."

"I'm sorry Ariana. I truly am," I said as I reached over and held her hand.

"I'm not. I'm surrounded by people who love me even if maybe she didn't."

"I'm sure she loved you," I consoled her.

"Then why'd she leave," she asked plaintively.

"Trust me Ariana; we're not always in control of our own destinies. She may have done it to protect you."

"From what?" she asked.

"I don't know but perhaps her sacrifice which also was your sacrifice had some noble higher purpose."

"Thanks Quentin, that was a nice thought. There is always hope, I guess. So what is it with you and Sharon?"

"I don't know but when I saw her I felt a connection that I'd never felt before. It was like she was my destiny only it didn't work out that way. Now I'm tied to her and in love with her and she is definitely not in love with me but seems to be warming up a little." I was rambling. "There's always hope I guess," I ended and we both laughed.

"Look, a falling star, make a wish! We both did. "Hope!" she whispered.

The next morning we headed back to my car where Sharon was waiting. When she saw us she seemed pissed off. "There you are! When you're finished with your little sexual dalliance the hermit wants to see us!" She turned and started to storm off in a huff.

"Excuse me, Goddess!" Ariana said in forceful voice. Sharon stopped in her tracks and turned to face us. "Begging your pardon, your grace," her voice was now soft and meek, "but you are terribly mistaken. Quentin and I slept out together under the stars, but nothing happened. He remains," she sighed, "hopelessly devoted to you!" With that she stormed off.

Sharon watched her leave with a bit of a surprised look on her face and then she turned to face me. "I'll be waiting in the dining hall!" was all she said and she turned and stormed off. How could two women be so mad at me when I didn't do anything!

Sharon was shocked when Ariana and Quentin came together and she wasn't very polite. As she walked away she thought, what was that? Clearly she let the ugly head of jealousy rise up but why? It's not like she and Quentin were a couple. But what really irked her was she couldn't figure out which upset her more, them spending the night together or Quentin's hopeless devotion.

It was a long quiet drive up the hill. I had taken a quick shower and felt a lot better until I got into the car with Sharon who eyed me suspiciously but silently. Tired of the silence I addressed the elephant in the room, so to speak. "Look Sharon, Ariana is my friend. She knew I liked to sleep outside and she came out and joined me. We talked, looked at the stars, and went to sleep."

"Is what she said correct?"

"Yes, nothing happened."

"No, I mean the other part. Are you hopelessly devoted to me?"

"I am devoted to you. Whether that is hopeless or not I guess is up to you." Then it was quiet for the rest of the ride.

Starshadow escorted us out to the deck where the hermit was waiting.

"Hi Zach, how's it hanging?" I joked.

"Hello Quentin. Start any peasant revolts lately?" He joked back.

"Sorry Boss, Shorty got me worked up. I was just hacking on them."

"No, don't worry about. Every group should question their own social order every now and then. You really shook a couple of them up, though."

"Why?"

"Because you were right! Your points were well noted. But your observations lacked one keen and crucial observation."

"I'm sure I missed more than one."

"Probably, but the one that I'm referring to is the fact that people are where they are because that's how you humans organize your societies. For reasons that Freud could best describe humans need someone at the top of the food chain to look up to and to aspire to be. If there is no one up there they will place someone up there."

"Makes sense to me. Anyway, I was just busting their balls, no harm meant. Frankly I'm surprised anybody listened to me, it never happened before!"

"You're the Champion and now you're on that pedestal. You are one of the Elite."

"Maybe, but I prefer sleeping under a tree thank you. So, any word on the big bad wolf?"

"If you mean the escapee, then the answer is yes. I believe we have located him in a place called South Central in Los Angeles."

"Doesn't sound promising. That's a tough neighborhood without demons and your pal!"

"Nonetheless it's time we plan our assault. Shorty's gone ahead to scout the location. You two need to practice with me until you're confident you can face the escapee. Once you have defeated him you can return to your lives."

"How Zach? Dude, I was a pacifist and now thanks to the champion my body count is worse than a 'B' movie! Can a whore go back to being a virgin? How do you return to innocence?"

"I can help there, if you really want that. When this is over I can wipe your mind of the whole thing, but everyone you've met along the way will be wiped away as well."

"Not much of a choice. No, I'll bear my burden. Beside, I'll probably die anyway." I said detached.

"There is that," he joked in a non-reassuring way

We spent the next few days practicing our mind blocking techniques. I repeated the multiplication tables hundreds of times and found that the technique was easy until I tried to fight. So then I sparred with Zach, who was very good with a sword, while I tried to keep him out of my mind. It was hard but with effort I got better at it. More importantly I began to get a feel for what it felt like when Zach broke through."

"Zach, how the hell do you people function if you're going around reciting numbers or poetry in your head?"

"Quentin, life in my world is hard and dangerous because almost anyone can control a mind, but over the centuries we have developed a series of protections and disciplines to let us know when our minds are being touched."

"Teach them to me!" I asked.

"I can't." He sighed.

"Why not?"

"It takes years to perfect the techniques."

"So go into my head and program me!"

"What?"

"Go into my head and program me. Look, it's pretty simple. Go in, make a few adjustments and then when I face the bad guy at least I'll be on even ground. Think you can swing it?"

"I'll have to give it a lot of thought. It's possible but dangerous, yet novel. Most people aren't comfortable with the idea of me monkeying around in their heads."

"How about for starters we don't use the term 'monkeying around'! The thing is Zach, if you wanted to mess with my head you could have done it at your leisure. I'm not asking for an advantage, just an even playing ground!"

"I'll give it some thought. Now back to work!"

Like any other skill, practice makes perfect and after long days of practice I was pretty much able to function normally while reciting the math tables. But my big worry was that during battle my mind was making dozens of calculations every minute as I sized up opponents, chose appropriate weapons and looked for an opening. So with the hermit's permission I had Jake round up five of his best swordsmen and had them surround me and attack while the Hermit attacked my mind. It was ruthlessly hard but by the end of the second day I was happily reciting math tables while I defeated the swordsmen. The hermit was impressed and so were Jake's swordsmen. I felt a lot more confidence.

Finally the Hermit relented and after gaining my consent he entered my mind and went to work. I could tell by his presence that he was working as lightly as he set up what he called warning beacons.

"This is how we protect our children," he explained, "and we carry these beacons inside our head for our entire life. Over our lives we modify and strengthen them but they are the core of our defense. For us there are various levels and depths of beacons so that we can let people into our minds deeper and deeper and still be protected. What I'm doing is setting those beacons up in your mind to alert you when an attack is being made. Your defense will still be the numbers, but these will at least let you know when you're being probed and will certainly alert you to an attack. When he was done it was clear after we tested it that he had been successful. He probed me and attacked me over and over until the beacons became undeniable. When triggered I immediately went into numbers mode. It worked and I was glad as I felt it might be an important tool in the fight ahead.

Sharon trained as well but had to be talked into the idea of having beacons placed. Or I should say the Goddess was not comfortable with adjustments being made to her ancient and precious mind. The hermit said that because the Champion saw it as a weapon he was more likely able to accept it, but the Goddess resisted until the Hermit pointed out that if she didn't have any defenses, she could be controlled by the escapee which would be worse. Finally Sharon relented and had the beacons placed and after practicing admitted that she felt more confident that she couldn't be surprised.

That night I was shocked and surprised to find Sharon approach with her own pillow and sleeping bag. "Mind if I join you tonight, as friends." She added.

"Sure," I said as I led her to the glen where I had been camping.

"Nice spot," she said as I laid out the tarp and placed the sleeping bags on it.

It was a moonless night and the sky was full of stars. We sat on our bags and faced each other and I didn't know what to do. God she was beautiful even in the dark, I thought but I didn't want to piss her off so I whipped out a joint. "Smoke?" I asked as I hit the joint.

"Sure," she said as she took it and took a deep hit. We smoked the joint in silence and after her third hit she lie down and stared at the stars as she exhaled the smoke. "I never knew there could be so many stars when I was young. We lived in San Diego and there were too many lights to see many stars. This is magnificent."

"You should see it above ten thousand feet while on top of a dome in Yosemite. You can practically read by the starlight! I saw falling stars that looked like flaming bowling balls."

"I'd like to see that! Still, this is pretty amazing."

"So are you!" I said quietly.

"Please stop, Quentin. Can't we just be together," she said sadly.

"Sorry. So how about a couple of tales from the goddess? Six thousand years should have produced some good stories I'd imagine. Maybe one of the stories should give us insight into the escapee."

"Certainly Champion, but my stories are your stories. What type of story would you like to hear?" she asked.

"Preferably one in which the Champion survives!" I said and we both laughed.

"You know many of the stories but rarely the way they're told. Centuries after it happened when I read Le Morte de Arthur, Sir Thomas Mallory's tale of King Arthur I almost vomited."

"Not a fan of Arthur?" I asked.

"Talk about a total cluster! For some unknown reason, those people could not keep their lust in control! I was the Lady in the Lake and handed Uther Pendragon the magic sword Excalibur to defeat the escapee who was running around having a field day raining chaos on the poor helpless people. Instead, he uses Merlin who was a powerful moron to steal Lord Gorlois's wife and throw the whole world back into chaos not to mention getting himself killed. So when Arthur was the king I sent the champion to aid him and I had great hopes for success until that damn blond came along and stole his heart. Lancelot could have been one of the great champions instead of just a jerk."

"Lancelot was a jerk?" I asked.

"Worst kind of Frenchman. He was arrogant, cocky, and so handsome it was frightening. Despite what the legends say he seduced his best friend and liege's wife. Guinevere was so pious on the surface yet had the morals of a goat in rut when she thought no one was looking. They ruined Arthur and the Kingdom and if the escapee hadn't been killed by marauding Saxons who knows what would have happened."

"Wow, now that was a story." I said.

"It was a mess and almost a disaster."

"I always figured the whole story to be depressingly stupid."

"They usually are a muddled mess. Hopefully this time things will go smoothly. That happens sometimes."

"So who am I talking to now?" I asked.

"It was the goddess' story but my voice," Sharon answered.

"So Sharon, how are you holding up? You seem to be under a lot of pressure as the Goddess. Sorry if I added to that." I said.

"Thanks for asking Quentin. Sometimes it's a lot but the Goddess bolsters me when I need it. It really isn't a burden, it's a pleasure. I feel like I'm doing something important."

"I feel like I'm locked in a bad dream. You're the only good thing about it!"

"Thanks. Don't worry it will be over soon and you can go on with your life." She said.

"What about you?" I asked. "What will you do?"

"I don't know Quentin. I've been working at staying alive up to this point. But I like it here so I might stay. You'll be welcome as well, I'm sure."

I wasn't so sure but I kept it to myself. "We'll see. At some point I have to get on with my life or at least maybe my journey. I'm not looking forward to the day I have to come to grips with all that I have done."

"I understand, but you did what you had to do to survive. Just tell yourself you had little choice in what you did.

If you didn't do what you've done I and many others here would be dead and that has to count for something."

"It does, but only time will tell if it's enough. Good night, princess." I said as I closed my eyes.

"Good night Quentin," she said. She was gone in the morning.

Sharon lay there listening to Quentin's gentle snoring. The truth was she didn't really know why she was there. She didn't mind sleeping outside but preferred a nice soft bed. But she thought it might be nice getting to know Quentin a little and she was surprised when he kept the focus of the conversation on her. She didn't need to be the Goddess to feel his pain and she wanted to soothe him but remembered what the Goddess had said. The problem was any kind of affection she showed him at all only raised his hopes and increased his devotion, a devotion that could quite possibly lead to his death. A death that she knew she would feel guilty about.

The next morning at breakfast I was downright shocked to see Rikki having breakfast with Jake. When she saw me I smiled and her face lit up! I didn't expect her to jump up and hug me, but I appreciated it.

"I wondered when you were going to get your sleepy head up!" She teased.

"Rikki! What a pleasure! How are you?" I asked. She looked great.

"Can't complain. Jake here says you've been busy and might need a re-load, on all fronts!"

"I did manage to get into a few scrapes." I said humbly.

"A few scrapes? You saved everybody's collective ass up here and a few of them, like Jake here, actually appreciated it."

"I couldn't have done it without you." I said.

"Aw shucks! Anyway, it's good to see you in one piece. Rumor has it that Shorty owes you as well?"

"Not in Shorty's eyes, I'm guessing! I see Shorty as more of a taker than giver."

"And you'd be right," Jake laughed.

After breakfast I fetched my weapons bags and they led me to the barn where a large truck was parked. Rikki unlocked the door and raised it and inside it was filled with guns and ammo.

"Unpack your stuff on these tables," she gestured to a couple of tables that had been set up. "I'll inspect them all for you. You know, guns aren't really meant to be used all that much. Daddy used to say that the more times you use a gun the more likely it is to misfire. When a gun is in a firefight it can get real hot, as you well know, and heat is metal's worst enemy. Daddy said it isn't necessarily the number of times a gun is fired as much as it's the length of time it was fired. He's seen guns used in combat get warped barrels the first time they were used, or overused, he used to say."

Rikki chirped away as she carefully but quickly stripped and inspected each of my weapons. "They're pretty clean, good work Quentin."

"So do you give all your customers this service?"

"Just the ones I like, sweetie, and those that are going to save the world!" She teased as she slipped another large baggie of weed into my pocket.

"So, Quentin, how did you come out west?" Sharon asked as we headed down the long driveway finally on our way.

"Lost in America I guess you could say." I responded.

"Sounds, like a promising career," she teased. "So, where do you see yourself in five years?"

I was surprised by the personal nature of the question as Sharon had always kept things on a professional level before. "Truthfully, I don't know. One of the reasons I'm on this trip was to find the answer to that. My dad always asked me what I was going to be when I grew up as if what I did was who I was. I think who we are doesn't have to be identified by what we do for a living. I hope that whatever I'm doing in five years I'm as happy as I am when I'm with you."

"Why do you always do that?" she said angrily.

"What?"

"Just when we're having a nice talk go and make it about your feelings about me."

"I'm sorry," I said. "So what about you? What plans did you have before getting hijacked by the Goddess?"

"Me? I was working as a graphic artist doing layouts for an ad company. I belong to a gym that I rarely went to except when I felt guilty about not using my membership. I had a small group of superficial friends who met pretentiously on Sundays for brunch where we picked at each other like crows."

"Any serious relationships?" I asked.

"They're all serious, at least at first," she joked. "Yes, I've dated but never really thought about getting married or anything. What about you?"

"Once I connected with someone, at least for a while. But she was older and had a daughter and I wasn't anywhere close to being able to deal with that."

"Don't you like children?" She asked.

"No, you don't understand. I really liked it being with her and her daughter. Almost too much! I was only eighteen and not ready to support us all but I started thinking of myself in that way. That wasn't what she wanted. She wanted another baby she could use to keep her welfare checks coming in."

"Yikes!"

"Yeah, she was afraid I'd try and stick around and do the right thing and that wasn't what she was looking for. Truth is I couldn't provide for her as well as the state could. So she left me and found someone else to impregnate her."

"You're probably better off in the long run," she said. I had no answer to that.

She changed the subject and we talked about movies, plays, and a dozen other topics as we killed time on the long drive to LA. I quickly discovered that Sharon was as beautiful inside as she was outside and my love for her deepened maybe because for a second I felt like I had penetrated her force field and touched her heart. I felt almost hopeful about our new friendship and was extra careful not to compliment her too often.

It was a long drive through the valley as we made our way to LA and we stopped at a nice restaurant for dinner as we hit the outlying suburbs. Sharon slipped off to call Shorty and let him know we were here while I got us a table. Then we had a lovely dinner. We talked about food and our favorite restaurants as well as vacations we had taken as kids. In this environment with the goddess and champion out of the way, I found it easy to talk to her and easier to really start to fall for her. Then Shorty called back and it was all about business between us.

Every time Quentin complimented Sharon it made her feel even guiltier which made her get even more irritated with him. It didn't help that they were driving south towards the enemy and the moment when the boy might actually have to die. Do or die had a whole lot more meaning when the stakes were actually death. But when it was just them together driving they relaxed and were able to talk about normal things. Right through dinner, it seemed like for just one day they were normal people, maybe on their first date. It felt like that and it was actually quite nice. But in the back of her mind, she held her guard high as she could not forget where they were going and what the Goddess had said. Could she send him to his death?

"I think we should go light and move fast," I said. We had met Shorty at a sleazy motel.

"Trust me, buddy, don't go near that place unless you're well-armed." Shorty offered and Sharon agreed. So we compromised and loaded ourselves down with hidden weapons. I carried two swords, a sawed-off shotgun on my back and two-shoulder holstered forty-fives and two nine millimeters in a second sling under my baggy hoodie. I had a full set of throwing knives as well as some other weapons and back up ammo stashed as well. Sharon wasn't as heavily armed, but she was not without her own defenses. For all his interest in our armaments, Shorty himself was lightly armed.

According to Shorty, he was able to get close to the escapee because he pretended to be a hired gun and the escapee wasn't using his powers on those who would sign up for duty willingly. I still kept one eye on him as he could have been adjusted upon his arrival. His plan was to walk in and walk right up to the bad guy based on his report that things were pretty lax security wise with most of their effort being trying to keep all the different gang-bangers from killing each other. It sounded thin, but what the hell. At this point I just want it to be over.

As soon as it was dark we loaded into my car and headed out. Shorty gave us directions and had me park on a side street so we could approach on foot. At the last minute, I gave each Sharon and Shorty a spare key to the car.

"What's this for?" Sharon asked as I gave it to her.

"Just in case," I said.

"In case of what?" she asked.

"Just in case I don't come back," I said quietly. That seemed to upset her a little and that lifted my spirits.

"Does it have gas?" was all that Shorty asked.

"Half tank?" I smiled.

"Gas?" Sharon asked.

"Yeah! If we have to make a getaway it's nice to know we won't have to stop at the first gas station!" He smiled.

"You've done this a lot?" She asked.

"Enough to know that you hope for the best and prepare for the worst. Now, stick close and don't even look at the other gang-bangers. I'll get you in and close but then I've got to split."

"Why?" Sharon asked.

"I'm in deep cover. Hermit says if this fails he'll still need me to keep tabs on the bad guy. So until he's done for good I have to play my part."

"Great!" Sharon sulked.

"Okay, let's get moving." After one last check we headed down the street. I was worried about my car in this neighborhood, but hopefully we wouldn't be gone too long.

I felt like every nerve in my body was receiving information as I approached the guarded entrance. I counted steps from the corner of the building to get an idea as to the building's size. My eyes darted right, left, up, and down as I took in everything. I felt like a cat about to prance, all coiled up, and ready to strike.

"Relax Quentin," Shorty answered.

"Sorry," I mumbled as I realized I wasn't attacking but infiltrating.

"Who's that with you Shorty?" the guard asked.

"Two new soldiers, bosses orders."

"Oh yeah, says who?"

"Says me," Shorty said with a cold smile on his face. "Don't fuck with my bounty!" he sneered. The guard looked at him and then at us.

"Okay. Head to the check-in desk and sign them in. Nice bounty Shorty."

"No shit! Any dinner left?"

"How the fuck would I know? Piss off!"

We silently entered the building and the first thing I noticed was a stench from a combination of weed, stale beer, cigarettes, urine, body odor and dozen other smells. The air was heavy with it. My eyes darted right and left and my hands were loose and ready to draw. I could see the check-in table leading into a large room and just one person who was asleep manned the table. We quietly slipped around him and entered the main room which was a large warehouse with cots spread around clustered by gang affiliation. As my eyes adjusted to the dim smoky room I could see at least a hundred people lying and standing around. Small groups were dancing while others just killed time playing cards or shooting the shit. Mean-looking mercenaries in camouflage fatigues carried heavy weaponry and stood sentry throughout the room to keep warring gangs apart. The whole scene was rather peaceful if you ignored all the guns lying around.

"Straight across the room is the canteen where they sell cigarettes and shit like that. Just past that is a hallway and that's where you're headed. He'll be in the room at the end of the hallway. Be careful." Then he disappeared into the crowd. We casually strode across the hall walking down the crooked paths between the various groups. We tried to look as bored as everyone else and I was surprised when Sharon held my hand. My heart raced for a second until I realized it was just her cover.

"When are we going to go home?" she whined like a valley girl.

"Soon, baby, soon!" I said pretending to soothe her.

"You said that last week!" she whined as we passed one of the mercenaries who was looking at us strangely. I rolled my eyes at him and he smiled and let us pass by without stopping us.

When we reached the canteen I was surprised at how cheap the cigarettes were and bought eight packs, stuffing them into my pants and coat pockets. Sharon rolled her eyes at me and I shrugged my shoulders. "What? They were cheap!" I said.

We approached the hallway and once we had entered it my senses all came alert. All at once, I knew three things instinctively. One, that trouble was behind us and not at the end of the hallway! Two was that we were way under-armed to deal with the horde behind us. The third thing I realized was that we were screwed. Wherever this hallway leads us, it is not going to end well.

"We're in deep trouble," I said as I looked around for an escape. I could hear the voices rising and a crowd forming and knew that the way we came in was now closed.

Sharon froze and looked around. I could tell her own senses were on high alert as well. "Oh no, what do we do?" she said. "Mary, Mary, quite contrary..." her voice trailed off as I realized she was closing her mind. Twenty times twenty is four hundred, I chanted in my mind as I headed to the door at the end of the hall. The door was unlocked which I took as a bad sign.

"When we go through this door let it open as we stand aside, then follow me and go in low." We moved to either side of the door and I looked down the hallway. I could see that everyone in the big room was standing and massing by the tunnel and that an aisle had been left in the middle. And there walking down that aisle was Shorty standing next to what I believed to be the dark one. He looked more like a dance instructor than anything else. Our eyes met and he smiled. I'd have shot the bastard but a hundred guns were pointing at us.

"So, you finally made it! Too bad you won't live long enough to tell that old meddling fool that I am the bane of his dreams. Tell him my time is now and when the time is right I will come for him. But first I will lay waste to our home world and then I will crush yours!" He smiled again and simply pointed and the aisle disappeared with armed men and women running straight at us.

I opened the door and crouched as I moved into the room scanning the room as I did. The large room was empty except for a machine against the wall at the far end which took up the whole wall except for a seven by seven foot section in the middle that was filled with a mural of a forest scene. My eyes scanned the room for another way out and I was coming up empty. Sharon entered behind me and I closed and locked the door. I looked around but there was nothing to brace it with. In fact, there was nothing in the room but the machine. I could hear them pounding on the door and laughing which I couldn't quite grasp.

"Quentin, that's the portal!" Sharon said. I looked back at the wall and realized the mural could be seen moving. We walked over to the machine and you could actually smell the warm breeze that was causing the leaves to blow. "We have to destroy it!" She said. "It's operational!"

"I can blow it! I brought some grenades!" I said and pulled two out.

"Well at least we won't die in vain." She said grimly.

I had sworn to protect her and now it was just a matter of time until they came through the door. I studied the machine and picked two spots on either side of the portal to place the grenades. "We'll have ten seconds when I hit the fuses on the grenade to find cover. You should probably go to the far side of the room to the corner. When the door opens I'll use my weapons to take them down and maybe you can slip out in the confusion."

Sharon stared out in horror at the amassed army. Even the Goddess knew their goose was cooked. Quentin refused to give up and dragged them into the room only to see the portal. There was no way out and an army between them and safety. Quentin's offer to distract them while she slipped away was brave, noble, and laughable. There was not going to be an escape.

'At least we can destroy the portal which will slow him down,' the Goddess said to her.

She looked at Quentin and realized what the goddess had meant about him being expendable. What she didn't know until now was that she was expendable as well. What the Goddess had meant was it would slow him down long enough for a new Champion and Goddess to arise. The Champion and Goddess will go on but Quentin and I won't, she thought sadly.

All of this was for naught and now we'll be dead but the game will go on. She felt used and betrayed and the Goddess really had nothing to offer her because she was right. She and Quentin were both expendable. She understood that and accepted it as well, but it still pissed her off. "No Quentin, I'll stand by your side. I owe you that much."

There was a loud rumbling behind us and when we turned around the entire fucking wall was rising up and most of it was made of canvas. What the hell? The 'hallway' we walked down looked like it had been created just for us. Then it hit me, it had. Shorty had set us up. Whether he was under control or not, that little fucker set us up. And as I watched an entire army appear behind the rising wall I could see Shorty shouting out orders. I turned around and pulled the pins. "Ten, nine, eight," I said as my mind raced. They charged at once and I fired with both nine-millimeters singing in rhythm, but there were too many. Four...then it hit me. I grabbed Sharon's hand and yanked her close as I dove through the portal. There was a strange tingly feeling as if passing through a shower of sparks and then I dragged her to the soft ground and rolled to our left. One! The grenades exploded and when they did the portal closed behind us with a sucking sound. The portal was closed, we were alive, and we were no longer in our own world.

7

The second the portal closed I knew we were safe or were we? The battle was over but we were on the wrong side of things. First of all we were no longer in a room but on the edge of a dark forest overlooking an empty plain covered in grass and wildflowers. In the distance was a large body of water whose shoreline stretched beyond sight. I didn't know if it was a lake, an ocean or a sea but on its shore, there was a large town. I knew instinctively that eventually, we would probably end up there. A river south of the town and even with us was dotted with what appeared to be waterwheels. Sharon was sitting on the ground with a shocked horrified look on her face. That didn't bode well.

"Are you ok Sharon?" I asked tentatively. As I did my eyes scanned the horizon and forest looking for threats. There were none, yet. "Sharon, can you hear me?" She nodded and I dropped to a knee next to her.

"Sharon?"

"Oh Quentin," her voice rushed and panicky, "we're through the looking glass! We're not on Earth anymore! What are we going to do?"

"Survive for starters." As I knelt there I inventoried my hardware. Two swords, three knives, four throwing knives, a pair of forty-fives with six extra eight-round clips, two nine millimeters with four fifteen-shot clips, two hand grenades, and a pump action twelve gauge shotgun, shortened for traveling, with about three dozen shells. I had enough for a good fight, but after that, it was swords and knives. "What are you packing, Sharon?"

"Huh?"

"Weapons check, girl. We could be in hostile territory! Snap out of it Sharon!"

"It's not right Quentin. She's afraid!"

"Who?"

"The Goddess! She's terrified! She has no power here. She's blind and powerless and terrified. The best way I can describe it is that she's psychologically hiding in a corner. She's always been there, Quentin! Giving me strength, telling me what to do! Now it's just me and I don't know what to do!" She burst into tears. Great, Quentin thought sarcastically, this is a good start.

I pulled her into a hug and comforted her for a few minutes and as the tears slowed down whispered reassurances. "We're not licked yet, Sharon. But you need to pull yourself together and we need to move!"

"Why? Are we being followed?"

"Not that I can see, but it would do us well to not be where we landed if we were noticed. Now here," I handed her a bandana and she wiped her tears on it and I had the thought that I would save the bandana forever. Then she blew her nose in it and I changed my mind. I stood up and stretched and offered my hand to Sharon who took it and pulled herself up. She was clearly shaken and looked quickly left and right as she straightened her clothes.

"What happened?"

"We got suckered Sharon! Hard to say where the fix was put in but we were maneuvered into that warehouse and the attack was not meant to kill us but to push us through the portal. I wonder if they realized we would destroy it!"

"But why push us through?"

"I'm not sure. But you said the Goddess is still with you?"

"Yes, but pretty useless."

"Well, if we're still the Goddess and the Champion and we're here, then we're not there. That means the Dark One is free to do as he wishes, because as long as we're here, Zach can't summon the Goddess and Champion. That's why they weren't trying to kill us and only herded us. If they killed us the Goddess and Champion would be free to find new hosts. They needed us here, alive and stuck."

"Then what is he planning?"

"I'm guessing he is the bad guy Zach's been waiting for!"

"The Dark One?"

"A very good possibility."

"Why, Quentin?"

"Let's walk along the tree line towards that town and I'll explain," I said as I helped her up. "Now mind you, this is just a theory, but Zach never mentioned that the escapee would have the ability to open and close portals at will. He had quite an army and yet only used what he needed. If he opens a portal and unleashes them on this world, well, I don't know what will happen. But it's more than that. This is it Sharon, the one they've been waiting for, I can feel it deep inside. We're here for a reason even if we don't know what this is all about and we have to stick it out. But most of all we have to get back as soon as possible because our world needs the Goddess and the Champion."

"But how?"

"Now that's the question! I'm guessing the beginning to that answer lies in that town over yonder."

"So what's the plan, Quentin?"

"First I'll scout out the area and the town."

"We'll!"

"Huh?'

"We'll scout the town. You're not leaving me, Quentin, ever. We're not on Earth and until we get back I'm not leaving your side!"

"I would never leave you but it might be dangerous!"

"Maybe, but if it is we'll die together. You are not leaving me here alone Quentin, ever. I get separation anxiety just thinking about it."

"That's going to make going to the bathroom awkward!"

"Quentin!"

"Just kidding." I laughed and she joined me and it felt good!

"Is the Champion still in you?"

"I guess. It's not like he gives me orders and controls my movement. It's more like I just know more. Like I know I'm not in my own world, but everything I see indicates that this isn't that far from ours. For example, I've seen birds, flowers, trees, and the air is good to breathe, so I feel enough at home to assume that while there may be significant differences in our worlds, there are even more similarities."

"Of course around the next corner could be a thirty foot bear that eats us in one quick move." She smiled.

"Maybe, but I doubt it. There would be tracks! But your point is well taken and we must remember that even more dangerous than bears, there will be local customs, taboos, and myths and we will have to learn them and use them to our advantage!"

"But how?"

"How indeed, is the question? Right now our knowledge base is zero. Slowly we'll add data and hopefully, when we have enough we'll be able to act."

"What do we need to know?"

"Depends on where we're at! That's why we need data. First, we need to know the basics, what do they look like, what kind of clothes are they wearing so can we pass for one of them. If we can, we can learn more and hopefully find the right people."

"Who are the right people?"

"Anyone who can help!"

The town looked farther away than it had appeared and by dusk we were just pulling up parallel to it. It was still a good hour walk to the town so we rested for a moment. Lights came on all over the town as the darkness fell. The houses were widely spaced and not that different from our own homes at least in basic shape.

"Quentin, maybe we didn't leave Earth!" Sharon said timidly. "I mean that looks like a normal town!"

"Quiet Sharon, you're being silly. If we were on Earth the Goddess wouldn't be cowering!"

"Oh yeah."

"Now, we're going to go scout around but avoid all contact and get ready with your rhymes in case we meet anybody. We don't know anything about where we are so we have to be ready for anything!"

"It's like we're explorers or something!" Sharon said.

"Yeah, well you only heard about the ones who survived, so stay alert. What are you packing?"

"I still have a couple of knives, my sword, and two nine-millimeters with two clips each."

"Okay, not a lot, so use it sparingly and hopefully not at all. It's dark so we should be able to get pretty close without being seen, but if you see something get down fast! Okay?"

"Yes Quentin, I'll be good."

"If something happens and we get separated, meet back here."

"There will be no separation and that's final!"

"Okay, okay, let's go!"

We headed towards the town. Our pace was brisk and anxiety high, but the longer we walked the further away it seemed and we started to talk."

"Sharon, are you all right?"

"Am I all right? No Quentin, I am certainly not at all right'! I'm not where I belong and I don't know where in the hell I am or how to get back. I frightened beyond belief and to make it worse I have a basket case of a goddess hiding in my sub-conscience!"

"I know," was all I said but I did put my arm around her and pull her into a hug. "It's going to be all right Sharon. I'll take care of you and make sure nothing happens to you. It's my job, but I'd do it even if it wasn't. So relax and breath and we'll take one thing at a time. Okay?"

"Okay. Thanks." She broke off the hug and turned to walk. I took a second to catch my breath. I found that I liked hugging Sharon.

The town grew in size as we approached it about an hour after we had started. As we got closer details began to appear. The first thing we came to was a ring of fields, pastures, and barns that seemed to ring the town. As we got closer I realized that what we were seeing were a series of plantations, with large manor homes each with a series of stables, garages, barns and outbuildings built close but not too close to the main house. Their fields and pastures, some with animals, fanned out onto the plains. As we drew near we found a series of small shacks lining the fields. There was light coming from inside one of the houses so we edged closer and peeked through a dirty window.

A shabbily dressed man and a woman were sharing a meal at a small wooden table in the cheaply furnished cottage. I was struck by both the poverty they lived in and the happiness they shared. Clearly they were in love and I guess that was all they needed. I felt like they were lucky. Then they talked.

Thank god for the Champion, because I had no clue what they were saying, but apparently it was fairly close to ancient Greek which the Champion did understand. The woman spoke, "It was a good day of work in the fields today, Alex!"

"Yes Maria, the Master should be proud of us. We shall bring him a good harvest."

"That would make me so happy!"

"Me too! We are so lucky to work for the Master!"

"Yes we are!"

"I love your soup, Maria!"

"Thank you Alex!" she said and blushed. They took each other's hands and drifted off into silence.

A reconnaissance of a couple more abodes confirmed my earliest suspicions that these were basically workers quarters. I did the best I could to ignore their resemblance to slave quarters, but as we drew closer to the house I realized that I might not have been wrong. It appeared as if status was clearly defined in this society and the size of the house apparently was the measure of that status. The manor was huge and attended by dozens of servants. These servants were better dressed and seemed well mannered but the distinction between classes was obvious. From the looks of the local nobles there was little chance of us passing as one of them for they wore elaborate hairstyles and gaudy clothes, but the servants clothes and looks we might be able to pull off. Slipping back to the workers quarters we stole a set of clothes for each of us and disguised ourselves as locals.

    A series of nice cabins surrounded the manor and in front of them small groups of people sat around. They were better dressed and seemed to be somewhere between the poor field hands and the rich noble. The manor itself could best be described in earth terms as antebellum-like, but there were improvements that had been made with modern materials and artistic deviations borrowing from a half-dozen other architectural styles. As you approached the manor you found elaborate gardens, fountains, and pools. The front of the mansion had a long circular driveway that led to a road that seemed to curve from one end of the water around the city and back to the sea. As we followed that road we discovered that the next two mansions were similarly lavish. The second of the houses had a large tree in front and helping Sharon up I climbed high until the city lay out before me.

At the center of the town on the sea, there was a large castle-like structure with a tall parapet and even what appeared to be a drawbridge and moat. It was surrounded by a narrow ring of parks, gardens, and small farms that insulated it from the rest of the town. Quentin knew immediately that the parks were not decorative but defensive in nature. There was a clear field of fire surrounding the castle, which was built for defense a long time ago. A road ran along the water from each side of the castle and a series of concentric half-circle roads linked the two roads and in their arcs was the city. Additional roads ran out from the castle intersecting with the curved roads and creating a web effect, which created the blocks of the city.

From up there, it was hard to tell but it appeared that each ring had its own function. Surrounding the castle's green space was what appeared to be a series of municipal buildings. The next ring contained what appeared to be merchants, then manufacturing and eventually housing. The housing seemed to grow more crowded and smaller the closer you got to the center of the city. The only exception was along the harbor which appeared to be lined with docks, marinas, warehouses and dozens of boats, both commercial and recreational. About half-way from the sea to where we were there was a ten foot wall separating what was clearly the old section from the newer sections. Inside the wall everything was crowded and old and outside the wall everything was nicer and newer.

The city was a built for a fight to the death defense. The old wall that protected the inner city would have been easy to defend. But if the wall fell the city itself was built for defense. There were only six spokes of roads leading from the castle and while they were each a wide avenue, they would be easy to barricade. An aggressor would have to take each ring and pay the toll in blood for each one. When the last ring fell the survivors ran for the castle and would await their doom and hope to make their enemy bleed enough on the plains to weaken any attack. The parapet would give the defenders a good view of the field of attack and they could see any invaders long before they could attack. It was a well-defended city but once the outer wall fell it wouldn't be long before a siege would set in. And he had no idea how defensible it was from the sea.

One by one lights winked out throughout the city as the town slowly went to sleep. As it became quieter you could hear the occasional animal stirring, voices, laughter, and it struck Quentin how much like home it really was. But he still knew very little and needed information. The question was how do we get it? The only real information they had on the place other than what they'd seen with their own eyes and Zach's legend of the Dark One. Other than that we knew nothing of the customs or taboos of the area. My biggest fear was someone would find us, paralyze us with their minds, and then lope our heads off without a word!

I passed Sharon on the way down the tree and dropped to the ground. Sharon followed and dropped into my arms, only I lost my balance when she did and I fell to the ground with her landing on top of me. Giggling broke out from behind us and Sharon rolled off me; I sprang to my feet, ready to pull any number of weapons. Nineteen times nineteen equals three hundred sixty-one, I thought as I began to recite.

"That was funny!" a girl a little younger than our own age said in Greek as she came out from behind the bush. "What were you two doing in my tree?"

"This is your tree?" I asked, somehow in Greek, while I looked her up and down. She was dressed normally and not all frilled out like the nobles.

"Well, my Lord's tree! I'm Lystra and my father is head of the entire Globstell Plantation owned by Lord Maxillium, which you happen to be trespassing on." She said proudly.

"I'm sorry, Lystra, we were lost and looking for a way home."

"Lost?"

"Our master doesn't let us leave, but I was walking with my beloved here and we just lost track of time and everything."

"You're in love?" she smiled at Sharon who smiled back. I took Sharon's hand and kissed it. She didn't flinch!

"Yes and we just got lost in each other!"

"How romantic! You hardly ever hear about that anymore!"

"Haven't you ever been in love?" I asked tenderly.

"Me? Certainly not! I don't know how things are run on your plantation, but here at Globstell we are proper and organized. No, next year I'll come of age and appear before the master to be sorted out and then I'll begin my life! I've been trained as a house servant and hope I get assigned there, unless I'm chosen for breeding."

"Breeding?"

"Dad says I'm pretty enough that I may be blessed with one of the Lord's own! Wouldn't that be exciting?"

"So you'd get to raise the Lords child?"

"Raise? Of course not, I'm no lowly nursemaid! No I would be a breeder for as long as I could! If I do well and honor my Lord I may someday be allowed to have a child to keep as my own. It's a great honor here at Globstell to be given a child and rarely granted. Dad was honored with me for saving our crop when every other plantation failed. Globstell was greatly honored that year and Lord Maxillium was gracious and generous to all."

"Do you get paid for your work?" I asked innocently.

"Paid? Why? The Lord provides everything you could need! Doesn't yours?"

"Ours? Well yes, but he gives out special rewards if you doing something special or bring in a huge crop and then we can trade these awards for extra food or fancy cloth."

"Hmph! I said we were a proper plantation! We work for our Lord and he cares for us. We don't need anything more than he already gives us and we all work as hard as we can already to please him. I would be insulted to get paid! Well, as they say, 'Each Lord to his own way but your own Lord's way is the best way!"

"We have that saying as well." I added trying to grasp it all. "So what's your sorting out like?"

"I'm not sure but my friend Carol did it last year. She said that the Lord helps you discover your true desire. She never knew until that day how much joy she got from doing laundry and how much she loved Jerzkyck, the man she married shortly after her sorting."

"Did she know Jerzkyck before that day?"

"Of course, it isn't that big of a plantation. She just never knew how she felt about him before that day!"

Suddenly it all clicked and everything I was seeing fell into place. The slave quarters, the plantations, and why everybody seemed so happy to please their Lord. This society practiced mental slavery. Sorting out, arranged marriages and yet everything is perfect, it had to be the Lord manipulating their minds. Was this Zach's sad secret, I thought?

"Do you believe in people being able to read or manipulate your mind?"

"You mean like in the carnival show? Those guys are so fake! Can you read my mind?"

"Um, no."

"Well I can't read yours either! I never heard of such a thing.

"Let me ask you a question Lystra. Have you ever heard of the Dark One?"

She immediately made a gesture that resembled the Earth version of the evil eye. "Don't talk about such things in the dark!" she scolded. "Of course I know about him! I have the dream just like everyone else!"

"The dream?"

"You don't get the dream?"

"Um?"

"That's impossible! Everybody has the dream from the time they're little."

"What happens in the dream?

"He comes and with him comes evil and death and the end of times."

"What do you do in the dream?"

"I do like everyone else, I cower, and then I die! You really don't get the dream?" She looked at me strangely. Suddenly she looked at Sharon, "how come she never speaks?"

"She lost her tongue for being loud!"

"You're lying! That can't happen!" Lystra said obviously upset.

"He's just teasing!" Sharon said in perfect Greek. "I just prefer to listen and let Quentin do our talking." Lystra settled down a little.

"You two are strange. I'm leaving you now. Please leave our plantation or I'll call the 'Black Guard'!" Her hands were on her hips and she stood defiantly.

"Let's go!" I whispered to Sharon as we slipped down the road. After we had traveled a piece we cut back towards the forest and hurried to its cover. On the way we discussed many things including Sharon's sudden ability to speak Greek.

"When I heard you speak it I realized that the Goddess should have the same ability. So I kind of confronted her and told her to stop feeling sorry for herself. While she may have been lacking some of her powers, her knowledge remained and that I needed it now. I reminded her that over the ages she had dined with kings and queens from many different civilizations and if she could understand this woman would she please help me! And she did!"

"It couldn't have happened at a better time!"

"Quentin, what is this place?"

"Mental slave colony, I think. Really if you think about it, it's the perfect setup. I suspect that a good portion of the population doesn't have any mental abilities at all and the sorting out is more like a reprogramming. 'Welcome to Globstell Plantation Lystra. You're going to wash windows, marry Gary here, and be happy for the rest of your life.' It's slavery without resentment, Sharon. The slaves don't know they're slaves and are happy because they're told to be that way. Even the poorest field hand barely alive is happy because he has no choice. He'll die serving his Lord to just please him."

"It's horrible!"

"Is it? I wonder? I mean, everybody is happy, no one is bitching about his job, they probably have a zero divorce rate, no crime, and everyone is content. By our standard they aren't free but they don't know they're being controlled so they think they're free as well. They're free to be happy, we're free to deal with our misery and discontent because all our lives we're being told we can be whatever we want to be when only a few actually have the drive to make that possible! A man here can spend his whole life trying to grow the biggest potato he can and love doing it. At night he goes home to his loving wife and they spend their time blissfully because they've been told to. For them it's Eden without the snake and apple. Ignorance is bliss!"

"Are you serious?"

"Yes and no. I'm not saying its better; I'm just saying it may not be worse. Of course I'm speaking about the lives of the workers. And as any society, there is a social hierarchy and rewards increase with status, like Lystra's father being granted a daughter to raise for his service. The house slaves here are well-dressed, they look better fed, and probably lead decent lives. All in all life for the workers of this planet are probably more pleasant, albeit artificially so, than the lives of workers on our own planet! The nobles are a whole different story, though."

"Yes! They could stop it all!"

"Why? Hundreds of willing slaves falling over each other to fulfill your every pleasure and whim while women are waiting in line to 'breed'! I'm guessing they experience high productivity, no labor relations problems, and everybody has perfect job satisfaction. It's a well-ordered society and we should not be so quick to judge them."

"Still, it doesn't feel right."

"Not our world."

"You surprised me when you said we were in love," she said quietly.

"Technically I was only half lying!" I joked. "I was trying to think of a reason for why we could be lost. I saw a young girl and hoped that the attraction of the idea of romance to a young girl transcended any planetary or dimensional differences. I'm sorry if it made you feel uncomfortable but I didn't think you could understand me, either."

We were nearing the forest when a low horn note rolled across the plain. "Look!" Sharon pointed and a light appeared in the tower.

"Quick, into the trees!" I said grabbing her and running. It wasn't far and we both ran quickly and when we entered the forest we dropped to rest and catch our breath. I stared out towards town.

"Do you think she told her father about us?" she asked.

"I wouldn't doubt it. It could even be part of her programming. No sugar, my gut tells me we've stirred the bees."

"Do you think someone will come?"

"Depends on how sacred these woods are. But we better keep an eye out and be prepared to skedaddle if someone comes. But that could be hours from now. Look Sharon, why don't you sleep for a while and I'll wake you if someone is coming, okay."

"Only if you wake me and let me take watch so you can get some sleep as well."

"Deal!" I agreed. She placed her head in my lap. "What are you doing?" I asked surprised.

"Just making sure you don't slip off while I'm asleep!"

"Okay."

She lay there with her eyes closed and I stared at her beautiful face. A wisp of hair lay across it and I gently brushed it behind her ear. I was really surprised when she sighed. That was followed shortly by a gentle snore! I turned my attention towards the town and didn't like what I'd saw. The plantation we had just come from was awash in light and as I watched the ones on either side began to light up as well. One by one the plantations lit up and I was sure they were looking for us. But I also knew it would take them a while before they would come looking here so I let Sharon sleep.

I thought long and hard about this world and still couldn't decide whether it was better for the worker or not. As a human being from our world and an American in specific, I found the very idea of slavery repulsive and offensive to my belief in freedom. But it was nearly impossible to get around the idea that despite their lack of freedom the people seemed happy and content. How many miserable humans had he met who hated their jobs and lives? The divorce rate in America was around fifty percent. I'll bet its zero here, no matter how abusive someone might be. Then again, I suspected that domestic abuse, along with anything else that resembled crime or may upset the balance was simply not tolerated and when caught perpetrators were probably reprogrammed.

    The girl implied that each Lord had certain autonomy, but clearly there must be a central authority, probably centered in the castle. But her suggestion that her lord ran a proper plantation suggested the idea that there were ones run improperly. I surmised that the autonomy each Lord had was probably centered on how they treated their slaves and if they were anything like the old South was then the treatment of slaves was widely varied and determined by each master. In our own world corporate executives pay their employees an unlivable wage to support their own lavish compensation packages, so it wasn't hard to imagine some extravagantly living Lord starving his slaves to support his lifestyle.

    Only the slaves wouldn't know they were being mistreated and would be frightfully grateful for the pittance they lived on. A girl would be grateful for her Lord's attention instead of being angry and hurt when raped. Mind control was in some ways worse than rape. An evil or sadistic lord could visit any and all kind of mayhem on his willing victims who wouldn't even know they were being abused. God protect the poor bastards who lived on that plantation.

But as I watched the search continue, I began to see my mistake. The very act of two slaves sneaking off for an unauthorized tryst was probably practically treason in a completely controlled environment. The fact that we didn't share their collective dream probably made us even more frightening to them. Frightening enough to dispose of us when caught, I suspected. Sharon and I didn't fit into their neat little box and they certainly aren't going to like the news we were bringing, I thought. But Lystra's curl up in a ball and wait for Armageddon attitude did not bode well for any attempt to muster help either.

As soon as they passed through the portal Sharon felt different. For over a year she and the Goddess had been together and suddenly the Goddess pulled back. For the first time the Goddess was frightened and without confidence and it left Sharon feeling alone, vulnerable, and frightened. But Quentin was a rock and she looked to him for support. The Goddess hid deep inside her cowering and whimpering. It was very unsettling. Clearly they had been double-crossed and Sharon had thought they were dead when that fake wall lifted. It simply never occurred to her that they would push them through the portal. It happened so fast the goddess didn't have time to leave her. Sharon felt bad for the Goddess but was glad she hadn't left. If the Goddess withdrawing like this felt so bad she couldn't imagine what it would feel like if the Goddess had left. She realized that once again Quentin had saved her life and it was hard to not feel appreciation for what he did. Sharon wasn't sure about anything other than she had no intention of letting Quentin out of her sight

There was nothing she discovered on their trip to town that gave her any sense of security. On top of that she couldn't even understand what they were saying. When she realized that Quentin did she confronted the Goddess. 'Goddess! Wake up! I need you,' she shouted in her head.

'I don't belong here!" she answered in a panic! "We'll never get home!'

'Not if you don't settle down and focus. Can you understand this girl? Because I can't help Quentin if I don't know what's going on and if I can't help Quentin then we'll never get home! You've dined with kings and queens and you've lived for a long time. Your knowledge alone is also powerful. Can you understand what this girl is saying to Quentin?'

She could and suddenly Sharon could as well. That helped Sharon considerably get a grip on what was going on. As they made their way back to the forest Quentin explained all that he had learned before she could understand the girl. She really didn't like this world and couldn't believe that Quentin considered it well ordered. But she listened to him and as always he made sense. Still, she hated it here. When they reached the woods she laid her head in his lap to rest. No way was she letting him out of her sight!

The hunt went on for hours as a string of lights swept back and forth across the plantations slowly getting closer to the ring road. Sharon's snored gently in my lap and I spent most of the time staring at her face. Yeah, I could wake up to this every morning, I thought! But each time I looked up more lights were dancing and, by the looks of the lights, hundreds if not thousands of people participated in the search. By now poor Lystra's mind had been thoroughly and probably willing examined by whatever the Black Guard was and they were pondering her answers. I carefully reviewed everything we had said and saw numerous errors we had made. In fact, from the view of a controlled world, our simple act of trespassing was seditious and treasonous. Slaves simply didn't wander off here or fall in love for that matter. Or talk to strangers, I realized. I suspected that Lystra's master was livid when he found out that seditious slaves had wandered onto his plantation and spoken to one of his slaves.

Shit! I thought as I watched a light detach from the others and head in our direction. I nudged Sharon who groaned and then whispered, "Is it my watch already?"

"Quiet beautiful, someone's coming! We need to duck deeper into the woods!" They slipped deeper into the darkness, hid behind a tree, and turned towards the town. The light bobbed as it headed straight for us and we slipped deeper to avoid its light. The vehicle entered the forest and we drew back further until we came to a clearing and hid on the edges. It was cloudy, there was no moonlight so it was pitch black now and the light came up to us and passed us and as it did I saw a woman driving a small horse drawn buggy. She crossed the clearing and as she did I could make out a small log cabin on the far edge of the clearing. I could tell from the stumps that appeared in the light of the lantern, that many of the trees that were here were used in making the cabin.

For no reason at all I skirted the edges of the clearing and I slowly made my way towards the house. Sharon followed closely behind and by the time they had arrived at the cabin the lights had been turned on and the wagon was parked in front. As good a place as any to start, I thought, as I silently edged closer to the cottage. It was a simple log cabin with uneven logs and wide chinks. A large garden lie on the far side of the cottage and a woodpile lay against the wall. A small horse and buggy sat parked in front of the cabin and it had a metal box strapped to the back. The box was painted with daisies and a peace sign, which Quentin thought strange. How parallel were the two worlds? Quentin peeked around the corner to the front of the house and watched as the door swung open and bathed the front of the house in light. The woman came out and went to the box, undid the latch and opened it. She removed two canvass bags, closed the lid, and turned around in the light.

"Ariana?" I called out instinctively as I saw her face. She froze at my inquiry and then got wide eyed.

"You know my daughter?"

"Briana?" I asked as Sharon came up behind me.

"Yes! You're from Earth, home, aren't you?" She was excited.

"Yes, the Hermit sent us, can we come inside?"

"Please!" she said as she sailed in.

We carefully followed her in and ducked to get into the door. The cabin was small, just a room with a bed in the corner and a small table and chair. There was a large stone fireplace and a small stove.

"Hungry?" She asked as she pulled out vegetables and washed them in a pan with a pump. "Don't get water out here in the sticks."

"What's the city like?"

"Finian? Well, welcome to Yeshoe; it's like Earth, but weirder. I mean they have a few of the basic conveniences, but the people are weird. Some of them can read and manipulate each other's thoughts and the rest are their slaves. But the nobles can read and manipulate each other's minds and slaves as well and to be honest it drives them crazy. You won't find a more paranoid, useless group in your life, which makes sense if you're always questioning whether what you're doing is what you want to do or what someone else wants you to do. But don't worry because they can't read our minds. Drives em crazy!"

"They can't? Zach, the Hermit, said they could?

"I think he assumed that because he had that power on earth we would be susceptible to it here as well and I was terrified when I got here, but he was wrong!"

"How do you know?"

"Good point! If it's possible that they could adjust my mind then it would be safe to assume I wouldn't be aware of it. But I have also seen them try to enslave me and it didn't work!"

"Really?"

"Yep, after trying to find my way back I headed to town where one of the local plantation owners tried to turn me into a breed mare. I slapped him good and he was terrified and was going to have me killed as a spy. It was only when he realized that I couldn't read or attack his mind but I could kick his ass that he let me be." She placed a loaf of bread on the table. "Tell me about my daughter."

"She looks just like you," I said, "She's a beautiful, warm, funny, sensitive, woman who has helped save my life more than once as a healer. You will be proud of her and she'll be thrilled to find out that you're still alive, but we have to get back home first. Any ideas?" She sat in her chair heavily and looked down.

"I was hoping you'd know." She said and slumped.

"Don't worry, Briana," Sharon said softly. "We'll get back! I can feel it."

"How did you get here?" I asked Briana.

"I'm not quite sure." She admitted. "I was checking on this warehouse and somebody threw me through the portal. I woke up on this side and waited a long time for the portal to re-open. Finally I walked to town but they're a most unfriendly lot, as I told you. My status as unclaimed and uncontrollable left a bad taste in the city leadership's mouths because things here are well ordered and organized and clearly I didn't fit in. Things weren't looking too good for me when I met a Noble woman and when she realized that she couldn't read my mind or control me and that I couldn't read or control hers, we became immediate friends."

"She stood up and claimed me and that was enough to simmer things down for me. I had some jewelry that I traded for seed, food, and supplies and came out here and built this cabin. I grow vegetables and sometimes trade them in the town for what I need. They have stores but they're not like ours. There's not a lot of trust in this world so people mostly take care of themselves."

"Sounds kind of gloomy?" Sharon asked.

"It is! It's beautiful but these are paranoid superstitious people. I live out here because they're afraid of these trees."

"Why?" Sharon asked.

"The woods are pretty scary, especially at night. But mostly because they are also inconveniently clairvoyant!"

"Inconveniently?" I asked.

"Yes, or perhaps I should say uselessly clairvoyant. Either way it's pretty much the same. They've all seen the horror of the final battle and the vision includes strange horrible creatures of all types rushing though a portal in the trees so they don't come near the trees. They don't want to face the end."

"Why don't they pull together and prepare?"

"It's too late! You have to understand Quentin that this civilization is older than even our own. Great cultures have risen and fallen mostly because they all have this amazingly reckless power to change each other's minds. Over the millennium people have used that power for good and evil too many times and consequently there is no longer any trust in this world. They wouldn't rise up for a cause because they have historically done so only to find the cause was just someone stronger than they were manipulating their minds for their own reasons. Finian, the town nearby, was built as an outpost to protect the land from this common nightmare, but instead of drilling and preparing they await their demise. I think they see their role as the sacrificial lamb whose death will warn the others. Not that they'll be any better at defending themselves."

"Zach made it sound a lot scarier!" I laughed.

"Well I'm not sure the Hermit knows, Quentin. He's been gone a long time and if the local history books are right magnificent civilizations here have risen and fallen in his absence. I think he assumed that since in our world they could read and manipulate our minds that such would be the case here. But he was wrong." She grew silent and the look on her face suggested that wasn't the only thing the Hermit had been wrong about.

"The history of this world is no different from our own with the exception that their greatest weapon has always been their mental abilities. Ambitious men have trained armies of men willing to fight to death for their lords because they have no choice and others have raised armies to stop them. But I doubt if any noble was ever killed in any war except perhaps as a punishment for losing. Every war on this planet has been fought with slaves. Everything you see on this planet was built by slaves. I doubt most of these nobles even wipe their own asses without a slave holding the paper!"

"Quentin says that it works." Sharon offered.

"He's right, if you're willing to dismiss the concept of free will. Everybody is happy because they have no choice. But we were born with free will and I think we can all agree that we would actually rather be miserable than be happy slaves."

"Touché! But my point about it working was that these people didn't know any better. If your mind wasn't resistant to control, right now you'd probably be raising a brood of young and happier than either of us could imagine and married to some stud who works hard for his master and loves his wife."

"True." She admitted.

"And you wouldn't even know what free will was at all, just how much you're grateful to the Master for your life! But that's on paper." I smiled. "What's the real scoop? You've already mentioned a few frisky nobles who started wars, so it occurs to me that each plantation could be the noble's personal freak show."

"Yes and no. Each plantation takes on a bit of the character of the owner, but there are also strict rules in the treatment and behavior of their 'workers'."

"Is that where the 'Black Guard' comes in?" I asked.

"How'd you hear of them already? You work fast! Yeah, they're the badass brains of the lot and act kind of like cops."

"So they protect the rights of the workers?" Sharon asked.

"Not likely," Briana laughed. "No they protect the colony from disorganization."

"Disorganization?" I asked.

"Yes, as in anything that threatens the status quo is bad. And with a hundred slaves for every noble, any noble who can't control his slaves is punished, up to losing them all, and it's the 'Black Guard' who is expected to deal with it."

"What's their power?"

"They're just really good at breaking down a noble's mental defenses and adjustments can be made."

"So what do they enforce?" Sharon asked.

"You can basically do anything you want to do with your slaves as long as you keep them under control. There are also minimum calorie requirements, housing requirements, sanitation requirements, and that type of thing mostly to avert plagues or diseases that could spread. But if you or your slaves cause any kind of trouble the Black Guard swoops in and everybody gets an attitude adjustment."

"How can that happen if everyone is happy?"

"In the past some nobles have dallied with the idea of feeling guilty and done things like paid their employees and freed their slaves. They don't last long. When the slaves were freed they went running to their neighbors looking for work. The neighboring lords were not amused and sent for the 'Guard'. They came and the next day everything was back to normal."

"Normal?"

"Yep! They fixed the noble and he fixed his people under their watchful supervision and the next day you'd never know there had been a problem. Neat, efficient, and scary as hell!"

"To us, Briana, but it seems the way of the world here."

"True, but it's a bully's world."

"It is that, but I've been thinking and it seems as if it couldn't be any other way. When a portion of the population has a significant advantage over another part they're bound to eventually use it to their advantage. So basically the ones with no talent were doomed to their station no matter how the society organizes. What is free will if you can't trust what really is your will anyway when it could be somebody else's? Societies tend to organize to solve their needs and I'm guessing that happily mind controlled slaves was the best way they could come up with dealing with the fact that not everyone was created equal."

"Aren't they?" Sharon asked.

"By our standard we're all equal, but not here. Here, those without the power are one evolutionary step down from the nobles and treated as such. Without actually knowing so, I'd bet that a noble's own son could be a slave if he doesn't have the power and likewise a field worker's child could become a noble if they received the gift!"

"And you'd be right, Quentin! The gift is everything."

"On our own planet stronger races have enslaved weaker ones and each and every one of them knew they were a slave. These people don't know they're slaves and they live their lives in happy, loyal ignorance."

"It may seem better but I'm all for the grind of our own dirty little world with all its unhappiness." Briana said.

"Me too," Sharon pouted.

"I didn't say it was better, only better organized. Speaking of which, could they be convinced to fight?"

"Not a chance! Oh, they might send the servants they could spare with axes and shovels to fight with but weapons are forbidden here because of the fact that any work force can instantly be turned into an army if they had the weapons."

"That would be useful right now?"

"Trouble?"

"Quentin thinks the Dark One is really coming this time,"

"Really? Why?"

"Because we're all here!" Sharon said. "I am the Goddess and Quentin is the Champion and we're trapped on this side. Without us the Dark One can gather his army at will. We can't stop him because we're stuck here."

"Shit!" Briana said.

"Yeah! So who's the keeper of the myth?" I asked.

"The myth?" Briana asked.

"The end of world myth," I asked. "Apparently they all dream of it."

"They do! It's like a collective hallucination and they have it just often enough to keep it in the back of their minds. They know it is coming and because they've all had the dream they assume it to be a sign of the end of times." Briana answered with disdain.

"Maybe not, but it will be if there is no one here to defend this place. What did Lystra say, Sharon, that in her dream she cowers and waits to die?"

"Something like that." Sharon agreed.

"Sounds about right." Briana shrugged. "They've accepted the inevitable. You show up telling them that the Dark One is coming and they'll all collectively groan, close shop, and wait for the end."

"We have to try?"

"There are some, the 'Riders', who don't live in the cities and are rumored to patrol the forest looking for signs of portals, but they are more of a myth from the old times than flesh and blood."

"That sounds promising, mythical beings!"

"Then there's the Black Guard! At least they'd make us forget our troubles!" Briana offered frustrated.

"I thought you said they couldn't control our minds?"

"True, but they can kill us and wouldn't hesitate to do that if it kept the peace even if you were their only hope."

"We may be. Nonetheless, we should report the rising of the Dark One to the authorities."

"The authorities?" She laughed, "I'm sorry Quentin but that's not quite how it works here. Authority here is exercised by each Lord who controls a portion of everything. Each lord is responsible for everything in his borders from the castle to the ring road. In the castle lives the administrator who is one of the Lords who serves a five-year term. The administrators are encouraged to do a good job by having their family members distributed amongst the other lords as hostages. The hostages are well treated because the lords don't want to piss off the administrator who can sick the Black Guard on them and the administrator treats the lords fairly to protect his family. The children are educated and raised alongside the hosts own and are well provided for. The administrator is permitted periodic visits with his wife, children and other family members. After five years a new administrator is chosen, new hostages taken, and the old administrator's family is returned to their plantation safe from service for another generation."

"Wow!" Sharon said.

"So what does the administrator do?" I asked.

"They have a few functions. He and a slave pool of administrative assistants that are programmed to have undying loyalty to whomever the Administrator might be maintain communication and oversee commerce with the other collectives. The trade centers on luxuries, as each collective is required to maintain self-sufficiency for essentials. But just like on Earth, resources are not equally distributed and each collective produces a few select and tradable items that the administrator trades through other administrators, who each have a hostage of each others."

"Really?"

"Yes, the castle is basically a luxury prison for all the hostages of the other administrators. Basically they're a twenty-four hours, seven days a week party as everyone is treated like royalty and every Lord in the collective contributes to their support. Inside the castle there is your typical romances and court intrigues, but they have no voice or power and are forbidden to meet with the Administrator. To keep it that way, they live in separate parts of the castle and can only make contact during state ceremonies. The hostages are also forbidden to meet with the local lords lest one gain influence through the lord. So the hostages, isolated from all others, spend their days eating, drinking and fooling around with each other while slaves cater to their every need and whim. Because the collectives have varied cycles there are always people coming and going."

"Who watches the lords Plantation while he's the Administrator?" Sharon asked.

"The plantations have been in operation for centuries and pretty much run on their own and at least one competent family member is left behind while the Black Guard keeps an eye on things. They too are sworn to loyalty to the administrator, but their commitment is more like religious since their minds are free from control. Basically they're the mind cops and they're good at what they do. But their loyalty has definable limits as they refuse to be used as political pawns. Because they maintain the right of refusal, in some ways they really control things and they have one job, maintain the status quo."

"Sounds like being chosen as an administrator is a nightmare!" Sharon said.

"Not really, Sharon, It's actually a great honor and boon because even though your family is scattered for five years and you don't get to see many of them, you are rewarded by receiving a larger share of the collective's proceeds for the entire five years you're in office. If the Administrator is good and keeps the economy healthy he usually clears enough money to keep the family in comfort for a generation."

"Clearly the structure doesn't really allow for expansion, so how do the Lords control and appease their offspring?" I asked.

"The hostage idea has caught on and when the Lords aren't being the Administrator they use their families as guarantees for everything from contracts to peace agreements. Every plantation resembles the castle on a smaller version as the Plantation owners host their competitor's family members as hostages. Actually I think the practice is at the center of the social life here. And don't forget that each Lord controls dozens of businesses and while slaves do most of the grunt work, someone has to run the businesses so many family members are trained in the family trade. But you're right; the number of lords is fixed as is the number of plantations so only one person can inherit the title from each Lord, usually the oldest son. In the old days wars were fought over succession, but the Black Guard would never permit that now!"

"It sounds like the Black Guard is our best hope for the upcoming battle." I mused.

"Are you kidding me?" Briana laughed. "No, I can see you're not. Let me tell you something about the Black Guard. Without their mind powers, they are about as scary as a Girl Scout troop. Remember, they're chosen for their mind controlling abilities and not for their fighting skills. They range from children to old people and everything in between. They dress tough and act tough and when you can bend someone's mind to the breaking point you are tough, but I scared the shit out of them when they couldn't control me. They would be less than useless in a fight without their powers and they would be powerless against an army of humans."

"You know Briana; none of what you're telling me is encouraging." I joked frustrated.

"Sorry Quentin, but 'you're not in Kansas anymore' as the saying goes."

"No shit!" Sharon added as she brooded.

"So if the city is useless and the guard is useless then our only hope for help would be this third group you spoke about." Sharon reasoned it out.

"Only they're ghosts, or at least no one has seen them. It's rumored they are some ancient society left over from the old days that patrol the forest looking for signs of portals. But as I said they're more mythical than anything else."

"Any way to contact them?" I asked.

"I think they have to find you!"

"Great!"

That night Sharon and I slept next to the fire. I wanted to sleep outside but Sharon insisted I join her on the rug and then when I did she rested her head on my shoulder, spooned with me, and pulled my arm around her. Once she felt safe she fell right asleep and left me to deal with the feelings I was experiencing as our bodies touched. Ever since we had crossed over I had been feeling a connection to her that I had never felt before. I actually started to believe she might be warming up to me. Clearly we were entwined like lovers and that was a start. I wondered if the lack of presence from the Goddess was allowing the real Sharon to come out, but no matter what the reason, I was making progress. I slept great considering how I was feeling inside.

Sharon could sense that the Goddess was listening as Briana and Quentin talked but she remained quiet and withdrawn. Briana was just as pretty as her daughter Ariana and Sharon could understand how Quentin might confuse the two of them. As they talked she was tired, scared, and doing the best she could to put up a brave front. But without the goddess she was just Sharon again and that did not leave her feeling confident. She had resisted Quentin for weeks now and had to admit that she slept well in his lap. Of course she was exhausted, but still, it was nice when he brushed the hair off her face. As the evening wore on she insisted that Quentin stay with her as she was frightened to be away from him. She didn't want to be alone in this world like Briana had been for ten years! As they lay together on the soft rug she put his arm around her and snuggled against him and just before she fell asleep she felt the safest she'd felt in a long time.

8

It didn't take the 'Riders' long to find us. Apparently our little disturbance in the village was enough to alert them that we were near and it wasn't a long stretch to tie us to the only other stranger in this strange land. By late morning they had surrounded the clearing and a cold hard knock came at the door. I was instantly armed as Briana called out! "Who is it?"

"I am Chocztal, leader of the Riders. Your home is surrounded. Bring the strangers out and no harm will come to you."

"I am Quentin, Champion of Earth, and it is you who I seek Chocztal. May we meet under a banner of peace to discuss grave news?"

"Let us meet." He said and I took a deep breath and walked out. I was armed for bear and had a sword in each hand and I noticed they each had a weapon, mostly swords or spears in their own hands. I had insisted that Sharon and Briana stay inside but both were armed. It was at best a shaky truce.

When I got outside I was facing a tall, handsome, blond-haired, sun tanned god who resembled a Venice Beach weightlifter, only you could tell he'd gained his strength the hard way. There was a cold steely look in his eyes, but I also saw fairness. "That's far enough. Lower your weapons and I grant you peace." I lowered my weapons and his men did as well. "I am Chocztal, leader of the Riders, protectors of the realm."

"I am Quentin, Champion of Earth and I come in peace but with dark tidings. The one you call the Dark One has risen and he is preparing an army to attack." The men mumbled and groaned at the news. "Because I and the goddess are trapped here, we cannot stop them from our side, which means we must stop them from this side and we seek allies in our endeavor. Will you aid us?"

"We must. When is this attack due?" He asked.

"Any time now. We must be there when it begins or all will be lost. Can you detect the openings?"

"We have been tracking the one in this area since Briana arrived. Where did you come through?"

"A couple miles south of here."

"Briana came through right here. That's why she built her house here, to wait for it to reopen."

"Come Chocztal, let us all sit and think this through. Call your men in and let them drink at the well and fix their mid day meal while we talk."

"Agreed!"

When we entered the cottage he stopped in the door as his eyes adjusted to the light. When they did he was staring into Sharon's eyes and she was staring right back. My heart dropped a foot when I saw the look in her eye.

"Are all the women on you world as beautiful as these two?" he asked.

"Only the ones who hate me!" I joked but was feeling very vulnerable. It was junior high and high school all over again as the girls both fawned over the tan, buff, handsome warrior. Once again I watched the girls go for the rugged handsome man over me and it brought back terrible memories and feelings of inadequacy. We sat at the table and after providing food and wine the girls joined us.

"This is Sharon, Goddess of Earth."

"Well named," he said as he kissed her hand, "for she looks like a goddess." He was smooth and she was eating it up.

"Whatever. Look Chocztal, trouble is coming and we need to be prepared. Can you find the breach in time before he attacks?"

"We know it is this area but we only have your two openings to go by."

"Okay, well, let's go over the facts. Briana, what time did you go through the portal?"

"About midnight," she answered.

"And what time was it here?" I asked.

"About the same."

"Same with us. We came through about three PM and it seemed as if it was pretty close."

"I don't understand your point." Chocztal seemed confused.

"Let me show you." I cleared part of the table and took some beans from the table. "Let's say this bean is here where Briana came through, and let's say this bean is where the portal was when we came though." I placed two beans six inches apart.

"So I still don't see your point."

"It's only a theory, but let's look at the beans differently. This bean is midnight and this bean is three PM." Then I carefully laid out a total of twenty four beans, marking the original two. "Wouldn't you say that dawn would be the best time to attack and if so the portal should open somewhere between these three beans!" I was proud with myself and Chocztal stared at it a long time and then smiled.

"Quentin, can you find these places in our forest?"

"It'll take me a while and I'll need some help, but yeah, it's just algebra."

"I don't know what this algebra magic is but if you can find the portal, we can close it!"

"Not so fast Tex, we have to get back through it before you seal it."

"But an army will be coming through it. To re-enter the portal you'll have to fight them back."

"I didn't say it was going to be easy." I said.

"You really are a warrior!" He said to me admirably.

"I better get to work. Sharon, are you coming?" I asked.

"I'm good Quentin." She said and I realized that the no-separation rule no longer applied. I stormed off in a huff.

Jesus! Sharon thought when the most gorgeous man she'd ever seen in her life walked through the door. Chocztal was an Adonis and even Briana's jaw dropped open as her tongue hung out. Seeing that Briana was interested in him triggered something deep inside of her, and when he flirted back she felt almost giddy inside. The man was a walking calendar pin up muscle man. In fact she had a picture of a guy who looked a lot like Chocztal hanging on the wall in her bedroom for years. When she was introduced and he kissed her hand she tingled with excitement as she realized that this hunk of a man was hitting on her.

She couldn't help but stare at him as the boys talked and she grew annoyed at the way that Quentin was showing off his knowledge, trying to show Chocztal up. It was clear that Quentin was upset and maybe a little jealous and that bothered her as she had said over and over she wasn't interested in him that way. That way? She suddenly realized that she was interested in Chocztal that way! When Quentin announced that he was going to go look for where they came across and that Chocztal wasn't going to go she figured that would be a good time to get to know the young stud better.

They lent me a horse and sent some men with me and I took off along the woods at a gallop mostly out of anger. I was always losing out to some big strong guy and I was a little tired of it. I let the horse run and felt the wind in my face and knew that the tears in my eyes weren't all caused by the wind. I used triangulation to find the approximate spot and then Chocztal's trackers helped me find the exact spot where we came through. We drove a stake in the ground there and then I tried to figure out how to measure such a vast distance.

The only accurate measuring device I had was my pace. I knew that a relaxed step of mine measured exactly three feet. So I started walking and counting. After four hundred and forty steps I marked the spot and counted again while walking back. It came out pretty close so I figured we now knew the distance of one-quarter mile. Then I timed how long it took the horses walking a steady pace to cover the distance. After a few trips we had an average time and then we timed the trip back to Briana's. In the end the distance was four and a quarter miles. Divided by the nine hours it worked out to eight hundred and thirty one paces between each hour. By late afternoon Chocztal had men going in both directions placing time markers as we created a living clock.

Of course it was all a hope and a dream. The truth was there was ten years between Briana's and our emergence and the proximity could simply have been a coincidence. But it's not like I had anything else to go on. Besides I had to keep busy to keep from going crazy because in the short time I had been gone measuring distances Sharon and Chocztal had bonded. It tore at my heart when I saw them together and stayed away as much as possible. Given a horse I was allowed to join their patrols, which gave me something to do. But when I returned I saw them holding hands and it was more than I could take. I had to do something so I decided to practice my swordplay.

I started my warm up when Chocztal cockily suggested I try my hand against a real swordsman! Apparently he was the best swordsman in their camp and maybe the world his men bragged. I was angry and hurt and shouldn't have fought, but I wanted to wipe that cocky smile off his face.

"It would be my pleasure!" I smiled and sheathed my second sword. I only needed one.

He took his place across from me and drew his own sword. I looked over at Sharon and she was staring at him with lovelorn eyes and my anger grew. I tried to calm my breathing but it was hard to suppress the myriad of emotions that I was experiencing. We touched swords and then began to pace as we measured each other. He made a few classic moves, which I easily parried and then I made a few of my own and his arm was bleeding.

"A touch!" He admitted and his men groaned. Now Sharon was staring at me with hate in her eyes and things were worse. He lit into me with a flourish but I knew almost instantly that I was quicker, smarter, and more deadly than he would ever be. I touched him again and his men groaned and muttered amongst themselves. He was now bleeding from two slight wounds. I looked at him and realized that I wanted to kill him. He was every guy that got the girl I loved going back to junior high and just once I wanted to show the world that I was better. It was my chance.

Now I pressed him. I could have touched him a dozen times and killed him just as many but I was toying with my prey. His face was contorted in stress and sweat poured off him as he did everything he could to parry my blows. I was just getting ready to slice him again when I heard a voice in the back of my head say NO! I looked at Chocztal and he looked at me with the eyes of a man who knew he was beaten but who didn't know how to stop. I needed his help and the help of his men and if I beat him he would lose face and I would have to stand alone. I realized that if we were to win I had to lose.

We returned to fencing as I looked for the correct moment to fake my loss. Chocztal was at the end of his endurance and I hoped he didn't slip when I offered him my neck. It was done quickly and smoothly and no one knew I had practically placed my neck against his blade.

"I yield!" I announced and he released his sword and looked at me. "You are a great swordsman, Chocztal, thank you for the lesson!" I said and gathered my stuff up and walked away. I looked back to see Sharon fawning over his wounds but Chocztal stood there staring at me as his men congratulated him. Our eyes met and he sternly nodded at me and I knew that at least he knew the truth. Then I watched

Sharon kiss the wound I had given him and I had had enough. I headed behind the cottage and washed the sweat and blood spatters from my body.

"What the hell was that Quentin?" Sharon asked. "You're lucky he didn't kill you!" I laughed at that. "God you're acting like a jealous schoolboy. Grow up, why don't you!"

"I'm sorry Sharon. You're right, I am jealous. For weeks I've looked for any sign that you might give a shit about me and just when I think there's a smidgen of a chance, Hercules shows up and I'm chopped liver again. So yeah, I'm jealous and I'm hurt and you know what, I'm really tired. Good night!"

I turned and walked away into the woods. I only had my swords and knives with me but at that moment I didn't care. I was hurting so bad that tears streaked my face.

"Quentin!" Briana called and I turned. Sharon was gone. "Quentin, where are you going?" she asked as she caught up to me. "What's wrong honey? Are you mad because he beat you?" she asked and all I could think was how little they knew.

"No Briana, my hurt goes much deeper than that."

"Sharon?"

"Oh Briana, it's junior high all over again. Just when I think I might have a chance with her in walks the football player and my heart gets smashed. I can't take much more of this."

"You love her don't you?"

"Yes and nothing in my life has caused me more pain. I'm just sick and tired of not being good enough!"

"I'd be proud to have you as a son!" She smiled.

"Thanks. Look, I'm going to go spend the night by myself in the woods until I can get my head on straight. I wanted to kill that man today and he only wants to help. I need to get myself together."

"That's a really bad idea, Quentin; it's not that safe out here."

"You know Briana, I'm not sure if I wouldn't welcome death right now. Anything has to be better than the way I feel. But I'll be fine." I turned and walked away.

"Quentin!" she called out but I just kept walking and she turned and ran back to her cottage.

I walked a long time. I knew I needed to be far away from what was happening. The woods were actually quite beautiful I realized and as I walked I found my tension easing. My mind was racing at a thousand miles per hour as one part of me was wallowing in self pity while the other was trying to dig me out of the hole. It was easy to intellectualize it all as I could probably justify anything if given enough time, but the truth was that inside I was a mess and bleeding badly. Sharon's desertion had left me unsteady and sad and the quickness of it left me spinning

I had to find something to focus on so I picked up a foot long tree branch, pulled out a knife and started whittling it.

I found a nice clearing and sat against an oak tree and relaxed. The sun was setting as I shaped the wood. I didn't know I was making a recorder until I started hollowing it out. Somehow my hands knew what to do with the knife and wood and it wasn't long before it began to take shape. I had to make it in two pieces that I joined together but as the last remnants of daylight faded I tried it and found it didn't sound too bad. Then I played it, which was quite a trick since I had never played it before. Before long a slow melodic song came out of it and I realized I was taping into some memory of the Champions past. It was the perfect song for how I was feeling and I realized that I wasn't the first Champion who had felt the way I was feeling.

Sharon was pissed with Quentin for trying to hurt her dear sweet Chocztal. She was a little dazed by the day as she and Chocztal clicked on some romantic spiritual plane. In some ways he filled the void left by the goddess' withdrawal. He was also gorgeous!

"Your hands are so soft," he had said as he took her hand in his own and she didn't let go. They were large and rough, just like he was and she felt like she had fallen into some cheap romance novel. But when they touched there was electricity and her heart was stirring with the first pangs of love. They walked together through the woods as they held hands and talked and it felt so natural. The Goddess tried to warn her but after having been ignored for so long it was easy to ignore her right back. The only bad thing was that when they returned Quentin's face was all screwed up in anger and pain, which she couldn't understand as she had been clear from the beginning that she wasn't interested. So when he returned she made sure he could see that she was interested in Chocztal.

She grew even angrier with him when the two of them fought and she thought it was grossly unfair. Despite Chocztal's skill, Quentin was the Champion and was using his skills to hurt Chocztal just to get even with her. Quentin was acting like a jealous little boy and she was sick of watching him hurt the poor warrior. Then suddenly Chocztal's sword was at Quentin' throat and she smiled as Chocztal was declared the winner. That will show Quentin, she thought smugly! She made it a point to fuss over Chocztal's wounds and gave Quentin a dirty look as she carefully bound Chocztal's wounds. But she was angry and she had to say something to Quentin. Like the child he was he stormed off into the woods. She returned to the wounded warrior and gave him a big smile, but he seemed troubled. Briana returned and looked worried.

"Briana, where is Quentin? I would have a word with him." Chocztal asked.

"He's gone." Briana answered sadly. Sharon felt a stab in her heart she didn't understand.

"Gone? Where?" He asked and she turned and pointed deeper into the woods. "What? Why?"

"He said he needed to get his head on straight." Briana said.

"Don't worry about him Chocztal. He's always slipping off to the forest to spend the night." Sharon said unconcerned.

"Not in these woods! It is unsafe." Chocztal said in a panic. "We must bring him back."

"You won't find him, Chocztal. For good or bad, he's gone." Briana said sadly.

"I do not understand this."

"Quentin's just mad because you beat him in a sword fight and he likes me and I like you!" Sharon said surprised she said it out loud.

"Beat Him? I did not beat him. He took everything I could throw at him and I couldn't even touch him. He offered me his neck so that I could save face in front of my men." When he finished she just stared at him.

"Well then he's just jealous of us." She said.

"Us? You would choose me over him? Are you a fool or just blind?' He scolded her.

"That's what I wondered as well!" Briana offered.

"I can't help it Chocztal, but yes I did choose you over him. I can't help the way I feel." She smiled but a tear fell.

"Ah, sweet Sharon, I am touched and honored as I care for you too, but two worlds may die because of our foolishness."

"Quentin will be fine. He'll sort it out and be back in the morning with a smile on his face."

"I hope you're right," he said worried.

"If you're so worried why don't we go find him," Briana asked.

"To walk in the woods at night is to invite death. My men and I as well, would never attempt it unless there was no other choice. No, we must wait and pray that the Champion is delivered."

"Really? He's out there alone and you're afraid to go out there, even with your men?" Briana asked shaking her head. She sat in a chair outside her door and faced the direction Quentin had gone as the sun slowly dipped in the sky. The others went back to cooking their dinner.

Sharon wasn't sure what to make of it all. She surprised herself when she admitted that she had feelings for Chocztal and was encouraged by his reaction but maybe a little disappointed in his words. She really wasn't worried about Quentin, at least at first. He was always wandering off somewhere and could handle himself. Couldn't he, she thought?

As if on cue there was a piercing high pitched scream coming from the direction Quentin had gone. Chocztal and his men all jumped to their feet as one drawing their weapons and facing out from the clearing. "Build the fire and post guards. No one sleeps tonight men, the devil's butcher roams"

"The devil's butcher, what is that?" Sharon asked beginning to feel uneasy.

"It is a hideous creature that can walk on two or four legs. It has long talons and fangs and they all carry deadly poison. Few men have ever faced one alone and lived!" He said sternly. Just then an even louder and more menacing cry came from the direction of where Quentin had gone.

"Quentin!" Briana cried out as she looked in the direction of the scream and started crying. Chocztal and his men all stood at attention but they looked towards the sound and the looks on their face were not encouraging. Sharon bit her lip and thought about the last thing she had said to him.

The recorder made a marvelous melodic sound and the tune I played eventually lifted my spirits. I was still hurting but the woods seemed to restore some of my sanity. Once again I started to reorder my inner house as I justified and compartmentalized each hurting emotion. Sharon never claimed she loved me but to see her love somebody else, even if it was just a crush was more than I could take. Yet no matter how I tried I couldn't find a way to fill the emptiness in my heart. I was about to start playing again when I heard a noise in the woods that was really close. At once I rose and was on my feet with sword drawn and facing the direction of the sound. Then I heard two tiny yelps and a rustling of brush before two baby wolf cubs came bursting into the moonlit glen. They were running scared and looking back and one of them ran right into me. The other stopped in surprise and then hid behind me. The other cub got up, looked me up and down, and then scurried around behind me. I couldn't believe two wolf cubs were hiding behind my legs and acting so unnaturally.

Just about the time my mind began to wonder what they were so afraid of, it came bounding out of the woods.

It was on four legs but rose to two when it saw me. Each of his four legs ended with long sharp claws and its fangs looked equally deadly. Its hairy body was taut with muscle and on two legs he was taller than I was. It looked down at the cubs, then at me, as it let out a ferocious scream that scared the shit out of me and nearly deafened me. Then it attacked. I parried its claws with my single blade moving quickly with all my skill and then poked him with the blade. Greenish blood spurted from the wound and the creature immediately backed off. I was hoping it would go away once it was wounded but it paced back and forth while looking at me. All of a sudden it rose up and made a sound that sounded both desperate and terrifying. Then it did nothing but stare at me and if I didn't know better I'd say that it was smiling at me. I wondered why?

"What's happening?" Sharon pleaded.

"I do not know, I have never heard a cry like that." Chocztal said amazed. Then they all heard it. First one, then another, and another as the screams of the devil's butchers could be heard in many directions. Then they heard another cry coming from Quentin's direction and all the other cries responded. Chocztal lowered his head. "I believe Quentin has taught the first a lesson and he now calls his companions. It is hopeless for him. Build a bier to Bantu Banthe and ask him to receive the soul of a brave warrior," he ordered.

"What do you mean it's hopeless," Sharon said in a near panic. Briana came to her.

"Sharon, Quentin may have been able to defeat one Devil's Butcher and from what I saw of his abilities maybe two, but I heard at least a half dozen and no one could survive that. I'm sorry."

"He'll be all right!" she said and hoped deeply inside.

"No, Sharon, he will not. You sure have a lot of faith in a man you hold in such disdain." Briana sneered.

"Quentin's a lot tougher than he looks."

"No man is that tough, my little pumpkin. I count a dozen creatures. No man can survive that!" Chocztal said sadly.

"Quentin?" Sharon said under her breath as she looked towards the point where all the screaming creatures seemed to be heading.

I had no idea what this thing was or what she was doing until I heard the other creatures. The cubs heard it too and crowded my feet. The creature seemed to be in no hurry so I leaned down and talked to the cubs.

"I will defend you with my life but you must hide behind this tree and wait until I have finished. It will be an honor dying for such noble creatures as you pups. Now go!" I was surprised when they both left me and cowered behind the tree. I had just drawn my second sword and was warming up when I grew concerned as I began to count the number of cries responding to the first. Then they appeared in the clearing, one by one, until I counted thirteen of the smelly bastards. I was sad, angry, jealous ready to hurt something, and here was my chance. I had not killed the first because I wasn't sure they weren't some kind of animal operating on instinct. But facing thirteen I realized that their intent was murderous and that I had zero chance of surviving. I raised my swords.

"Oh Great Spirit, "I started. "Thank you for my life and for the lives of those that have given theirs so that I may continue. Thank you for the chance to die in battle for a just cause. Today is a good day to die!" It was the best I could do! Their response was that all thirteen rose up at once and cried out and the noise was deafening. I knew that it was designed to cause me fear but the battle lust was upon me and knowing I was going to die I never felt more alive. When their screams died down I made my own war cry, "ODIN!" I cried to the Norse god of war and then I attacked.

The noises grew closer to Quentin's location until suddenly it was quiet and everyone back at Briana's cottage looked west towards the silence. Then a sound that was nearly unbearable came out of the woods as all thirteen creatures screamed at once. Even the most stalwart of Chocztal's warriors shuddered at the sound. But what really caught their attention was the faint but discernible man's voice.

"Quentin's war cry. The battle has begun. Begin the prayers." Chocztal said somberly.

I had no plan other than I was going to be damned if I let them make the first move. No longer debating my enemy I knew that I had to strike hard and fast and so I did. I had killed three before they figured out what I was doing and then the battle really began. They converged on me but I was quick and effective, hewing limbs and heads indiscriminately. The first claw caught me on the arm and from the burning I began to feel I knew that there was poison. I figured I was already dead but I still had two pups to protect. Not knowing how long I had before I would be dead or paralyzed, I got serious, but also more cautious. My blades were moving in all directions and I suddenly realized that my sphere exercise was pretty close to what I was doing. My swords moved in a quick and almost circular pattern as I tried to parry blows from all directions at once. But when I saw an opening I took it and one by one I was carefully dispatching them. I took my second hit in the leg from one who fell on me as his head rolled away. I could feel my own blood running down my leg and the poison burning but looking up I could only see six left. The clearing was a mass of dead whatever they call these things and if the poison didn't kick in right away I might survive.

Then the poison kicked in and I laughed. Maybe it was my body chemistry, just slightly different from the natives, but I started getting kind of high off the venom. I had no idea if the euphoric feeling it was giving me was going to last or if I was going to die right away, so I took advantage of feeling good and attacked the remaining creatures. My swords were a blur as I slipped between them hacking at limbs and head. Then I faced one, the original one who was still bleeding. It let out one last scream and then it died. I was left alone in the silence and dropped to the ground against the tree. The two pups came out from around the tree and looked at me. I petted them each on the head and then they lay their heads on my lap and I let the poison take me away.

The noises coming from the woods were frightening but the longer they went on the taller and more focused Chocztal grew.

"What's going on?" Sharon asked.

"It is not possible," was all that Chocztal could say. More and more of his men had joined him and they were all staring in the direction of the noise.

"The cries lessen." One of his men said and Chocztal nodded grimly.

"Chocztal, what's happening?" Sharon pleaded.

"It appears your assessment of Quentin is correct. He is indeed tougher than he looks."

"What do you mean?" She asked.

"Few men have ever survived a fight with a single Devil's Butcher. It appears that Quentin has taken on thirteen and may be winning. The cries of the creatures lessen with each second. There, did you hear that. Only one is left! It is impossible!"

"Could they have run?" One of his men asked.

"I don't know, but if they did they would be screaming mad. Shh!" It was silent.

"Has he won?" Sharon asked.

"Oh my love, he may have won the battle, but not without being struck. Not against so many fangs and talons can we expect just one touch. No, I fear he lay dying right now. Tomorrow we will get him and honor him above all men."

"Tomorrow?" Briana screamed. "No, damn it, now! We should have all been there to help him. He shames us in his success and now you fear retrieving his body as he lay dying?"

"He is already dead, my lady. The poison is very effective and there is no antidote. Even if we reach him there is nothing we can do."

"We can say goodbye!" She said and turned and went into the house. She came out a few seconds later wearing her guns with Quentin's shotgun thrown over her shoulder. Then they heard a long plaintive and distinctive howl from a wolf. She swung the shotgun into her hands and chambered a round. "Oh hell no! Don't worry Quentin, I won't let the wolves take your body." She started around the cottage.

"Wait, I'm coming with!" Chocztal said.

"No baby maybe we better wait here." Sharon said frightened.

"Are you fucking kidding me?" Briana said in disbelieve. "Really? That boy saved your life at least three times and all you can do is break his heart, and then leave him for dead. You are a cold fish, honey. You stay with Chocztal, sweetie, Quentin doesn't need a girl like you in his life!"

"I meant that if we all die then the Dark One will win." She said hurt.

"Do you really think we have any chance at all if he's dead? You can't really be that stupid! God, what was the goddess thinking when she chose you?"

"Excuse me?" Sharon asked offended.

"You heard me girlfriend. I heard you tell Quentin to grow up. Well it's time you grow up too Missy! Do you really think you're here so that you and lover boy could meet? You're the goddess and the world that my daughter lives in is counting on you and while you and lover boy here have been playing house a real man just killed thirteen of the meanest creatures on this world. So why don't you go play schoolgirl with your new boyfriend while I go out and try and save the man who saved my daughter's life."

"You shame me with the truth." Chocztal said sadly. "Little Pumpkin is it true you owe Quentin three life debts."

"I don't know what a life debt is?" Sharon said flustered. Briana had shaken her to the core.

"Did he save your life three times?" he asked.

"Probably closer to five, but some of those times he saved a lot of lives and not just mine!" she said.

"Five? Five life debts? Your world must be very strange to take such a thing so lightly. In our world we take having one life debt seriously and will do whatever is necessary to be free from such a debt. Men, hurry, a real man is dying and we have been fools and cowards. Get torches!"

Sharon stood there stunned as everyone scrambled to get ready for the rescue mission. The idea that Quentin would die didn't occur to her. He had been through so much! And Briana was right, without him how could they get back. What's more, if Quentin is dead then the Champion is as well and it angered her that it was partly her fault. But he had stormed off and she was in the right! Emotionally she was a cyclone as her feeling of new love for Chocztal ran square into her fear that Quentin may have died. Goddess, she thought.

'Yes Sharon,' she said wearily.

'Could Quentin really be dead?'

'Yes Sharon, he could. I feel him out there but he is weak and getting weaker. We may have lost him." She seemed sad.

This was a whole different kind of death than the last time. I sat at the base of the tree and looked around me. The whole area around me was covered with dead bodies, carnage and gore. I checked my body only to discover that I had taken three hits, two from claws and one a bite on my arm. I could feel the venom entering my blood but was a little surprised to find out that it really relaxed me. I settled against the tree as my breathing slowed. I realized that death would not be far behind. I looked down into the eyes of the two pups and smiled. They looked deeply into my own eyes and seemed sad.

"I told you I wouldn't let them hurt you! Now run off, your mother is probably worried."

It won't be long now, I thought. I tried to think? I tried to think of something clever to say as my last words and laughed when I realized that the only ones who would hear them were a couple of wolf pups. No, I was going to die the way I lived. Alone!

The story continues in *Bargains:*

If this was dying it really wasn't so bad. The two pups remained with their heads resting on my lap and stared at me with soft gentle eyes. An eerie quiet hung over the glen and I was grateful for the peace and quiet. I was alone but had been most of my life, so I guess that was fitting. Now that the thirteen creatures were dead, I had time to appreciate the beauty of the world I was about to die in. To be honest it wasn't that much different than a forest in our own world and much like many of the places I had camped at in the last few months. I felt comfortable there and reasoned it really wasn't that bad of a place to die. As my breathing slowed and numbness spread around each of the wounds I sat back and awaited my death. Truthfully, as I sat there still stinging from Sharon's rejection, I was pretty much welcoming my now imminent death.

A lone female wolf entered the clearing and stopped right in front of me. I was unable or unwilling to move and she looked around the clearing and then at her cubs and then at me. Our eyes locked for a minute and then she raised her head and let out a loud howl. I had been planning on just slipping into death, but I was okay with being eaten by such a beautiful creature. One by one the other wolves in her pack answered and one by one they appeared in the clearing. Then he came, the Alpha male, and from the way he nuzzled the mother of the pups, I gathered the pups were his. He walked around the clearing sniffing the carnage and looked back at me often. Finally, he came and sat in front of me and bowed. Then he blew my mind!

"I am Lobo, head of the pack, and I name you wolf friend, oh noble warrior. You protected my cubs and we shall protect you tonight while the spirits come to you. My pups seem to have taken a liking to you!" Then I think he smiled.

"Thank you, oh noble creature, for not eating me, although I would consider it an honor to be eaten by such a noble pack if I had to be eaten." Okay so I wasn't quite right in my head and I was talking to a wolf, but it all seemed real. Then the wolf nodded and barked and the other wolves formed a circle around the clearing.

I thought I was tripping. I mean what the fuck was this, a Disney movie or something? So, imagine my surprise when I looked up and Buddha was sitting lotus style in front of me.

"Siddhartha? Is it really you?"

"Yes, my son. You know why I am here."

"Yes, at least I think I do. The four Noble Truths? Eliminate desire, eliminate pain."

"You understand me so well, yet listen so rarely."

"I know, but it's hard to live without love."

"Of course, it is," I looked up and Jesus had joined the conversation. "Love is the basis of all life. You know that Siddhartha. You didn't have to tell them you had achieved enlightenment, but you chose to share out of the love in your heart for all people. The human problem is that they confuse love and lust! Look, Quentin, you have the rare gift of unconditional love but you get lost in romantic love. Try to embrace the agape love and you'll have an easier time."

"Agape my ass!" A scruffy-looking Viking said as he appeared between them.

"Odin?" I asked.

"In the flesh!" He looked around. "Nice, thirteen beasts, not a bad night's work!"

"Odin?" I was trying to get my head around that.

"You called on me before battle and I came to make you an offer. You are perched on the edge of life and death. As you have previously stated that you liked the idea, if you wish and you are willing to walk across the Rainbow Bridge, I will welcome you to Valhalla. You can end your pain on Earth and we will drink to your honor. Come, my boy, hunt and fight with us all day and drink and wench all night. You'll forget your earthly troubles the first day!"

"Thank you, sir, but that would mean I'm dead and I don't wish to be yet. But thanks for the offer."

"Too bad, we could have used a guy like you." Then he disappeared.

Jesus and Buddha were still sitting across from me and smiling. "So, am I dead or hallucinating or what?"

"Probably a little bit of both and neither." Buddha smiled.

"Great, a Zen Koan, that's just what he needed," Jesus said smugly.

"What, did you have some great parable lined up?" Buddha laughed.

The next thing I know the two of them are arguing and then another man enters the picture. He is ancient, dressed in a simple tunic, an ancient leather jerkin, and carrying a round wooden shield and stone-tipped spear. He comes and squats between Jesus and Buddha, turns and looks at each, and then smiles and says, "Beat it!" They do and I'm left behind with the ancient warrior.

Made in the USA
Coppell, TX
29 October 2022